A VERY *Italian* WEDDING

BOOKS BY DONNA ASHCROFT

STANDALONES

Summer at the Castle Cafe

The Little Guesthouse of New Beginnings

The Little Village of New Starts

The Little Cornish House

Summer at the Cornish Beach Cafe

SCOTTISH HIGHLANDS SERIES

Summer in the Scottish Highlands

Christmas in the Scottish Highlands

Snowflakes and Secrets in the Scottish Highlands

Christmas Secrets in the Scottish Highlands

Winter Wishes in the Scottish Highlands

A Christmas Romance in the Scottish Highlands

CHRISTMAS BOOKS

If Every Day Was Christmas

The Christmas Countdown

The Little Christmas Teashop of Second Chances

DONNA ASHCROFT

A VERY *Italian* WEDDING

bookouture

Published by Bookouture in 2025

An imprint of Storyfire Ltd.
Carmelite House
50 Victoria Embankment
London EC4Y 0DZ

www.bookouture.com

The authorised representative in the EEA is Hachette Ireland
8 Castlecourt Centre
Dublin 15 D15 XTP3
Ireland
(email: info@hbgi.ie)

ISBN: 978-1-83618-881-0
eBook ISBN: 978-1-83618-880-3

For Erren and Charlie
My moon and stars
Remember to follow your dreams
and keep your hearts open
Oh, and read my books!
xxx

1

ROSE

Rose Loveheart shifted uncomfortably in the aisle seat on the aeroplane as she scrolled through the emails on her mobile, flagging anything that needed urgent attention. She frowned at the space beside her again which was still empty, despite a special call over the tannoy for a missing passenger ten minutes earlier.

Where was he? He should have met her in the airport lounge two hours ago. Ten o'clock sharp – she'd emailed and told him that he'd recognise her easily because she'd be wearing a cream linen suit. He'd even made a joke about carrying a rose.

Her mobile suddenly pinged with a new text from her assistant, encouraging her to switch off her phone. 'I can't, there's too much to do,' Rose grumbled, resuming her scrolling as Coco – who was in a dog carrier perched on her lap — let out a low growl.

Getting a cramp, Rose carefully tried to shift the dog onto another section of her leg. The snow-white shih tzu was a diva at the best of times, and being flown to Italy as hand luggage, secured in a pet carrier, definitely wasn't one of those. The air hostess had asked if she could put the dog under the seat a few minutes before, but when Coco had started to bark, she'd allowed Rose to keep her where she was.

'It's not dinner time yet.' She reluctantly put the mobile into the pocket of the seat in front of her where she'd already stored her small laptop and checked her watch. 'Won't be until we get to Italy.'

Rose patted a soothing palm on the side of the gauzy material hoping it might placate the dog. But the growl deepened until Coco sounded more like a grumpy bear than her best friend's bijou pet. She pulled her hand away in case she got nipped. It wouldn't be the first time. Dog sitting should really come with danger money.

'Are you the maid-of-honour-to-be?' A deep and decidedly sexy voice suddenly asked, making Rose flinch in surprise. She glanced up and felt something inside her chest perform a series of energetic bench presses. The man looming over her was gorgeous – with capital O, M and multiple Gs. Rose swore she could hear one of the air hostesses fan herself, while a woman a few rows in front let out an audible gulp.

He had incredible eyes. Some might have called them dark brown, but Rose thought they probably deserved their own Pantone reference. Or a special name, like one of those extravagant paints from Farrow & Ball – Roasted Coffee Bean, Mahogany or maybe even Bated Breath?

'Rose?' he repeated, looking a little confused. His flawless forehead wrinkled, drawing attention to tussled dirty blonde hair and a jawline that was so sharp he probably used it to slice vegetables. 'Rose Loveheart, right?'

Rose frowned, surprised by her body's visceral response – which for the first time in her life, she couldn't seem to control. 'Yes?' she said and shifted again when she realised the sound had come out as more of a husky come hither than a confirmation.

'I'm Ben Pearson, the best man. I heard you were beautiful.'

He grinned. 'I love the suit, it's very... cream.' His eyes twinkled as if he'd just flicked on a switch and her stomach performed an unexpected happy dance. Rose swallowed, she had to be careful. She knew all about men like him, but she wasn't about to let a pretty face get the better of her.

'You're late,' she said, giving Ben her disappointed glare. The one she usually reserved for clients when they refused to talk or grew distracted during one of their therapy sessions.

'I am.' His smile deepened and a dimple winked in his right cheek. Someone – on the aisle behind them this time – let out a throaty groan. Wasn't he going to apologise?

'Sir, please can you take your seat?' An air hostess appeared from nowhere and offered Ben a beaming smile.

He quickly scanned her name badge. 'Of course, Mandy. How lovely to meet you, and may I say that blue uniform really brings out the colour in your cheeks.' He grinned.

Mandy flushed. 'Um...' The air hostess looked flustered. 'If you could.' She pointed to the middle seat. 'I'd appreciate it.' The words came out breathy.

'Oh, Mandy, I would, it's just...' Ben turned his hormone-stirring gaze back to Rose giving her a jolt. 'I'm so sorry if it's inconvenient, but would you mind very much if we swapped? It's just, I don't think my legs are going to fit.'

He gestured to the middle seat next to Rose and then looked down, and she found her eyes following his gaze to dark jeans that hugged long muscular calves and thighs. 'Last time I tried to sit in the middle seat on a flight to Prague one of the crew practically had to rub me down with oil to get me out,' he joked.

Mandy let out a raspy chuckle before muttering something about being more than happy to help.

'Fine,' Rose murmured. 'But if I move, you'll need to hold the dog.' She offered Ben the carrier, and he took it without commenting. Then she gathered up her mobile, laptop and the handbag she'd stashed underneath the seat in front and carefully shifted into the middle one. The gentleman already sitting in the spot beside the window suddenly snorted and slid sideways, pressing his shoulder heavily into hers as he began to snore.

Rose sat statue-still trying not to disturb him in case he woke and wanted to chat. As soon as some people discovered she was a therapist by trade, they tried to hog her attention for hours. Not that she minded usually, but she didn't want anyone opening up with Ben next to her, listening.

'Let me help.' Mandy took Coco's carrier as Ben started to sit.

'Thanks, gorgeous,' Ben murmured, making Mandy simper again. Rose watched as he tried to get comfortable. His legs were so long he had to fold them into the centre aisle. When Mandy gave him back the dog, he winked and peered through the mesh.

'Cute,' Ben said as Coco shuffled closer to the opening so she could get a better look. 'Yours?'

Rose shook her head. 'Nope. She belongs to the bride-to-be. She's going to be the ring bearer – if she doesn't eat the rings first.'

Ben absorbed that information and clearly decided not to run with it. 'What's her name?'

'You can call her Coco. I call her *the Demon from Hell*,' Rose said sweetly, waiting for the shih tzu to bark, growl, or twist her claws in the net in an attempt to scratch Ben's striking face.

'Why?' he asked, sounding surprised.

Rose heard the thump of a tail fervently battering against the carrier's sides. 'Forget it.' She sighed, irritated that Ben's charms had worked so quickly on both Mandy and Coco. She'd never been able to bond with people or animals so fast. She searched in her handbag for her headphones and put them on before quickly finding a Mozart piano concerto on Spotify.

Then Rose shut her eyes, deliberately signalling an end to the conversation.

They didn't speak again until the plane was in the air and Mandy had served them both with coffee. Black for Rose, milk and three sugars for Ben – and biscuits on white china plates that, apparently, were usually reserved for the customers in first class. Ben had gifted Mandy with a barrage of gratitude until her cheeks had turned puce. The hostess had then found a treat for Coco, and the demon had offered her a rare tail wag too.

'I usually travel in business class, but all the flights today were full,' Ben confided to Rose, shifting in his chair so he could look at her. 'I appreciate you booking a seat for me.'

'These were the only two left on the one dog-friendly flight.' She frowned at Coco. 'Then again, that's what happens when you're asked to fly to Italy at the last minute to take part in an impulsive wedding.' Rose broke off a tiny piece of biscuit and chewed it slowly. It was mouth-wateringly good, so she nibbled a little more.

'You don't approve?' Ben asked, and for the first time since they'd met, he stopped smiling, although it didn't dim the power of those good looks.

Rose swallowed. 'I've known Luna since we were in school.' She paused. 'She's my best friend, the closest person I have in my life.' She thought about her parents and grimaced. She'd love to have a better relationship with them but... she sighed feeling a familiar ache. They'd never really treated her like a daughter, she'd always been more of a pawn in their crusade to hurt each another. But that's what happened when you married in haste. 'I don't want her to make a mistake. She's had a few near misses, people who've tried to take advantage. Her family are very wealthy.'

Ben stiffened. 'Marco isn't a mistake and he's not a gold

digger,' he said firmly, sipping some of his coffee, carefully hovering the paper cup over Coco's carrier. 'He's a good man. From what he's told me, your Luna is his perfect match. Love at first sight he told me.' His tone was surprisingly wistful.

'They met three and a half weeks ago. This was a business trip for Luna, so she was working most of that time,' Rose said, trying to keep the incomprehension out of her tone. Luna had said the same thing about love at first sight to her. But she'd said that before – and each time the relationship had ended in disaster.

'Have you told her how you feel?' Ben asked, looking amused.

Rose shook her head. 'It's a difficult subject to bring up on the phone. I thought I'd leave it until we were face to face. We've texted and emailed, and I'm planning to keep it that way until we can talk properly.' At least then she could look Luna in the eye and persuade her gently.

'Makes sense,' he said thoughtfully. 'Perhaps when you see them together, you'll realise you're worrying about nothing?'

Rose had to fight the desire to shake her head. 'You've known Marco for a while?' she asked, shifting her shoulder because it was beginning to go numb.

Ben nodded, shooting her another quick smile, clearly unable to stop his charm reflex, which told Rose everything she needed to know about how authentic it was. 'Since university. We work together too – have done for over twelve years.'

'Has he been married before?' Rose shot back, staring into his hypnotising chocolate brown eyes and swallowing.

Ben's smile grew brighter, lighting his face. He was clearly delighted with the interrogation. 'You'll be pleased to know there has not been a Mrs Marco Marino to date. He had a near miss too a couple of years ago. Someone who cheated, and it's taken him a while to get over that. That's why I'm so pleased to see him back on his feet.'

'I'm sorry to hear that,' Rose said softly. She'd seen enough heartbreak to know it could take someone years to heal.

Ben paused, the smile disappearing momentarily before it reappeared like a dolphin performing a spectacular somersault out of the sea. 'When he asked me to be his best man, I dropped everything.'

'I did the same for Luna,' Rose said. Her words were punctuated by a sudden bout of turbulence which made Ben's cup of coffee tumble from his hand.

'Damn!' he exclaimed as it somersaulted before landing upside down in Rose's lap, spilling the contents.

'Ouch!' she yelped, practically levitating as the hot liquid spilled onto her legs, seeping through the cream linen trousers and staining the material. She quickly grabbed the cup, righted it and handed it back to Ben, wincing as she stared down at her clothes.

'I'm so sorry, are you hurt?' he apologised, sounding upset.

'I'm okay,' Rose muttered as she tried to reach for her handbag which contained a bottle of water.

'But I've ruined your wonderful suit,' Ben said as the turbulence returned, shaking the plane, and the seatbelt sign was switched back on. Rose's neighbour grunted a couple of times, but thankfully didn't wake. 'I'll get the lovely Mandy to bring you something to clean that up.' Ben grimaced as he took in the dark stain which had travelled from Rose's knee to halfway up her thigh. 'If it's any consolation, I think you can pull it off.'

Rose grimaced. It wasn't Ben's fault, but the suit was ruined – worse she knew she was going to be stuck in it for the rest of the journey, if not until tonight. Unless she could change when they got to the airport?

'I don't think Mandy is going to be able to do much to help, and I think I'll be putting up with it rather than pulling it off. It's fine,' she muttered, finally getting to her handbag and grabbing the bottle of water so she could pour a little onto the stain. It didn't help.

'It really was an accident,' Ben promised.

'I know.' The stain wasn't deliberate, but Rose hated looking untidy. She brushed at the mark fitfully before giving up. Hopefully, this wasn't a premonition for how the rest of the trip was going to turn out.

Ben gave her a half smile. 'Well, I owe you. Feel free to drop something on me another time. Maybe at the wedding?' His eyes twinkled again, making the breath catch in her throat.

'I wouldn't do that.' Rose brushed at the stain again because she couldn't help herself.

'You were saying how you think the wedding's a bad idea?' he probed, probably trying to distract her from the coffee disaster.

Rose sighed, dragging her attention away from her clothes. It was pointless attempting to fix something that so clearly couldn't be fixed. She knew that from bitter experience with her parents. But she still ran her finger over the material once more.

'I just think...' She paused, choosing her next words carefully. If she could get Ben on side, it might be easier all round.

'It's all a bit rushed, don't you think?' she asked. 'I'm not saying they shouldn't marry.' *At least not out loud.* 'But I am saying they've only known each other for a few weeks.' A month if she was being generous, but Rose decided not to round it up. 'It wouldn't hurt to give it a little more time. I'd hate for them to make a mistake. They need to make sure they're really compatible. They haven't had a chance to find that out.'

They'd clearly hopped through multiple stages of the relationship ladder. They had to go back and start again, following Rose's strict 'Love Rules' which she used with all her clients. Luna also needed time to ensure Marco wasn't after her trust fund like a couple of her previous boyfriends – and they had to see each other through the lens of day-to-day life.

Ben's eyes filled with sympathy, and, for a moment, Rose lost her breath. 'It's difficult to stand back and watch friends find happiness when we haven't found it ourselves,' he said kindly, his eyes dipping to her bare ring finger as the plane bounced a couple more times. 'I understand that. I've been burned myself, but that doesn't mean it's not real for them.'

Rose jerked back and her shoulder collided with her neighbour's again. She held her breath when the man inhaled sharply, but he didn't wake up. 'I'm not jealous,' she grumbled, insulted. 'I'm happy being single. I'll meet the right person one day, but I'm going to wait until I know they're perfect.'

She wasn't going to let her guard down too soon either – and she certainly wouldn't be vaulting over all the careful stages of her relationship's development. When she finally let someone into her heart, it would be forever. There would be no chance of getting hurt, and no rushed weddings leading to a lifetime of chaos. She'd had a front-row seat to that already.

'Right.' Ben leaned back in his seat, holding onto Coco's carrier with one hand and gripping the now-empty coffee cup, looking thoughtful. 'So, what's your plan? Are you going to don a Bat Woman cape and storm the church shouting it's all a terrible mistake?' His smile told Rose he was teasing, but there was a look in his eyes that suggested if she tried, he'd be there to stop her.

She chuckled. 'That's plan B. I'm guessing it won't make it that far,' Rose admitted.

Ben's forehead creased and he pushed his cup into the pouch under his tray table. Then he poked a hand into the carrier so he could tickle Coco under her chin.

'I'm not sure you should do that,' she warned. The dog practically purred, and Rose sighed. If she tried to do the same, she'd probably lose a limb.

Despite being in the dog's life since the shih tzu was a puppy, there was no love lost between her and Coco. She had no clue as to where the creature's antagonism stemmed but it hurt. If only she had some Love Doctor rules to use on dogs.

'So, what's your alternative to the happy ever after?' Ben asked.

Rose shrugged. 'I'm just going to talk to Luna – ask her to wait. I've already reserved a venue for Christmas, close to where she lives in Brighton. It's a special place for her and her mum and they're very close.'

Ben's eyes widened. 'You don't hang about. I think the Marinos would be upset if the wedding wasn't held in Italy. Besides, the date is important to them.' He removed his hand from the dog carrier and shifted a little closer to her, his expression serious. 'I think it's only fair if I tell you that I'm going to do everything in my power to make sure this wedding goes ahead as scheduled. It's what Marco wants, so it's what I want too.' He drummed his fingers on the dog carrier.

'Well, I appreciate that, but I'm still going to try to get her to delay. It's for their own good,' Rose insisted.

Ben regarded her for a moment longer, humour now colouring his expression which had morphed from serious to amused at a speed that had Rose's head spinning. How was she supposed to read this man if his emotions changed so often?

'You know, usually my adversaries are ugly,' he muttered as his dimple reappeared.

'I don't see how that's relevant,' Rose spluttered. She was used to dealing with all kinds of people in her work, steering all types of odd conversations in the right direction. She had no idea how he had the power to turn her brain to mush.

'Hairy too.' Ben grinned.

Rose sucked in a breath. 'I'll try harder to look the part,' she muttered.

He eased forward, and his fresh masculine scent made her head spin. 'I'd rather you didn't.'

What was he doing? 'Are you flirting because you think it'll make me change my mind?' Her voice rose an octave as her stomach turned over like a washing machine heading into full spin.

Ben considered her question. 'Will it work?'

'No!' she said, sitting up straighter. It was time to put a stop to this. She was losing control of the situation, falling under his spell and that *never* happened. 'We're the best man and maid of honour, both travelling together to do the right thing for our friends,' she said firmly.

'Which means Luna and Marco will soon be married,' Ben teased.

'Which means Luna and Marco will be postponing their wedding,' she shot back.

Ben grinned and held out a hand. 'So may the best man win?' he asked.

'I think you'll find it'll be the best woman,' Rose countered, taking his hand and shaking it once.

Ben chuckled, his dimple winking at her charmingly, and Rose had to steel her insides as they started to fizz. He squeezed her fingers momentarily and she tugged them away from his grasp, shocked by the pure wave of lust that swept through her. 'I'm suddenly looking forward to the next few days even more,' he said as the glittering eyes came out to play again.

Rose leaned away and tried to get comfortable, wondering if she'd misjudged this man and whether the dazzling facade might just run a little deeper than skin. In which case, her quest to delay the wedding might be more challenging than she'd hoped.

'This is your captain speaking,' a female voice suddenly rang out, pausing until the chatter in the aeroplane died down. 'I just wanted to inform you that there's an ongoing incident at Pisa airport which means we're unable to land there at the moment.' Rose turned in her seat and caught Ben's eye as the other passengers began to complain.

'We can't land?' Rose twisted her hands together.

'Doesn't sound like it,' Ben said, looking unsettled for the first time since they'd met.

'We're going to circle the airport until we have more news,' the captain continued. 'For now, please relax while our attendants serve you with a complimentary drink. I'll tell you the minute I know more.'

'Relax?' Rose protested as her shoulders went rigid. A delay was the last thing she needed. She didn't want to spend any more time in this man's company than necessary. He was too confusing. Besides, she had to get to Luna as soon as possible to ensure the wedding got called off, and every minute was wasted time.

2

BEN

'I can't believe we got diverted,' Rose muttered angrily as she absently swung the dog carrier around her legs so vigorously that Ben wondered if Coco was going to get whiplash. He prised it from her tense fingers and watched as she sped up, marching along the cream and glass corridor towards passport control, overtaking at least a few dozen passengers on the way.

Ben followed amused. Rose was a vibrant, prickly dynamo. Exactly his type. Then again, there weren't many women in his experience that he didn't feel at least a modicum of fascination for. He just had no intention of letting it get beyond that again.

'That's what happens when there's a fire at the airport you're supposed to be landing in,' he said to Rose as he caught up, trying not to smile because he guessed it would irritate her. And while he relished watching the flickers of exasperation light up her blueberry-coloured eyes, they had a long drive ahead of them.

'Still, did it have to be Nice? It's miles from where Luna is!' Rose harrumphed as they joined the back of the queue of people, and she carefully opened her brown, leather handbag before pulling out a wallet of neat paperwork. Two large white envelopes fell onto the ground, and she quickly retrieved them and shoved them back into her bag looking perturbed.

She was remarkably uncreased – and despite the stain on her linen trousers, she looked perfect. Ben knew if he was dressed in the same, he'd look like he'd just crawled through a junkyard on his hands and knees — and that was without an accidental coffee spill.

He went back to studying Rose as she retrieved her passport and then Coco's paperwork. Her hair was blonde and styled in a perfectly set shoulder-length bob. Ben had watched, captivated, during the flight to see if even one of the lustrous strands had dared to move out of place. None had – and he'd enjoyed a short fantasy that involved mussing it with his fingertips before he caught himself and stopped.

She was a beautiful woman, but a little tightly wound. He could see that from the way her mouth pursed into a perfectly formed 'o' whenever she was concentrating. As if even the shape of her lips had to conform.

'It's going to take hours to drive to Bellemilia from here,' Rose complained.

'I called Marco when we landed, so he's aware,' he told her.

'When?' Rose's forehead creased and she glared at him suspiciously.

'While you were discussing travel options with Mandy.'

By options, Ben meant Rose had asked if the airline could charter a special plane to take them back to Pisa. She'd been serious too. Needless to say, the hostess hadn't been able to help, although she had offered them both another biscuit which unfortunately Rose had declined. Rose had been most put out when Mandy had offered him her phone number, though, so Ben had decided to put in into his mobile to rile her up a little more.

'Marco understands that we're going to be a little late and he said he'd change the booking for our hire car, so we'll be able to pick it up from here.' He paused and winced. 'He asked if we could make a short detour since it's not that far.'

'Not far from where?' Rose asked as the delicate bow at the top of her lip pinched, and Ben realised she'd found the time to apply a fresh layer of lip gloss, causing him to momentarily lose his train of thought.

'Um,' he croaked, a little surprised by his reaction.

'How far is this detour?' she demanded, narrowing her eyes. 'This isn't some devious plot to keep me away from Luna, is it?'

'Nope.' He chuckled. 'Although I probably should have thought of that. It's just a couple of hours out of our way,' he confessed. 'To a village just across the Italian border called, Neruno.'

'And what's there?' she snapped as Coco let out a rough bark from the carrier and Rose knelt so she could look inside. 'It won't be long,' she told the dog, her voice gentle. 'We just need to go through passport control, collect our luggage and then I'll let you get out for a while, it'll give me a chance to check my emails and talk to my assistant. I've got lunch and treats in my handbag. If you stay quiet, I'll give you some.'

'You think she understood?' Ben teased when the shih tzu growled and started to yap loudly, making Rose look around at the other passengers in the queue and wince.

'I should have remembered that demons can't be bargained with,' she ground out, rising to her feet and smoothing a hand over her trousers.

'Perhaps we should try one of those treats now?' Ben suggested as the dog's barks grew more frenzied.

She frowned. 'She's not doing as she's told. How's she supposed to learn?'

'It's up to you,' he said as the dog's barks intensified further.

Rose sighed. 'Knock yourself out,' she said, reaching into her handbag and handing him a tin. 'Just be careful if you want to keep those fingers. I expect Marco would prefer it if you had all ten. For the wedding photos,' she added with a smirk.

'So now the wedding's going ahead?' Ben teased and laughed when she huffed and turned away, before spinning back.

'You didn't answer my question,' she said, looking annoyed, as if she suspected he'd deliberately changed the subject. He dropped treats into Coco's carrier and the dog quieted down. 'About the purpose of our detour,' Rose prodded.

Ben stood, straightening his legs which were still stiff after being jammed into the tiny space on the aeroplane. 'We're going to pick up Marco's Aunt Aurora. She's a clairvoyant. Apparently, she predicted that our plane was going to be redirected and rang Marco last night to ask if we'd give her a lift.' He kept his face deadpan.

The look Rose gave him would have soured tiramisu, but the corresponding thump in his chest proved he was already half gone on this woman.

'You're mocking me,' she said sternly.

Ben shook his head, stifling a laugh. 'Wait until you meet her. You'll see.'

Ben watched Rose stare at the empty luggage carousel and shake her head for the twentieth time, looking around at the large, bright hall with high ceilings which had all but emptied of the rest of the passengers from their plane.

'Neither of them are here. How's that even possible?' she asked, pacing to the other side, perhaps to check if she'd somehow missed the two suitcases while the other travellers were gathering theirs. Ben frowned at his own small leather bag which had skipped off the belt first, feeling guilty.

'I think we might need to accept that your suitcases have somehow been misdirected,' he suggested tentatively as she turned and fixed him with her deep blue eyes. Somehow, despite queuing for an hour at passport control and waiting here, she didn't look tired. But it was obvious from the way she kept stroking the brown patch on her trousers, that the stain was bothering her.

She shut her eyes momentarily. 'What am I supposed to wear while I'm here? I've got nothing,' she asked when she opened them again. 'Most of my toiletries, clothes, even my phone charger is in my suitcase. Not to mention all my files.'

'I've got a charger, some toiletries and a spare T-shirt you can borrow,' Ben offered.

She winced. 'I'm not sharing your toothbrush,' she said stiffly, looking down her nose at him. 'I've no idea whose mouth it's been in.'

'Just mine.' He shrugged, trying not to be offended. 'Alternatively, we can see if there are any shops open in Nice after we pick up the car?'

'I'd rather get on with our journey,' Rose said. 'I'm sure my luggage will turn up by the time we get to Luna.' She glanced at her outfit looking worried. 'I suppose I should go and report the suitcases missing.' She sighed wearily. 'With any luck, they've somehow found their way to Pisa instead. Lucky them.' With that, she took off.

The queue to report the missing luggage was long and it took almost an hour for Rose to fill in the relevant forms, including details on exactly which clothes and toiletries they contained. Ben was impressed by Rose's recall because the list was both extensive and expensive – she even knew to the penny how much everything was worth. He was quite taken aback by how many suits she'd packed, though.

Then they'd had to queue for the hire car, while multiple passengers fought to secure themselves last-minute transport. Ben was grateful Marco had called ahead, otherwise they might have ended up with a scooter or something equally unsuitable.

The garage was almost empty by the time they were led to their car.

'It's small for three people and a demon with an ego the size of Rome,' Rose observed as she paced around the cherry red Citroën C1, frowning while Ben fiddled with the keys.

'I expect the choices were limited today. I'm happy we have a car at all,' Ben said as he opened the boot. 'And I think we might have to thank our lucky stars that your luggage went missing.' He put in his bag which – despite its size – took up most of the tiny space. Hopefully, Aurora would be travelling light, or one of her spirits would have to arrange some kind of astral luggage transportation.

'We'd have managed somehow,' Rose muttered, looking upset.

'If your suitcases do turn up, I might have to share your wardrobe,' Ben joked, pointing to his small leather bag, hoping he might elicit a smile from Rose who was looking glummer with every minute that passed. 'I'm guessing it's a lot more glamorous anyway.'

She gave him a tired frown. 'I have a Chanel skirt that would suit your colouring, although...' Her eyes skimmed down his length and he felt an immediate burst of heat. 'It'll depend on if you've got the legs to carry it off.'

'Better not risk it,' he said, a little off balance. 'I think it'll be best to put Coco in the back.' He watched as Rose opened the door and secured the dog carrier with a seat belt, ignoring the warning growls.

Coco had been given a twenty-minute reprieve while he'd been queuing for the car and had enjoyed a joyful frolic on a small patch of airport grass. Rose had produced a collapsible dish out of her TARDIS-like handbag and had fed and watered the shih tzu, proving she wasn't as immune to the dog's charms as she made out. Especially considering she'd produced a fluffy toy for her to play with. Perhaps the prickly ice princess did have a heart?

'I'll drive,' Ben offered as he noticed Rose glance at the driver's seat and her forehead crease.

'I can do it. You gave the car hire company my licence too,' she shot back, folding her arms.

'I'm sure you can.' He shrugged as he squeezed himself behind the steering wheel, shuffling back and forth, trying to adjust his legs in an effort to get comfortable. The space was small, and he grimaced as his whole body protested. 'But I know the way to Aunt Aurora's, so I might as well drive us there at least. If you want to take over after that...'

Rose looked a little nauseous, and Ben wondered if there was something she wasn't telling him.

The journey started out well. It was beautifully sunny once they got out of the garage, and he put the air conditioning on full. The roads were busy, but nothing Ben couldn't handle, and he relaxed into the drive, admiring the blue sky and pretty red rooftops on the vibrant white buildings as the road took them upwards, affording them a variety of breathtaking views.

Rose sat ramrod straight staring at the road, seemingly ignoring the broccoli-shaped trees and glimpses of sparkling, azure sea as they flashed past. Instead, she sucked in sharp breaths whenever any cars got within metres of them. After twenty minutes, she opened her handbag and swallowed a couple of pills.

'I get car sick,' she explained when she realised Ben had noticed. 'I was in an accident in Paris when I was a child and whenever I've been in a car abroad since... well...' She straightened her shoulders, shrugging off the confidence, as if by the sheer power of will, she could erase the memory or her reaction to it. 'I'm fine. It's nothing to worry about,' she added after a brief silence.

'So,' Ben said after a pause, deciding to change the subject because she was obviously uncomfortable about sharing her vulnerability. 'Tell me about Luna. How did you meet? If we're going to be alone in a car together for –' He glanced at the sat nav. '– almost three hours until we get to Aurora's, we might as well make the most of it.' He hoped it also might distract her from the other vehicles. The roads were only going to get busier from here.

Rose considered his question for a moment. 'I suppose there's no harm,' she said with an air of someone who wasn't sure she was doing the right thing. 'Luna and I met at Roedean School in Brighton when we were eight. I was a full boarder and she stayed a couple of nights a week. We hit it off and I often used to stay with her family in the holidays. We've been friends for over twenty-three years.'

The air in the car had grown heavy, and Ben wondered what Rose had left out. He could almost feel the weight of the unsaid words – the burden of emotion that hadn't been shared. 'You were young,' he said as he changed lanes. 'Were your parents abroad?'

He saw Rose shrug. 'No, they were in the UK. I wanted to stay at school.' She didn't elaborate. 'Luna's father died when she was in her early teens,' she continued. 'And she was left a trust fund, which she'll inherit in just over nine months. She almost married someone last year. Turned out he was hoping for an injection of cash for his family's business.'

Ben nodded slowly as he absorbed that information. No wonder Rose was worried about Marco. In the same position, he might have the same concerns.

A mobile beeped and Ben saw Rose wince. 'It's my mother,' she explained. 'She wants me to call her so she can ask—' She pursed her lips looking unhappy.

'You can call her now if you like,' Ben offered. 'Is it important?'

'She thinks it is.' She shook her head. 'I'll wait and ring back when we arrive.'

He watched as she picked up her handbag and played with the two crisp white envelopes he'd seen earlier, before placing them back inside the bag and zipping it up.

'You mentioned Luna was close to her mother?' he asked. Marco had shared basic details about his bride-to-be, but there were plenty of gaps he'd like filled.

Although all he really cared about was whether she was going to make his friend happy – and so far, she had. He saw no reason in trying to find cracks in something that on the outside at least, looked ideal. Marco deserved the perfect relationship, and Ben was determined to make sure he got exactly that.

'Deborah Kennedy is an amazing woman,' Rose answered, her voice filled with a sudden burst of warm affection that made something inside Ben's chest heat. 'She's a marine biologist, stationed on an island somewhere off the coast of Scotland. I can't remember exactly what it's called.' She paused. 'Luna and she talk every day – depending on phone signals. Luna told me Deborah is coming to the wedding – she's bringing her grandmother's necklace with her. I've no idea when she'll actually arrive. Travel can be tricky – it's a bit of a trains, planes and automobiles experience and that's before you add in the boat journey.' She winced.

'I'm sure Marco will make sure she makes it on time. He'll do everything in his power to ensure Luna is happy,' he promised.

'I think this might be out of his hands. That's what happens when you rush into things without thinking about the consequences.' Rose gazed out of the window as the vibrant purple lavender that edged the road obviously caught her eye.

'What does Luna do?' Ben asked, pleased that the tension he could see in Rose's shoulders had begun to ease. Her leg wasn't bouncing either.

'She runs a herbal tea business. She grew it from nothing and now she sells to teashops and hotels across the world. It's very successful. It's why she's been in Italy. She has a warehouse in Europe,' Rose said, turning back to him, her voice filled with pride. 'Tell me about Marco. You said you worked together?'

Ben nodded. 'We run an architectural company based in Bristol. We met at university.' He overtook a couple of cars and heard Rose's sharp, peppery intakes of breath. 'Are you okay?' He couldn't stop himself from checking.

'I'm fine,' Rose said wearily, before lapsing into silence. 'Have you met his family a lot of times?' she asked once the traffic around them had eased.

'Yep, loads of times,' he told her. 'I'm like part of the family – his parents joke I'm their second son.'

Ben had no family of his own. His parents had been quite elderly when he'd been born. A happy accident, his mother had once told him, although he wasn't sure his father had agreed. They'd died within a few weeks of each other when he'd been at university. It had been a terrible time, and he'd been inconsolable with grief. For a long while, he'd been alone.

Until the Marinos had taken him under their wing. Which was yet another reason why he wasn't going to let this wedding get messed up. Family is important to Italians, he already knew from the burst of excited WhatsApp messages that they were all beside themselves with excitement about the upcoming nuptials, eager to embrace their new daughter-in-law. It had been the same when he'd got engaged…

He shook his head, dismissing the memory.

'Tell me about them,' Rose demanded. 'I don't even know what Marco looks like.' She tapped her fingers on her thigh looking tense.

Ben reached into his pocket and pulled out his wallet,

holding onto the steering wheel with one hand and eliciting a new gasp from Rose. He handed the wallet to her without taking his eyes from the road. 'There's a photo of all the Marinos in the front, you can take it out.'

He waited while Rose did as he'd suggested. 'Which one's Marco?' she asked after a few moments.

'He's standing in the middle, wearing the dark blue suit. He likes to dress up,' he told her. 'Even while we were at uni.' Marco had drawn a lot of comments from the lecturers, but he'd won his fair share of admiration from the other students too.

Rose sniffed. 'Luna prefers casual, she thinks casual clothes give more away about someone's personality,' she muttered without irony. 'Who else is here?'

Ben knew the image off by heart. He had another copy at home, but carried this one wherever he went. 'The woman on the right, dressed in the—'

'Bright pink dress,' Rose filled in.

'Yes, that's Marco's Aunt A who we're going to pick up.' He saw her squint at the picture. 'Next to Aurora, you'll see her sister – Marco's mother – Elena.'

'She's very beautiful,' Rose commented, although her tone suggested there might be something wrong with that. 'I'm guessing the man on the left is Marco's father?'

'Yep. Leonardo Marino, he's a good man,' Ben said, smiling. 'He's not into suits but likes white shirts and chinos. His father, Marco's nonno, Cesare – that's Italian for Caesar – is beside him.' He pictured the older man's face, which was wrinkled from a lifetime spent in the sun. He was still handsome, and, in the picture, he was grinning. Ben knew he hadn't had a lot to smile about recently, though.

'And the older woman?' Rose asked after another moment of silence.

'The one with the big smile is Isabella Marino, Marco's

nonna. She's...' He had to search for the right words. 'A tricky woman sometimes, but she has a big heart. In many ways, she runs the family or at least she keeps everyone in line.'

'Does she keep you in line?' Rose shot back.

Ben grinned. 'She tries. Isabella taught me how to make the perfect pizza. She also told me how to impress women in Italy.' He frowned, slamming his foot on the accelerator and overtaking a car as it slowed, before pressing his palm on the horn.

'Did she teach you how to drive too?' Rose asked, her voice breaking as she clearly tried to hide her panic.

'Sorry, I tend to get carried away when I'm over here,' Ben said, slowing and allowing a couple of cars to overtake.

Rose folded the photo carefully and placed it back in his wallet. 'Tell me more about the family,' she said. 'Are they close?'

'Yes, very. They own a restaurant in Bellemilia, did Luna mention that?' he asked as soon as the road was clear again.

'She said something about it. She also told me we'd all be staying together in the family house.'

'You don't sound very happy about that,' Ben said.

'In my experience families can be complicated,' Rose said. 'I'm concerned they'll be a distraction. I want Luna to really think about what she's doing without the added pressure of people who might not have her best interests at heart. She can be a bit too trusting sometimes.'

Ben bristled. He couldn't help it. 'I think you'll find the Marino family are just as infatuated with Luna as she is with Marco. They're good people,' he added. 'The best I know.'

'I'm sure they are,' Rose said gently. 'But that still doesn't mean this marriage is a good idea. Wed in haste, repent at leisure is a mantra I share with all my clients.'

'Clients?' Ben asked as a car came up behind them at speed and overtook before weaving back into the same lane, forcing him to apply his brakes again. He saw Rose grip the edges of her seat and swore he could hear the enamel chipping off her teeth. In the back seat, Coco let out a yip. 'I'm sorry,' he muttered.

'While it's tempting, I'm not blaming you for other people's driving.' Rose shook her head and reached into the back so she could pat a hand on the dog carrier, muttering sweet nothings under her breath, and getting a growl in return. When she turned back, she folded her arms.

'You were about to tell me about your clients,' he pressed, partly to take her mind off the other cars and partly because he wanted to know. If he understood Rose better, it might be easier to convince her to let Marco and Luna's wedding go ahead without interference.

Rose sighed. 'I'm a psychologist,' she said. 'I specialise in working with people on improving their relationships. Some of my regulars call me the Love Doctor.'

Well, that explained a *lot*.

'I see,' Ben said. 'Then I'm surprised you're so against what is so clearly a love match.'

Rose snorted. 'I think I need to meet Marco before I can make a decision about that,' she said. 'I'm not against love, but I am against any connection that doesn't go through the proper format.' Her voice was clipped. 'In my experience that's only going to expose people to a lot of future pain and Luna doesn't deserve that.'

Ben remained silent as he tried to work out exactly what that meant – and what might have happened to this woman to make her so suspicious. It was usually easy for him to get people – especially women – to open up. He was about to ask more, but another car sped past and Rose let out a curse. Then she pulled her earphones out of her bag and put them on before shutting her eyes. 'I'm going to try and get some sleep,' she muttered.

Ben remained silent, absorbing the pretty views as they sped towards Italy. But his mind was whirring.

How many more surprises was the woman going to deliver

on their journey? And why – despite their opposing views – with every additional moment they were together did he like Rose a little more?

3

———

ROSE

Rose felt a palm tap her shoulder and jumped in surprise as she stirred from her nap, stiffening immediately as she tried to work out exactly where they were.

'We're here,' Ben said helpfully as she looked around, blinking. The sky was blue, so she knew it was still daytime, but the motorway and deluge of fast cars were all gone. Instead, the Citroën was parked in front of a gorgeous golden-stone villa with a pretty matching veranda bursting with multiple clay pots of pink and white flowers that spilled down their sides.

'Where's here?' Rose croaked, clearing sleep from her throat as the oval wooden front door of the house suddenly flew open and a woman with a bright pink silk scarf wound around her hair and an enormous pair of Jackie Onassis-style sunglasses came bursting outside, beaming.

It took Rose a moment to recognise Marco's Aunt Aurora from Ben's photo. She was probably somewhere in her late sixties. Despite that, her curvy frame was encased in another extravagant, multicoloured dress, with pink and blue sequins sewn across the collar, cuffs and hem. The style was eccentric and very avant-garde. Rose took a moment to absorb the overall effect – lamenting the sorry state of her trousers again – as Ben hopped from the car and met Aurora at the bottom of the veranda's steps. Then he picked her up and twirled her around, his face a picture of pure pleasure.

Rose sat back and watched. She was suspicious of anyone who wore their heart on their sleeve so obviously as Ben. He seemed determined to flirt with everyone – from Mandy to the woman in passport control to the man who'd led them to the hire car. Even Coco wasn't immune.

But those bright smiles and easy conversation surely hid something – like vanity, a lack of self-esteem or a fear of commitment. She guessed it would only be a matter of time before his shiny surface began to dull, and she'd get to see below the surface where the real Ben lurked. That's what her rules were designed to expose. Over time they left no stone unturned, no chance for people to commit to a relationship they – or their children – would ultimately regret.

She opened the door and carefully prised Coco's carrier from the back seat, checking on the dog who was still fast asleep.

'*Bello!*' Aurora trilled as Ben finally stopped spinning and put her down. 'It's so good to see you in the flesh. It's been too long.' Her accent was all Italian, but she spoke in perfect English – probably for Rose's benefit.

'It's only been two months,' Ben laughed, blossoming with pleasure.

'I saw you coming an hour ago in my crystal ball, so I made sure I was packed and ready to leave.' The woman quickly skirted the car and swept Rose into a hug without introducing herself. Rose found her nose pressed into the woman's dress and smelled cherries and incense. She tried to pull away, feeling awkward. She wasn't used to such open affection. 'And you must be the friend of our Marco's *sposa*!' Aurora bellowed as she finally released her.

'She means his wife,' Ben translated as he wandered around the car. 'I know it should be fiancée, but in four days...'

'You speak Italian?' Rose ignored his assumption that she wouldn't be able to persuade Luna to postpone the wedding.

'Isabella taught me that too.'

'Ben is a man of many talents,' Aurora said affectionately. 'Although his manners could do with some work.' She pouted as she widened her eyes at Rose, clearly indicating she expected to be formally introduced.

Ben flushed. 'I'm sorry,' he said. 'Rose Loveheart, please say *ciao* to Marco's Aunt A.'

'Hello,' Rose said stiffly.

'It's Aurora Gallo,' the older woman expanded, offering Rose her hand, which she took. Then the older woman turned it over and began to study Rose's palm muttering as she nodded. 'I'm sure Ben's told you I'm a clairvoyant. I'm also Elena's older sister. That's Marco's mamma, you'll see the resemblance when you meet.'

'Ben mentioned that,' Rose told her.

The older woman narrowed her brown eyes as she looked up from Rose's palm. 'You have an interesting future,' she murmured. 'And the power to smash a vulnerable heart,' she declared as she let go of Rose's hand and winked at Ben.

'I would never...' Rose began. She'd seen far too much of that in her life.

'My tarot cards predicted we might have two romances instead of one this summer – and now I see why. You have a clear palm,' she told Rose. 'A solid line indicating one marriage. When I read your cards, I'll tell you if it'll be happy.'

Rose winced and Ben shook his head. 'I think you'll find Rose is trying to take the number of romances from two to zero.'

He picked up Coco's carrier and walked towards the villa leaving the verbal landmine he'd just thrown to explode.

'Is she?' Aurora asked, sounding more delighted than concerned. 'The cards didn't mention it, so perhaps she'll change her mind...'

Rose didn't bother to argue. She wasn't going to get into a squabble with Marco's relatives about the speed of the nuptials. Hopefully, this whole thing could be handled quickly once she met with Luna and they'd had a chance to talk alone. Then they'd be making their way back to England.

'Is it okay if we put the dog in your garden before we go? She's been stuck in this thing for hours and I've an inkling she'd like to stretch her legs,' Ben said.

Coco let out a delighted yip and Rose saw the carrier bounce as the dog scrambled to the front flap, trying to get out. She couldn't help being both impressed that the man had thought about Luna's pet's needs — and guilty because it should have been her.

'Of course! How thoughtless of me.' Aurora threw up her arms flapping her triangular billowy sleeves which glittered like gold in the sunlight. 'You should all come in – have a glass of wine and freshen up. I'm packed, but I might throw in another couple of outfits. I heard from my sister that the restaurant has a new chef and I do love making Aldo jealous.' She waggled her eyebrows as she overtook them and skipped up the stairs to the veranda, while Ben waited for Rose.

'Aldo?' Rose asked.

'I'll let Aurora explain.' He shook his head. 'She has an interesting take on romance and she's always trying to fix people up,' he confided as they walked side by side. 'I'm looking forward to seeing what you make of each other. Perhaps she might even teach the Love Doctor a thing or two...'

Rose doubted anyone could teach her about love. She'd been through heartbreak, marriage and multiple divorces, and that was just as a spectator to her parents' relationships. Still, she wasn't going to explain that to Ben.

The villa was gorgeous inside with high ceilings and large windows which had all been shuttered because it was the afternoon – although the grey marble floors still shone under the lights Aurora suddenly clicked on. The whole place felt gorgeously cool compared to the dry heat in the driveway, and Rose took a moment to enjoy it as she looked around. Aurora pointed to the garden, and Ben nodded and took Coco out of the carrier and disappeared.

'Please can I use your bathroom?' Rose asked as her attention caught on the stain on her trousers and she winced. 'I had an accident on the plane.' She flushed as she realised what she'd implied. 'Not *that* kind of accident, someone spilled coffee on me.' She pointed to the brown blob. 'And my suitcases have gone missing, so I can't change into fresh clothes. I thought I might try to clean this off.'

'Sì, of course!' Aurora declared. 'But *un momento*, I've plenty of clothes and –' she studied Rose, '– you're not quite the same size, but I'm sure it'll work. I'll get you something of mine to borrow.'

'Oh I couldn't,' Rose said forcefully. The clairvoyant's clothes were extravagant, and she didn't do colour or glitter. Ever.

'I insist!' Aurora said, leaving Rose in the hallway as she disappeared up a swirling marble staircase at a jog. Rose heard her chattering to someone a few moments later, but when Aurora appeared again carrying a number of colourful dresses under one arm, she was alone.

'Is everything okay?' Rose asked as Aurora handed her some dresses, keeping a few extra colourful ones for herself.

'You should change,' the older woman said. 'There's a bathroom over there.' She pointed to the back of the hallway and then went to get a large suitcase from where it had been left underneath the stairwell. She opened it and shoved the new clothes inside.

'Did I just hear voices?' Rose asked as she balanced the outfits on one arm and heard the dull ring of her mobile which was still in her handbag. She recognised the ringtone as 'Heartbreaker' by Pat Benatar – which meant her father was calling.

Rose ignored the call – she didn't have time to speak to him now. Had no idea what to say to him or her mother. The two envelopes were still in her handbag waiting for a response, and she had no idea what to do.

'Don't worry about the voices. That was me talking to Aldo. I'm sure he'll chat with you when we're in the car,' Aurora said as she wheeled her black suitcase towards the front door.

'In the Citroën?' Rose echoed. She hadn't been expecting more company in the small car. Ben hadn't mentioned any other passengers, and she wasn't even sure how they were going to fit Aurora's suitcase inside, let alone another man.

'Go and change.' Aurora wafted a hand towards the bathroom. 'I'm sure we all want to set off soon. We've got an engagement party to attend!' She grinned.

Rose nodded and looked through the dresses, choosing the one with the least glitter on it before hanging the others over the wooden banister at the bottom of the stairs. Then she headed in the direction Aurora had pointed. She didn't want to change, but she didn't want to remain in the soiled suit either. She prided herself on her neat appearance and didn't want to turn up at the Marino home in dirty clothes.

Perhaps if she washed the trousers and laid them out in the Citroën for the rest of the journey, they'd be dry by the time they arrived? Feeling better now that she had a plan, she went to the bathroom.

Rose emerged ten minutes later carrying her damp trousers and wearing a pink dress with a flowing skirt and billowing sleeves that covered half of her hands. The top of the dress slid down her shoulder and she pulled it up feeling self-conscious. The outfit was a tiny bit too big, too long and way too extravagant, but at least it was clean and she wouldn't be wearing it for long. Her luggage was bound to turn up soon. She paced the hallway, searching for Ben and Aurora.

She could see Ben was still in the garden, and he was throwing a ball to the demon, who was clearly besotted with him. Bemused, Rose watched them play for a moment, a little hurt by the way the shih tzu was behaving. For some reason, animals didn't warm to her, no matter how hard she tried with them, and she had no idea why. She was rigid with her rules and pets liked boundaries.

Why were people like Ben adored by everyone without even trying, was it just his pretty looks? She didn't know him well enough to judge but couldn't help finding it irritating.

Aurora began to chatter to somebody again, and Rose spun around searching for her. She spotted an open doorway on the other side of the stairs leading into a dim room.

She silently made her way towards it and peered through. Aurora was sitting in the half-darkness at a round table covered in a blue lacy tablecloth. In the centre of the table was a huge, shiny crystal ball.

'You wish to see my office?' Aurora exclaimed when she spotted Rose. 'Oh!' she gasped as her eyes lit. '*Bellissima!* My dress suits you. I knew it would. You can keep it; I predict there will be plenty of opportunities for you to wear it in Bellemilia. Keep the others too, and I have more you might have need of.' Rose didn't comment and Aurora turned back to stare in the glass ball. 'Come, come.' She waved when Rose didn't move.

'Okay.' Rose took another step into the room, trying to ignore the full skirt as it swished around her ankles. 'This is not what I expected,' she confessed. 'Then again I've never visited a clairvoyant before.'

Aurora nodded. 'You expected red tablecloths, flickering

candles and ghosts shrieking *boo*?' She chuckled, signalling at Rose to take the seat on the other side of the table. It was dim in the room, but her eyes gradually adjusted so she could see past the shadows to the furniture.

'Yep,' she admitted. 'I think I expected to see ghouls too.' She giggled for the first time in what felt like days – but it sounded odd. Then she pulled out the chair Aurora had indicated and sat. 'Is there a secret compartment or a passage in here. I'm sure I just heard you talking to someone. Was it Aldo?' She looked under the table but found nothing but wooden legs.

'*Sì*.' The older woman nodded. 'It is Aldo.'

'Where is he?' Rose asked, twisting around to check the room thoroughly.

'You won't be able to see him, *cara*. He's a spirit.' Aurora quirked an eyebrow when Rose widened her eyes. She should have expected that, the older woman had talked about ghosts, but it was still a shock. 'You don't believe in them?' Aurora asked.

'I only believe in what I *can* see – I'm sorry.' Rose put her hands flat on the table as an urge to fiddle with them overtook her, suddenly aware Aurora's gaze had grown more intense and she was trying to read her.

Isn't that how clairvoyants knew so much about their clients? It was similar in her job, analysing people – although she never had to resort to making things up. Psychology was a science – a series of rights and wrongs, black vs white. There was no room for fantasy or wistful imaginings.

'Ah. Yet you believe in love?' the older woman asked, gifting her with a smile that wasn't malicious. Instead, it was filled with understanding, and it was clear she wasn't trying to catch Rose out.

Rose frowned. 'That's different,' she said. Although she had no idea how to explain why it was.

'Because you believe. I know trust is an issue for you,' Aurora said, nodding at the globe.

'That's not true.' Rose's stomach bunched and she worked hard not to appear affected by the clairvoyant's observation. She trusted people – she couldn't think of any examples right now, aside from Luna. But she did.

Aurora nodded as if she knew exactly what Rose was thinking. 'Perhaps you'll believe in a little more after this trip. Don't you British often say that there are more things to heaven and birth…' she added mysteriously.

'I think you mean there are more things in heaven and earth,' Rose corrected.

'Exactly.' Aurora smiled before leaning forward and staring into the shiny glass ball. 'I see great things for you…'

'A tall, dark and handsome stranger?' Rose quipped, aiming to lighten the mood, as her mind flashed up an image of Ben with his sharp jawline, haunting eyes and kissable mouth… She cleared her throat.

'*Si.*' Aurora's eyes widened. 'Perhaps you have a little of the gift too?'

'I'm sorry, I don't think…' Rose wafted a palm at herself.

'I know, but you will,' Aurora said with a grin, then she cocked her head as if listening to something. 'Aldo says we should leave soon or we're going to get caught up in something on the roads.' She stood suddenly and Rose got up too, watching as Aurora turned towards the wall on her left and tugged out a hidden drawer.

She grabbed a large canvas bag, a pack of what looked like tarot cards and a pair of reading glasses before popping them all inside the bag. Then she gathered up the crystal ball and placed it inside too, topping it all off with a bottle of water and a red lipstick.

'Come on, *cara*,' she said briskly. 'Let's go and find Ben. Your future awaits.'

Rose followed shaking her head. Her future involved persuading Luna to postpone her marriage to Marco, then getting them both back to England before her friend could change her mind. Then her life would return to normal.

There were no tall dark or handsome anythings in her future, she was sure of that.

4

———

ROSE

'I honestly think you'd be more comfortable if you were in the passenger seat,' Rose said again, shifting so she could see Aurora, who'd insisted on sitting in the back of the Citroën with Coco's carrier balanced on her knee. They hadn't been able to put the dog on the seat because Aurora's suitcase was too large to fit into the boot, so Ben had squeezed it in beside her – but it had taken up almost three-quarters of the space.

That did, however, mean Rose had been able to leave her wet linen trousers draped over Ben's bag in the mostly empty boot – which meant they'd probably be dry by the time they arrived in Bellemilia. So at least there was going to be one win.

'I'm okay, *bella*,' Aurora soothed again, patting her red fingernails on the carrier, eliciting an odd purring sound from Coco, who'd totally fallen for the older woman.

Rose's mouth pinched. She had no clue why the dog hated her so much, while she seemed to be having a lovefest with everyone else in the car. Surely animals were supposed to adore the people who took care of them – and wasn't she the one who'd been feeding and watering the demon for the last three weeks?

Ben drove over a bump and Rose's stomach pitched. She immediately shifted to face the front, ignoring the tingles of fear as they vibrated across the surface of her skin.

She'd been twelve when her father and mother had been arguing during a family holiday in Paris. They'd been driving around the Arc de Triomphe. Distracted, her father had gone the wrong way and someone had hit them, making the car roll. Her parents had filed for divorce a few months later, putting an end to the turbulent marriage.

Rose wasn't sure why she hadn't been able to get over the accident. But every time she got into a vehicle abroad and the driver headed onto what she considered the wrong side of the road, her whole body began to tremble. From that point onwards, Rose had tried to avoid being in a car at all. When she went abroad, she opted to stay in locations as close to an airport as possible, then travelled on trains. So until today, the phobia hadn't been a big problem.

She gritted her teeth and squeaked as a car swung out of a side road ahead, forcing Ben to slam on the brakes.

'You should go right.' Aurora pointed a finger towards a turning in the distance and tapped Ben vigorously on the shoulder.

'That sat nav says left,' Ben muttered, pointing to the colourful monitor on the dashboard which was ordering them to do something in Italian. Rose didn't understand the words, but the arrows on the screen were telling them to take the next fork on the left.

'Aldo says right is the better way.' When Rose twisted around to look at the older woman, her eyes were shut and she was muttering in Italian. 'Yes, right and then left. He says it should add –' her forehead creased, '– no! cut, at least an hour off our arrival time,' she promised.

'Aldo,' Ben said carefully. 'I wasn't expecting him to join us on this trip. The thing is Aunt A.' He paused, clearly searching for the correct thing to say. 'We're already going to be four hours late to Bellemilia. I'm not sure we want to risk another detour.' His tone was all reason, and Rose wondered if it would work on the older woman, guessing that Ben was used to getting his way with the opposite sex. 'I texted Marco and the family are going to delay the engagement celebrations. We don't want to be too late, or we might miss them completely.' Ben's tone was pleading now.

Rose sighed – Luna had told her something similar when they'd texted earlier, but she'd hoped to catch her friend before the wedding celebrations progressed any further. An engagement party filled with friends and family would only make it more difficult for her friend to back out or delay.

If they were late... Well, it was going to be awkward enough, and postponing their conversation was bound to cause even more upset. Rose was all about creating a win-win solution. The Marino family would surely understand where she was coming from if she approached the situation calmly and without emotion – sticking with a head vs heart approach. It was the best way to avoid chaos.

'All the more reason to take my *cut short* then, no?' Aurora asked, getting the words muddled again. Rose saw Ben's shoulders stiffen and waited for him to argue. She knew in the same position her father would have insisted he knew best and her mother would have exploded, choosing the opposite route because she couldn't bear to agree with him. The whole thing would have caused a silent rift that would have lasted for days. Instead, Ben shrugged, proving he was even more laidback than she'd first imagined. Was it real, or would his gentle geniality turn out to be a mask?

'Turn right here,' Aurora ordered as they drew closer.

'Turning now.' Ben steered them into a narrow road framed by lofty golden buildings which ran parallel to one another. Most had washing lines, which were full of colourful clothes that had been pegged out in the sunshine, strung between the high up windows. The socks, pants and T-shirts looked like odd-shaped flags. 'I hope Aldo's right about this shortcut,' he said gloomily.

Aurora chuckled. 'Trust me, *cuore mio* – my heart,' she translated for Rose. 'I trust him more than your Google Maps. Besides, he's being most insistent – I think there's going to be some kind of delay on the route you were going to follow, and we don't want to be late, do we, *pulcino?*' This time, Aurora spoke into the carrier which was still perched on her lap, and Coco made a cute chirping sound Rose had never heard.

'Does that mean dog?' she asked.

'No. Little chick,' Ben explained. 'Aurora likes to give everyone their own unique nickname.'

'Once I get to know them properly,' the older woman told her. 'This one's feathers get ruffled easily.' She smiled as she reached into the carrier and gave Coco a gentle stroke. 'But underneath she's as soft as one of your English runny eggs.'

'Right,' Rose murmured, drawing out the word. As far as she was concerned, the demonic shih tzu was more hard-boiled than soft to the core, so she'd stick with her nickname.

Ben nodded. 'Aurora's names are usually perfect. I don't know how she gets it so right.'

'The spirits guide me,' the older woman said mysteriously.

What had Aurora called Ben back at the villa? *Bello.* Rose picked up her phone and searched, noticing the battery was fading. She'd spent too much time fielding emails on the plane. The word meant handsome, which she probably should have expected. Unfortunately, the moniker didn't tell her anything new about him.

She stared out of the front window at the empty road. If a car was travelling the other way, there'd be no chance of avoiding it. Her heart thumped against her chest, registering her growing anxiety.

'Tell me more about yourself,' Rose croaked, aiming to distract herself as Ben took a left onto another narrow street. She could see wide fields of vibrant green grass and rust-coloured mountains in the far distance and hoped that meant they'd leave the village soon.

Hopefully, away from civilisation, the roads would be clear. For a moment, Rose wished she'd said yes to the glass of wine Aurora had offered her back at her villa. If she had, she'd have been able to probably sleep all the way to their destination, or at least it would have been easier to relax.

'You know I'm a clairvoyant, but I used to work in Vegas in my younger days,' the older woman told her. 'I began as a magician's assistant, but after a near-death experience when I was almost sawn in half, I began to hear my ghostly friends on stage, so I started to perform alone.'

Rose shifted her gaze to Ben and pulled a face, wondering if Aurora had fabricated the story, but he didn't look at her. 'You hear lots of voices?' she asked carefully. She'd had a client once who'd said he could hear his mother talking to him – which had been a huge problem for his wife. Especially when he'd insisted on criticising her cooking before telling her the comment had nothing to do with him. After months of therapy, he'd finally admitted that he'd lied. So they could eat less vegetables, apparently. The marriage hadn't survived the revelation.

'I have Aldo with me always, and a few who appear from time to time when they're needed.' Aurora waved a hand as if talking to random voices was the most normal thing in the world.

'Did you know these people when they were alive?' Rose asked, curious as to whether the older woman really believed her story, or if the fairy tale was simply an attempt to deal with a trauma from her past.

'*Sì*, some. Aldo is my husband.' She tapped a hand to her chest as her expression darkened. 'He accidentally fell into a well and passed away on our fourth wedding anniversary.' She cocked her head as if listening to someone. 'Aldo thinks he was pushed by our *postino* because he was in love with me.' She flushed. 'But—' She tutted. 'I think he just had too much Chianti that afternoon.'

'Your ex gives you advice?' Rose steered them expertly towards a new topic. She didn't want to get caught up in a marital disagreement about cause of death.

'He is not my ex,' Aurora said archly. 'But *si*, he does give me guidance, he's very perceptive.' Aurora glanced at Rose and her eyes glittered as she moved her gaze to the back of Ben's neck. '*Very* perceptive.' She sighed. 'So have *you* ever been married?' The older woman waved a finger at Rose.

'No,' she said firmly. She couldn't even imagine it. Probably because the right person had never come along.

Aurora nodded. 'I was twenty-three when Aldo won my heart.' She grinned. 'He says I was *bellissima*, and impossible to resist. How old are you?' the older woman pressed. 'It's not me.' She tapped a fingertip to her temple, her forehead creasing. 'Aldo is asking. Forgive him, he's nosy.' Her smile was affectionate.

Rose widened her eyes. She wasn't used to being on the other end of questions and wasn't sure if she liked it. Especially when she was being quizzed by a so-called spirit.

Then again there was no harm in telling Aurora more about herself. Perhaps if she did, she could get her on side with her plans. Maybe Aurora would talk to her nephew and convince him not to be in so much of a hurry?

'I'm thirty-one.'

Aurora hummed. 'And our Ben, he is thirty-two, so you are perfectly matched.' She smiled and Rose decided not to rise to the comment. 'What do you do?'

'I'm a relationship psychologist. A Love Doctor,' Rose told her. 'I give couples and single people advice.' She waited for the older woman's reaction. She was never sure how people would feel. Some tried to quiz her, others laughed. Many told her she was too young to have enough life experience to guide anyone on a romantic path. Especially since she'd never been married.

Little did they know her whole life had been about giving relationship advice. Acting as a buffer. She'd probably been the only seven-year-old in history to be used as an emotional sounding board. To have spent more of her life soothing and advising her parents on their various relationships than the other way around.

'Aldo, I think that's, what do you say? *Too merciful,*' Aurora muttered, her cheeks pinking underneath her makeup.

'Do you mean personal?' Ben asked. 'What does he want to know?' He sounded amused.

Aurora tutted. 'Aldo wants to know if Rose has had any serious relationships. It's okay if you don't want to answer. It is *fine,* Aldo,' she added in a stern voice.

Rose considered the question. Did she want to share? Was she giving away too much insight into her life? Then again, she doubted Aurora meant any harm; she was just being friendly, getting to know the family guest. 'I've had a few,' Rose admitted. If you counted going out on sixty dates with someone as serious. Which was entirely dependent on how good the dates were. Not very, it had turned out.

For an uncomfortable moment, Rose caught herself hoping Aldo couldn't read her mind before she dismissed the notion. He obviously wasn't real.

'A few?' the older woman queried, leaning forward, still balancing Coco's carrier on her lap.

'Yes,' she said tentatively, breathing in the scent of cherries. 'I mean, I haven't found the one yet. But I know what I want, and I believe in taking relationships one day at a time. There's no hurry. That just leads to chaos and bad decisions.' Something she knew a lot about. Did she sound defensive? Rose schooled her expression into one of tranquillity.

Aurora nodded and her attention drifted back to Ben. 'Sì.' Her forehead scrunched. 'But sometimes taking things slowly leads to mistakes anyway.'

'Aunt A,' Ben warned, and Rose wondered what she was trying to say.

Had Ben got himself into a bad relationship and been hurt? She studied his profile, but his expression remained blank. It was unlikely a man like him would take love seriously enough for that.

Aurora shrugged. 'You have –' She waved a palm and put her other hand on Coco's carrier to stop it from toppling. '– rules?' The skin on her forehead smoothed as she found the correct word. 'Forgive me. Sometimes, I don't understand everything I'm being asked. My English is good, but Aldo's is not and he's trying to stick with it for you.'

'There's no need,' Rose muttered. It's not like she could hear what he was supposedly saying.

But how did the older woman know about her rules? Rose frowned. Perhaps Ben had mentioned something when they'd been speaking in Italian? She nodded. That made sense.

'The word rules is correct,' she said as the car got to the end of the narrow street and continued onwards, finally leaving the buildings behind. Rose felt her chest release as they headed upwards, into the hills, in the direction of the mountains where the cars surrounding them gradually thinned. Perhaps Aldo's *cut short* had been a good idea? She let herself relax another notch.

'Tell me about them,' Aurora said as Coco began to bark. '*Pulcino*. You must be uncomfortable in this tiny prison. *Ti lascerò uscire.*'

'Aunt Aurora, letting her out is not a good idea,' Ben said urgently as the older woman unzipped the carrier.

'Ben's right. She bites,' Rose exclaimed as she realised what Aurora intended to do.

'You both have so much in common!' the older woman trilled as the demon shot from the carrier and immediately scampered onto the top of Aurora's suitcase and barked delightedly. Rose inched forward, away from her, aware Coco's teeth were close to the back of her neck. 'There, she's so much happier!' Aurora said.

'I think she might be the only one,' Rose muttered. Ben chuckled and she wondered if he'd heard.

Aurora smiled as Coco adjusted herself so she could see out of the window, her tiny tail flapping with pleasure. The older woman tossed the empty carrier onto the parcel shelf and gave Rose her full attention again. 'It's a long journey, why don't you fill me in on the details?'

Rose kept a careful eye on Coco as she answered – who knew what the demon was going to do next. 'My rules aren't easy to understand if they're taken out of context,' she explained, worrying about sharing her life's work with Ben and Marco's aunt.

'Don't you have them written down?' Ben queried, slowing as the road narrowed and the tarmac began to get patchy, which meant the vehicle began to shake.

'I have a folder, but it was in my suitcase. I remember them of course,' Rose said as the car rolled over some rocks and shuddered violently.

'Aurora, are you absolutely certain this is the right way?' Ben sounded worried.

'Aldo is sure, and his directions were always *magnifico*,' the older woman insisted, waving a hand. 'Everything he does is,' she purred, turning back to Rose. 'Let's start with your favourite rule if you know them all by heart, *cara*.'

Rose gripped the door handle to stop herself from being thrown around the car as it went over another bump. Her stomach did a series of slow somersaults before she steeled herself to continue. 'I need to preface this by saying I've been a therapist for almost eight years,' she said, her voice trembling. 'My success rate with steering relationships in a more positive direction is second to none.' Which was true – unless you counted her parents; a failure she lived with every day. She thought about the two envelopes in her handbag and winced.

'Aldo tells me you are *very* good,' Aurora said and then fell silent, giving Rose the chance to speak.

She sighed. 'My first rule – and the most important one – is that my clients need to have shared interests,' she said, thinking about her parents again. The only shared interest they'd ever had involved her, or complaining about each other, or their various divorces. Although both of them had moaned about their new spouses with equal gusto, so she supposed that could be considered having something in common.

They'd always been the poster couple for what not to do in a relationship. The warning that had helped her to develop and craft her rules. Her life's work was about ensuring no one else went through the same pain.

'It's what will get them through difficult times,' she continued. 'For instance, Luna is passionate about tea, it's her business. If Marco is too, then that will be an excellent start.' Rose knew nothing about Luna's fiancé. His hot drink preferences would be one of the first things she'd ask.

Ben snorted. 'Marco thinks tea tastes like someone washed their feet in hot soapy water, then decided to drink it.' Rose stiffened. Her worries were clearly founded, and this would be one of the first things she'd raise when she met with Luna. 'He's a coffee man. Milk and two sugars. I am too.'

'Perhaps he should be marrying you then,' Rose said darkly.

'Sadly, I'm not his type,' Ben quipped. 'Too hairy, apparently.'

'Tell me another rule,' Aurora said before Rose could

counter. She turned around and saw the edge of the older woman's mouth twitch as she digested their interplay.

Rose opened her mouth just as her mobile began to ring again, chirping 'Heartbreaker' so loudly that Coco began to bark along. 'That's my dad. I need to get it. I can't really ignore him again.' She shuffled through her bag until she found the phone. She didn't want to answer, but he'd keep calling until she did.

'Dad,' she said into the mouthpiece, twisting her body away from Ben and Aurora towards the window, letting out a surprised gasp as she noticed the view. She'd been so caught up in their conversation and her fears about being in the car that she'd barely looked at their surroundings.

The sky had changed while they'd been travelling. The deep cloudless blue had given way to lively oranges, filled with streaks of brilliant red as the sun had begun to dip lower in the sky. It was now a vibrant semi-circle sinking into the top of one of the mountains. The whole thing made a stunning picture, one she wished she had time to enjoy.

'Rose!' Her father's wail dragged her back to the conversation. 'Where are you?'

'I'm in Italy.' Rose braced herself.

'Why?' he snapped.

'It's a long story.' She knew her dad didn't care. She leaned back in her seat and rolled her shoulders, feeling the tension that had begun to ease during the journey return.

'You received the invite to my wedding, though?' he checked.

Rose sighed, frowning at her handbag where she'd put the two envelopes, noticing her leg had started bouncing again. 'I did.'

'Then why haven't you responded?' he barked. 'You're usually more efficient with your paperwork.'

Rose bit her lip and shifted further around. She didn't want to share her business with Ben or Aurora, but it was difficult not to in such a confined space. 'Do you realise that you've booked your wedding on the same day as Mum's?' She pulled a face. 'Within an hour of the ceremony and a four-hour drive away.'

Had her father realised? Rose hoped not. But she was used to being put in the middle of their relationship, having to deal with the emotional pull from both of them. But she had no idea what to do in this situation. How to navigate it without hurting either of them.

'A mistake,' her father said sourly. 'But you're coming to mine of course?'

'Dad, I don't know,' she said. She hadn't even met his new bride – he'd barely been divorced three months, and she doubted this marriage would last any longer than his last five. 'How well do you know your fiancée?' she asked.

'Enough to know she's the love of my life,' he gushed. 'Rose, I know you won't let me down. I'm going to need you there on the day. You always give such good advice.'

Advice he never followed. 'I need to talk to mum first,' she said. 'Is there any way you can shift the time, or date so I can go to both?'

'Absolutely not, I'm not changing anything for that woman —' The car made a suddenly loud crunching sound before it started to wobble, and Rose's stomach lurched. 'Dad?' she squeaked as the phone lost signal, and she put the mobile down and grabbed the door handle trying not to panic.

'Dammit,' Ben said, steering them carefully off the unmade road onto a patch of spiky brown grass. He climbed out so he could check the car, and Rose saw his mouth pinch. 'Looks like we've got a flat,' he said dully.

'Aldo, you didn't warn us about this!' Aurora complained, hugging Coco to her chest as she peered out of the window.

Rose got out of the car and looked around. The sun was almost hidden by mountains now. How long would it be until it was fully dark and how late were they going to be now?

'Can you change it?' She paced to where Ben was standing. The tyre was pancake flat, and they obviously weren't going anywhere until it was changed.

'Yes.' Ben wiped his hands on his jeans and went to search in the boot. Rose followed, trying not to notice the way his T-shirt rode up, exposing some of the tanned muscle of his back as he bent so he could get a better look. He really was perfect – she'd never responded so viscerally to anyone like this.

Rose had experienced sexual chemistry in the past, but it had never been this strong. She hated the chaotic churning in her stomach, the lack of control in her mind. She could have blamed her feelings on the stress of the drive, but knew it was Ben.

Perhaps having these feelings for him would help her to understand her parents and their multiple marriages better? Clarity on their behaviour might teach her how to deal with them in the future — and it could help when she spoke to Luna later.

Ben turned to hand her the damp linen trousers so she could hang them over her arm. She watched him put his bag on the ground, unable to tear her eyes away as he moved to search again. The light from the evening shadows coloured the planes of his face, making him seem almost otherworldly. She cleared her throat and stepped away, fighting an urge to fan herself like one of the women on the aeroplane.

'The spare will be in here,' Ben said as he stripped the carpet away from the bottom of the boot, exposing a wheel and tools.

Rose heard the sound of a door opening, and when she turned, she saw Aurora had got out and was carrying Coco. 'Aldo says we're not far from a hotel,' she said. 'Perhaps there will be someone there who can help.'

'We won't need them,' Ben said calmly, drawing out the wheel and a bag of tools, his muscles flexing in the dim light.

'Do you need any help?' Rose asked as Aurora drew closer. Coco barked and leaped out of the older woman's arms. As she did, her claws somehow caught on the edge of Rose's trousers, yanking them out of her hands.

'No!' she yelled as the trousers landed on the floor with the dog touching down on top. As if Coco knew how distressed Rose was, she began to trample on the material, driving it further into the dust.

'She's just playing,' Aurora said indulgently as Rose bent to rescue her slacks.

'She did it on purpose,' she grumbled, grabbing Coco's collar and moving her carefully so she could retrieve the trousers. 'I'm going to have to wash them all over again.' She examined the dirty material and whimpered.

Aurora swung Coco back into her arms. 'Don't worry, *cara*,' she soothed. 'I've got plenty more dresses in my suitcase that you can borrow.'

'Well... okay...' Rose swallowed. *Dear God,* she needed her suitcases to turn up now. She watched Ben wheel the spare around to the driver's side, before checking her watch. They were going to be late and even when they did arrive, she'd be wearing an oversized, sparkly dress. It would take a miracle for her suit to be wearable for the party now. No one was going to take her seriously when her top started to fall off her shoulder or she tripped over her skirt.

Ben let out a sudden, loud curse. 'The tyre's flat!'

'Which is why you're changing it,' Aurora said reasonably.

'I mean the spare one is too.' Ben sounded annoyed.

'It can't be,' Rose stuttered, moving closer to Ben who was now prodding at a hole in the tyre with his finger. 'We need to get help,' she said.

Ben pulled his mobile from his pocket and frowned at the screen. 'Do you have signal?'

'I lost it when I was talking to my dad, but I'll check.' Rose went back to the car and collected her mobile from her bag, then her heart sank. 'No.'

'Do you have a phone?' Ben checked with Aurora.

'I don't need one, *cara*,' she said, hugging Coco.

'Aldo doesn't happen to have a direct line to whatever the Italian equivalent of the AA is, does he?' Ben joked wearily.

'No. But he suggested we walk. To the hotel.' The older woman pointed to the narrow track leading away from them in the direction they'd been driving. 'Hopefully, someone there will be able to help.'

Ben sighed before turning to Rose. 'I don't think we have much choice,' he said, before going to pick up his bag.

'Let me get some essentials from my suitcase!' Aurora yelled, bolting to the car with Coco still under her arm. Then she retrieved her bag with the crystal ball and added a couple of clean dresses and some other bits.

Rose watched them as they began to walk and shook her head. This visit was turning into a disaster. They were going to miss the engagement party, and by the time they arrived, it would be harder than ever for her to convince Luna she was making a mistake...

5

———

BEN

'I'm so sorry, there's no one here to help with the car.' The woman behind the counter of the hotel gazed at Ben adoringly before frowning at Rose and Aurora looking less than impressed. Then again, after an hour's walk on a hot, dark and dusty road, he knew they all looked unkempt.

'Well, when will someone be here to help?' Rose grumbled.

'He'll be here, *mattina* – in the morning,' the receptionist told her slowly, as if she were talking to an idiot, in a mixture of Italian and English.

'Surely you have a number for somebody who can come now?' Rose asked, dismissing the receptionist and turning as if she expected Ben to have a repairman on speed dial and glaring when he shrugged, making him choke down a chuckle.

She was so uptight; he'd never met anyone who needed to let go so much – and there was something about her that made him want to be the one who set her free.

Then again, he had a history of falling for the wrong women and he wasn't going to do it again. He was all about casual these days, and Rose clearly wasn't a woman who'd consider anything like that. She'd probably tie him up in rules before they were even allowed to kiss.

'I've got the paperwork from the car,' he told her. 'I'll start by calling someone from the hire company to see if they can help. Why don't you both see if you can find us something to eat and drink while I try?'

Aurora nodded and Rose pursed her lips as he paced towards the front of the hotel with his mobile. When Ben returned ten minutes later, they were sitting in the reception area in round orange seats surrounding a coffee table, and there was a spare chair ready for him. On the floor, Coco was eating from the bowl Rose kept in her handbag.

'The kitchen's about to close, but they're going to rustle us something up at astronomical expense,' Rose told him, her mouth pinching into an unhappy line.

'Rose is *allarmante*. Scary,' Aunt A translated with a girlish grin. 'The woman was unable to refuse her – which is good because Aldo tells me the chef here is *magnifico!*' She swished her glittery skirts as she crossed her legs, and chuckled when Rose pulled another face.

Ben was beginning to suspect Aurora enjoyed winding Rose up as much as he did. She hadn't given the spiky Love Doctor a nickname yet. Was she too difficult to read or was Marco's aunt waiting for something, another spooky sign perhaps?

'I'm afraid the car company can't get anyone here until the morning either,' Ben told them, scratching his fingertips along his scalp, which felt gritty and hot after the long walk from the car. He needed a shower, preferably a cold one, or better, a long, hot soapy bath. Maybe Rose would offer to scrub his back? He glanced at her. *Maybe not.*

'Where are we going to sleep?' Rose asked, looking dismayed, her face paling despite the fact that her cheeks were endearingly pink from the recent exercise.

'We asked about rooms, but there aren't any available. The

receptionist says we can't sleep here – although if you ask, she'll probably offer to share her room with you.' Rose took a moment to turn and glare at the woman with an intensity that might have scorched snow if there had been any. 'And there isn't another hotel for miles. What are we going to do?'

'Aldo says not to worry, all will be taken care of.' Aurora, looking relaxed, wriggled her middle and index fingers mysteriously.

Rose pulled a disbelieving face, just as the phone rang at the reception desk and the woman answered and began to speak in rapid Italian. Ben couldn't make out all the words, but Aurora started to nod and smile.

She'd always claimed she could commune with spirits, and until this moment Ben had taken her words with a pinch of salt. Marco had never questioned his aunt's talents, but Ben had always thought that was more about family loyalty than anything else. But after today, he was beginning to wonder if perhaps Aurora did have a gift, after all. Then again, if she did, why hadn't she warned him about his ex?

He watched the receptionist smile at him as she put down the phone, and he wondered briefly if she was indeed going to offer to share her bedroom with him. Then he saw her tap something into the computer before shimmying out from behind the desk, just as a waiter emerged from another doorway.

He carried a large white plate filled with bruschetta, mozzarella balls, olives, cheeses and various breads. Ben inhaled the mouth-watering aroma and his stomach grumbled. The man placed the plate on the coffee table without comment before ceremoniously whipping out smaller plates, napkins and cutlery. Aurora immediately grabbed a dish and dug in. 'Do you have wine?' she asked cheerfully, and the waiter nodded without smiling, then disappeared.

'We have two twin rooms available last minute. They are connected by a shared bathroom – we normally reserve the rooms for families, but we will make an exception for you,' the receptionist told Ben, completely ignoring Aurora and Rose.

'Why is the accommodation only available now?' Ben asked, curious as to why they hadn't been vacant earlier.

'What is the saying you English use?' Aurora queried as she swallowed three olives in quick succession. 'Something about looking at a gift horse and a mouse?'

'Mouth,' Rose corrected as she added a couple of tiny pieces of food to her plate. 'Don't look a gift horse in the mouth.'

'Why would you ever want to do that?' Aurora barked as she fed a piece of chorizo to Coco who gobbled it with gusto, somehow avoiding the older woman's fingers.

Ben heard Rose sigh.

The receptionist echoed her. 'The people who had reserved the rooms just called to say their plane was diverted and they can't get transport here tonight.' She smiled shyly at Ben. 'This is a lucky break for you, no?'

'Perhaps they were sent to Nice too,' Rose muttered darkly. 'I suppose we should be grateful we made it as far as here. Even if my suitcases got lost and the car's as useless as a chocolate teapot.' She looked around, her expression anything but thankful.

'Chocolate teapot? But it would melt, *cara*—' Aurora glanced up, her forehead squeezing in confusion.

'Do you want the rooms or not?' The receptionist complained, directing her question to Rose.

'*Sì*,' Aurora said quickly, nodding vigorously. 'We will take them both.' The woman smiled and winked at Ben, then she headed towards the counter.

'Who's going to sleep where?' Rose asked roughly, glaring at Ben with distrust.

'Of course, you will share with me,' Aurora soothed. 'But I apologise, *cara* – I talk in my sleep. To Aldo and other...' She wafted a hand. 'Friends. I can't help myself.' She mimed zipping her mouth up before unzipping it again and shaking her head.

Rose shrugged. 'That's okay. I think I could sleep through anything at the moment,' she said wearily. 'I'm sure it'll be fine. I'm just a bit worried.' She glanced down at her dress looking startled, as if she was surprised by what she was wearing. 'I have nothing to wear to bed. I can wash my trousers again ready for tomorrow.' She eyed the linen trousers which she'd laid over one of the orange chairs and grimaced. After being trampled on the ground by Coco, Ben suspected they needed CPR to revive them rather than a quick rinse in the sink.

'I have a nightdress,' Aurora said, eyeing Rose speculatively. 'It's very sexy, and I've always loved orange silk.'

'I have a T-shirt you can borrow,' Ben chimed in, guessing the no-nonsense Love Doctor would prefer to wear something less glamorous, and trying not to picture her in seductive nightwear.

'You've already loaned me enough of your clothes,' Rose said politely to Aurora. 'Thank you, I'll take the T-shirt,' she told him.

'*Buono*. I have a new dress for you to wear tomorrow, though. I insist.' Aurora grinned when Rose paled. She turned to Ben, '*Bello*, you take Coco to your room.' She pointed to the dog. '*Pulcino, mi raccomando*. I've got my eye on you.'

'Just make sure she doesn't try to eat you while you sleep,' Rose whispered.

'She'd do that?' Ben gaped, watching the dog bolt down the rest of her food enthusiastically, suddenly worried. It was only when he caught the hitch of Rose's mouth that he realised she'd been teasing him. It came as a surprise; he hadn't seen a hint of humour from her until now. He liked it – which was not a good sign.

'We should go to bed,' Aurora said, swallowing another piece of bruschetta before rising.

'I'm just going to eat something first,' Ben said, watching as Rose bent to pet the dog, who immediately yapped and tried to bite her hand. She looked hurt, but the emotion was wiped from her face so fast he wasn't sure if he'd imagined it.

She pointed to the dog carrier and bowl. 'Good luck,' she said lightly before following Aurora.

When they were halfway to the reception desk, the waiter appeared with a bottle of red wine and three glasses. Aurora grabbed them. 'I'll leave your drink in your room, *bello*,' she promised as the receptionist gave her a key.

Rose was about to follow but suddenly stopped. 'I need to speak to Luna.'

'I'll see you in the room,' Aurora sang as she disappeared through a door leading to the bedrooms.

'You want to talk to her now?' Ben asked.

Rose nodded. 'I was trying not to speak with her until we arrived. But we need to tell her that we're not going to make it to the engagement party tonight.' She checked her watch and winced. 'We're already late, I can't believe I forgot until now.'

'I already told Marco we weren't going to get there. After I called the car hire company.' His friend had been worried at first, but when he found out what had happened, he was more relieved that they were all okay. He'd been a little concerned when Ben mentioned Rose's intention to convince Luna to postpone the wedding. But Ben had told him not to worry. Even though he had no idea how they could stop her from carrying out her plan.

Rose frowned. 'What did he say?'

'That they were going to postpone the engagement party until tomorrow, so we can all be there.'

Ben saw Rose's eyes flicker and wondered if she was pleased. Tension tightened his shoulders – this whole situation was playing into her hands. Delaying the party meant she'd have time to speak with Luna and encourage her to postpone the wedding before it got too far.

He'd had a chance to see her in action now. She was demanding, persuasive and tenacious too. They were qualities he admired. But if Rose set her sights on Luna, would she be able to convince her friend to delay the wedding? Should he be taking the threat to Marco's happiness more seriously? He frowned. It would be easier to see Rose as the enemy if he wasn't attracted to her. He shook his head – he was an idiot, and he needed to pull himself together.

'I could call her now,' she said thoughtfully.

'Marco said they were going to have an early night,' Ben lied. It was an impulse; one he wasn't particularly proud of. He felt bad, but Marco had sounded so happy on the phone. If Rose spoke to Luna, the bride might start to have doubts. But surely once Rose saw the happy couple together, she'd rethink? Which meant he was going to have to try to stop her from talking to her friend this evening. Whatever it took.

'But it's not that late...' Rose said, checking her watch again.

'Italy is very romantic and they are engaged...' Ben trailed off, hoping Rose would fill in the details for herself. When she did, her blush was swift and he rocked on his heels, shocked by the intensity of his reaction to it.

Rose gulped as heat travelled down her neck. 'Fine,' she croaked. 'I'll call tomorrow.' She tugged her mobile out of her bag. 'If I can find a phone charger, that is – I'm almost out of battery after the journey and speaking with my dad. My charger is in my suitcase.'

Ben thought about the charger in the bag currently hitched over his shoulder. 'I left mine in the car, and as you know, Aurora doesn't carry a phone,' he said.

Was all really fair in love and war? He hoped so, but that didn't stop him from feeling guilty. 'If you switch yours off, you can save your battery and charge it tomorrow.' That way there would be no chance of her calling Luna before the morning and no chance of her friend getting in touch with her either.

Rose stared at him for a beat, and he felt a flush begin to form at the back of his neck. Could she see he was lying?

She finally nodded. 'I suppose.' She sighed, then fiddled with the side buttons on her mobile until the screen went blank. Then she turned and headed after Aurora, leaving Ben wondering why he felt so bad.

6

BEN

Ben lay in one of the double beds staring up at the ceiling of his hotel room. He'd drunk the glass of red wine Aurora had left, taken Coco for a quick walk and switched off the light ready to sleep. But his mind was whirring, thinking about all the things that had happened today. About how he'd lied to Rose about the charger, already warned Marco about what she was planning to do. He knew he'd done the right thing – protected his friend from the humiliation and pain of a wedding being cancelled. But he didn't feel good about it.

Coco shuffled on the bed beside his feet. He'd tried to move her onto the floor multiple times, but the dog kept hopping back onto the mattress and snuggling in. In the end he'd given up – the shih tzu was stubborn and he had to get some sleep. The car hire company had told him they planned to send someone out early to fix the tyre. Which meant he'd have to wake, dress and walk back to where they'd left the car to make sure someone was there.

He heard a soft knock on the door leading to the bathroom and waited for beat in case he'd imagined it. The knock came again, and Ben got up and pulled on the jeans he'd dropped on the ground before unlocking it.

'Sorry.' Rose looked embarrassed when he swung it open. The bathroom was large and the stark light from the overhead bulbs lit up the white T-shirt he'd loaned her. It swamped her and made him wonder what was underneath. Ben swallowed and met Rose's eyes just as he heard an odd noise. It could have been someone moaning, but surely a human couldn't sound like that?

'What's that?' He looked around the bathroom. Did the hotel have rats? It might explain why the receptionist hadn't wanted to rent them these rooms at first. Maybe she'd made up the story about the previous booking but had taken pity on them?

Rose glanced at the door which connected to her bedroom. 'Aurora,' she whispered, blanching. 'She's been at it since we went to bed. She's either snoring, talking or shouting and she hasn't stopped.' She let out a long breath as the clairvoyant yelled something in Italian. 'I thought I'd be able to sleep through it, but—'

'Aldo, you need to stop doing that, *dolcezza*,' Aurora bellowed, her words audible this time. 'I know we're married, *caro...*'

'It wouldn't be so bad if she was only shouting in Italian, but for some reason she keeps switching to English, probably because she's been talking to me all day,' she grumbled.

'I see,' Ben said as Rose let out a forlorn sigh. 'You want to come in?' He took a step back, unsure if she'd agree, even less sure if he wanted her to. He could smell strawberries and wondered if it was her shampoo. 'It's just Coco and me. No ghosts or wild parties I'm afraid.'

'I'm disappointed, seems I might have got you all wrong.' Rose gave him a half smile as her eyes skimmed the room. He hadn't turned on a light, but there was enough coming from the bathroom to illuminate the two double beds and bedside table that separated them. There was also a small wardrobe and a dresser covered with cream doilies. 'Oh,' Rose said, striding to pick one up and switching on a lamp. 'My grandmother used to have loads of these.' She held it up to the light. 'Mum used to put them around our house until Dad threatened to burn them.' The look of enchantment on Rose's face evaporated as she recounted the memory, and Ben got a glimpse of an emotion he couldn't quite read. He took a step towards her, before he caught himself and stopped, gulping down his need to soothe. He wasn't looking to bond with this woman.

'Do you still have the doilies?' he asked instead, injecting his voice with a teasing tone, trying to lighten the mood.

'I've got a few in my loft,' she said, looking sad. 'Mum took them with her when they divorced, but her third husband hated them and tried to throw them away. I managed to rescue a few when she agreed to dump them for him.' She frowned. 'She tends to be very pliable when she's in her honeymoon phase.'

'Is she still with him?' Ben asked.

'No.' Rose sounded amused. 'She's on husband number six. At least she's about to marry him.' She looked perturbed.

'You don't like him?' he asked.

Rose sighed. 'We haven't met. Mum enjoys a whirlwind romance, so there's not usually time to meet the daughter before the confetti gets thrown.' She paused. 'I'm sure he's perfectly nice – and probably wrong for her. I expect the marriage won't last. It's a pattern I've grown used to. But I'll be there to pick up the pieces until the next man comes along.' She winced.

How would it feel to be constantly caught up in other people's relationships? Worse, to be a shoulder to cry on one day, and dismissed the next? And why didn't Rose just walk away?

'Aldo, stop tickling me!' Aurora exclaimed, and Rose

widened her eyes and quickly went to shut the door to the bathroom, instantly muffling the shouts.

'I'm sorry,' he said.

'It doesn't matter.'

Ben decided not to ask for more details. The more he knew about this woman, the more he seemed to like her and he really didn't want that. Distance was the only way to handle his attraction. Although that was going to be difficult if they were sharing a room...

'Actually, I'm sorry.' Rose suddenly shook her head. 'I know this is an imposition.' Her eyes shifted to his unmade bed before they shot back to him. 'I tried to sleep in the bathroom, but...' She glanced at the bed on the other side of the room which hadn't been touched, her expression filled with longing.

'You're welcome to stay in here with me.' Ben shoved his hands into the pockets of his jeans, suddenly realising he wasn't wearing a shirt. Had Rose noticed? He swallowed before nodding at Coco. 'At least we'll have a chaperone.' His voice was rough.

'I'm not sure I can rely on the Demon to save me – or you for that matter.' She winced. 'Besides, that's not a problem. I'm not your type and you're definitely not mine.'

Rose's eyes skimmed his chest, and Ben could have sworn they lingered, making him wonder if she was telling the truth. He wanted to ask why he wasn't her type. Why she thought she wasn't his, but knew that would be a terrible idea. Surely it would be easier to keep his attraction in check now he knew they were on the same page.

He felt a prickling sensation under his skin, and turned abruptly so he could tug out a fresh T-shirt from his bag before pulling it on. At this rate nothing would be clean when they got to Marco. He winced – what if one of his friend's relatives offered to share their wardrobe with him?

Rose cleared her throat when he turned back, perhaps realising she'd been staring. Ben wrapped his arms around himself as she began to pace. The air in the room had grown hotter since they'd shut the door, despite the fan spinning above their heads. Why did the atmosphere suddenly feel heavy and why was he finding it so much more difficult to breathe?

This is exactly what he'd spent the last two years trying to avoid. Keep things light, don't let anyone get the upper hand was his mantra. So, why was his body ignoring all that excellent advice?

Rose pushed her hair from her shoulders as she turned around. It was mussed from when she'd been lying down, but the *just-got-out-of-bed* vibe looked surprisingly good on her – and was having the oddest effect on his ability to listen to his misgivings and do the right thing.

'You can take that bed,' he said gruffly, pointing to the other double.

'Thanks.' Rose sounded breathless. She hopped in and lay on her back, then pulled the covers over herself, tugging them up to her nose, her fingertips gripping the edge of the sheet tightly.

Ben went to switch off the lamp and quickly shrugged off his jeans before climbing into his own. Then he lay staring at the ceiling – how was he supposed to get any sleep now?

After a few moments, he heard a muffled shout.

'I'm now realising why the Marinos always put Aunt A on the top floor of the villa, far, far away from everyone else,' he muttered. Rose snorted out a laugh and Ben found himself chuckling too before they both lapsed into an awkward silence.

'Do you think my suitcases will turn up?' Rose asked suddenly.

Ben winced. 'I'm not sure,' he admitted. 'I lost my luggage on the way to Italy three and a half years ago and it never arrived. I had to claim everything on insurance.'

He frowned. He'd packed an engagement ring ready for a

proposal that he'd been planning for months, and he'd had to claim for that too. Now he wished he'd seen the fact that it went AWOL as an omen and called the whole thing off.

Instead, Marco had insisted on taking him to a jeweller in the village where he'd found the perfect replacement. Ben shook his head. He could have saved himself a lot of heartache if he hadn't bothered.

Rose sighed.

'I'm sure Luna will be able to lend you something. Failing that I've got at least one more clean T-shirt.'

'Luna is tiny, the only thing I could borrow would be her socks,' Rose grumbled. The bed creaked and he guessed she'd turned to face him. The breath lodged in his throat.

'I'm sure Aurora has plenty more dresses for you to borrow,' he said, and grinned.

'That's what I'm worried about. It's very generous of her, but the style, all those colours and glitter, it isn't quite my thing...'

'Perhaps you could work together at the wedding. You can give advice on love and she can predict if it'll work out.' He was joking, but Rose didn't laugh. 'Sorry...'

'Not everyone believes in what I do,' she said quietly.

He frowned. 'I didn't say I didn't believe in it.' He sighed, suddenly wanting to make amends. He hadn't been trying to insult her; he'd just wanted to make her laugh. 'If I'd hired you two years ago, you might have saved me from making a big mistake.'

Ben shut his eyes, reliving the moment when he'd been standing at the end of the makeshift aisle the Marinos had set up in their garden. Waiting for his fiancée, Sophia, to join him. She'd been late and he'd been so nervous, but excited too. Marco's father, Leonardo, had given him a high five trying to get him to smile and Marco had started to look concerned.

Ben let out a long breath, feeling a wave of grief wash

through him. He hadn't thought about that moment for a long while and didn't particularly want to think about it tonight. Especially not now he was back in Italy and about to attend a wedding in the same place. He didn't want to relive those feelings – he was over them and on a new and better path.

'What happened?' Rose asked carefully.

Ben pulled a face. He hadn't meant to share. He didn't give pieces of himself away anymore. It made it easier to stay intact. But he'd started this conversation, and he knew Rose was too tenacious to let it go. She proved that a few moments later when she cleared her throat.

'I was jilted, at the altar,' he said bluntly, keeping his voice clear of emotion.

'I'm sorry.' She sounded like she meant it, and Ben wanted to bat the words away. He wasn't looking for sympathy. He didn't need it. He'd got over what had happened and changed. He wasn't looking for a happy ever after anymore. At least not for himself.

'That's okay. She did me a favour.' He grinned into the darkness, injecting his voice with enough levity to prove he was telling the truth. 'We had a big party afterwards, no one was standing by the end.'

He'd made sure of it. He'd laughed and joked his way through the whole event – proving to himself and everyone else that he didn't care. Fake it till you make it had proved an effective blueprint to dealing with a shattered heart. One he'd continued to use until all that fakery had morphed into truth. 'The food was amazing and the cake was better. I sent my ex a slice, it was the least I could do.'

She'd responded with a pretty note in her best handwriting, apologising. Telling him she wasn't ready, that she'd realised she didn't want to marry him. That she'd been infatuated, because of his looks.

Shame she'd only found her voice a few minutes after the wedding march had started playing.

Something seemed to wedge itself in Ben's throat and he cleared it away with a cough, moving his leg in case it woke Coco and she wanted to go out. He'd welcome a walk around now. Didn't want to stay in the room with the truth spinning between them like a plate about to come crashing down. He was about to get up when Rose spoke.

'My parents got married after meeting on holiday thirty-two years ago.' She paused, perhaps in an attempt to stop her voice from wobbling. 'It was a mistake, but by the time they got back from the honeymoon, my mother was pregnant with me and they decided to stick it out for a while. For my sake. They stayed together for thirteen miserable years and they've both remarried more times than I care to remember. None of those relationships have worked out either.' She sounded bitter. 'I'm truly sorry about what happened to you. Your ex should have told you earlier – I can only imagine how much that hurt, but...' She sighed. 'Do you ever wonder if she did you a favour?'

'Every day,' Ben replied. 'I got to keep the presents, so I won't need a new toaster until after I retire.'

Rose didn't laugh, but Ben could almost hear her mind whirring and wondered if her next question was going to hurt. 'So your mother is marrying again?' he said, before she could ask him anything.

Rose fell silent. 'Yes.' Her voice was matter of fact. 'Actually, both of my parents are planning their next wedding – on the same day, as it happens.' He thought he heard her gulp in the darkness and recalled the broken pieces of the conversation that he'd overheard in the car. 'I'm supposed to choose. It's like a game they play. Who gets to have Rose today? I don't know why, but they enjoy hurting each other.'

And in the process, they hurt Rose. 'What are you going to do?' Ben asked.

'I've no idea.' She sounded unhappy.

'You could miss them both?' he suggested, wondering why a woman like Rose would allow herself to be manipulated.

'If I go, I'll be able to give at least one of them some advice, see if this time their marriage might be different.' She sighed. 'If I don't try, what does that say about me?'

That you've learned some things aren't your responsibility, Ben thought. 'Is that why you're so against Marco and Luna marrying?' he asked.

Rose sighed. 'I don't want to see anyone make the same mistakes. It leads to a constant cycle of unhappiness that's difficult to break. It's better to get it right from the start. Why choose to be with someone who might not be right for you? I like to think of it as putting down the right foundations. You do that when you build a house—'

'That's true,' Ben murmured, thinking about his plans at work, how a building always needed the right roots. 'Bricks shouldn't move once you cement them in; unfortunately, people change and grow.' Or they hid things from you and moved the goalposts so you didn't know where you stood.

'If the foundations are right, they can change together.' Rose sighed again and the sound merged with the fan, joining with another shout from Aurora, creating a chorus of anguish that Ben didn't know how to feel about.

Then his mobile beeped, alerting him that the battery was going flat.

He'd meant to charge it earlier, but he'd got distracted by the wine, Coco and then Rose's visit. 'Sorry that's my phone,' he said, patting the ground in the dark, searching for his charger which was already attached to the plug adapter and ready to use.

'What are you going to do? You'll need your mobile tomorrow,' Rose asked, sounding worried as he found what he needed and plugged it into a socket that he'd spotted by the bed earlier.

'It's fine, all sorted.' He lay back and heard Rose let out a sudden splutter of air.

'I don't believe it!' She clicked on the lamp and Ben shielded his eyes from the light as he sat up and turned to face her. Rose was sitting up in bed staring at him, her eyes wide and burning with anger.

'What is it?' he asked as Coco woke too and began to growl.

Rose threw back her covers offering him a tantalising glimpse of bare leg before tramping around the bed and pointing to his charger. 'You had one here all along.' She folded her arms. 'Why would you...' She trailed off as her face transformed from confused to annoyed. 'You didn't want me to talk to Luna. That whole story you spun about Italy being romantic.' Her jaw dropped and she shook her head, looking upset.

'I—' Ben blew out a breath, scratching a hand over his forehead. 'It was just a white lie – all for a good cause.' He winced, suddenly embarrassed – why did allocating an untruth a colour make it less of a betrayal? 'I just thought it would be better if we waited until we were all together. I didn't want you persuading Luna to postpone the wedding without Marco being there,' he explained, trying to sound reasonable.

She glared at him, her eyes sparking pure fury. 'Yet it's okay for you to speak to Marco?' she asked, her voice icy.

'It's not me who's trying to cancel the wedding,' he blurted, caught off guard and regretting the counter as soon as he said it.

Ben knew he'd said the wrong thing when Rose reared back and gave him a look of disgust.

'And yet you seem so determined that it goes ahead,' she shot back. 'Why does it matter to you so much? Is there something about Marco you're not telling me?' The pitch of her voice had changed, grown fretful.

Aurora punctuated her words with another loud shout and Rose let out an angry hiss, before marching to the bathroom door and pulling it wide.

'I think I'll take my chances with the ghosts. It beats sharing a bedroom with a snake.' she said before turning back to him and narrowing her eyes. 'Looks can be deceiving. I'm not sure why I forgot that.' Then she walked into the bathroom and slammed the door.

Ben stared at it for a moment wondering how trying to do the right thing for his friend had put him so firmly in the wrong – and more importantly, how he was ever going to get Rose to trust him again.

7

ROSE

Rose was furious. She'd let her guard down. Had begun to believe that perhaps Ben was a decent man, one that she could trust – but now it was clear he was her nemesis, right to the very marrow of his deceiving bones.

She'd kept her eyes shut for most of the journey to Belle-milia, refusing to communicate with him but responding to Aurora whenever she commented on the view or shared funny anecdotes from Aldo. It might have been childish – more like the way her parents sometimes behaved – but she couldn't seem to help it around him. Forget the power of pheromones, Ben Pearson was more like her own personal kryptonite.

She was so disappointed. She'd begun to like him and that was something she rarely allowed herself to feel. Then again, it was probably for the best. They'd get there soon, and she couldn't allow herself to lose focus even for one second. Luna's future was on the line.

'We're here,' Ben said, sounding relieved as he stopped the Citroën in front of a cream stone restaurant with a sign indicating they'd arrived at La Marina.

Pots of fragrant olive trees and barrels of pink hydrangea

lined the large patio and steps leading up to the entrance. People were sitting at the wooden tables in the sunshine eating pizza, fresh salads and large plates of pasta, and Rose's stomach grumbled as she got out of the car and caught a whiff of the delicious food.

There'd been no time for breakfast this morning, and the receptionist at the hotel had begged the chef to at least provide a picnic for Ben. But even a flash of Ben's gorgeous smile hadn't persuaded the chef, and Rose had briefly pondered what was wrong with him. She might not trust Ben, but that didn't dim the power of his extraordinary good looks.

Through the entrance of the restaurant – which was framed by a rustic archway decorated with apricot pansies, magenta dahlias, and purple snapdragons – Rose could just make out a room filled with yet more chunky tables, chairs, shimmering glasses and sparkling cutlery. Soft music was playing, giving the buzzy restaurant an authentic and relaxing feel. Almost every seat was taken by a customer; most chatted or laughed while they tucked into the wine and food. She could feel the warm ambiance from where she was standing by the car and suddenly wished she was sitting inside.

She moved to the other side of the car and saw an open doorway leading to a terrace at the far end of the restaurant. A single empty table had been laid with glasses, plates and fresh cutlery. Knobbly, leafy trees hung over the table that would shade the patrons from the midday sun. Rose wondered if the table might have been set for them.

Luna suddenly bounced from the right of the entrance, followed by a dark-haired man wearing a navy suit.

'We've been tracking you for hours!' her friend exclaimed, tossing a strand of white-blonde hair from her oval face as she grabbed Rose and gave her an enthusiastic hug, beaming. 'Only you could take this long to get to my wedding,' she teased, pulling away so she could look Rose up and down, her heart-shaped mouth pinching. 'What are you wearing?' she asked, her face a picture of confusion as she took in the azure dress Aurora had insisted Rose put on this morning. Since her cream linen trousers would need an act of God to get clean after Coco had trampled them, she hadn't had much choice.

The dress was sparkly, with a long flowing skirt that she'd tripped over more than a couple of times. It had a low bodice that, because it was a little too big for her, exposed her collarbone and far more of her chest than she'd have liked. 'You look stunning!' Luna declared, hopping up and down, her delicate lace dress fluttering around her knees, as she took Rose in.

'I do not and this is not mine,' Rose said firmly. 'I texted you when we arrived in Nice to say my suitcases went missing, remember? They still haven't turned up.' She fiddled with the soft material of the sleeves self-consciously. 'I borrowed this from Marco's aunt.'

After finally getting to use Ben's charger in the car, she'd phoned the airport to see if there was any news about her luggage, only to hear the staff were still looking. They were very apologetic, but Rose suspected they weren't confident they were ever going to arrive.

'Of course!' Luna blushed as Aurora stepped out of the car and, holding Coco under one arm, gave the younger woman a hug. 'I'm Luna Kennedy,' she said.

'Indeed, you are. I will read your palm later, *cara*, but I can already tell that you are the perfect fit for my nephew. He can be a little inflexible at times, and I can tell you are going to be quite the antidote.' She grinned. 'My husband, Aldo, thinks you're delightful too.'

'He always agrees with you,' Ben said with humour. 'Funny that.'

'Where is Aldo? Didn't he come?' Luna asked, looking towards the back seat of the Citroën.

'He is with us in spirit,' Aurora said mysteriously, wafting a hand as she handed over Coco.

'Ah.' Luna nodded as she took the dog and Rose realised that she'd probably already been tipped off about the clairvoyant aunt. 'Of course. Nice to meet you, Aldo.' Luna spoke into the sky and then turned back to Aurora. 'I'd love a reading; Marco and his family have told me how talented you are.'

'Of course, *cara*,' the older woman promised. 'You and Rose are the first on my list. We will start with my crystal ball. That's the easiest way to tell if your marriage will last – and how passionate and fruitful it will be. Or...' She winked at Rose. 'If there is a new love on the horizon.'

'We should do it tonight!' Luna gushed.

Rose coughed. The reading sounded like a terrible idea. Yet more fictional promises when her friend needed to focus on cold, hard reality. Rose also suspected Aurora had set her sights on getting her together with Ben – and she had no intention of engaging with that fantasy. The man spelled TROUBLE in sparkly capitals.

Luna pressed her nose into Coco's fur. 'I've missed you,' she purred to the demon, stopping momentarily to give Rose a cheeky grin. 'Did you two make friends over the last few weeks?'

'We have a new understanding,' Rose said dryly. 'Involving her ignoring me and me not turning her into a winter coat.'

'I know you love each other really,' Luna snorted. 'You're just too stubborn to see it.' She let out a sigh as she perused the dress Rose was wearing again. 'This is making me rethink your outfit for the wedding.' She took Rose's hand. 'This is a much more feminine look for you. More like my style.' Luna pointed to her own sheer, floaty skirt. 'You seem more approachable – you're more likely to find yourself a husband if you dress like that.'

'I have no intention—' Rose shook her head. She was used to Luna winding her up about her lack of love life.

Her friend grinned cheekily, her skin pinking under her tan. Usually, Luna looked pale – a result of all the hours she spent working on her tea business, toiling over emails late into the night. But she looked less stressed, happier than Rose had seen her for a long while. It was a good sign, but it might just be the result of time in the sun – it wasn't necessarily Marco's doing.

Her insides tightened as she imagined how hurt Luna would be if their romance fizzled out, or if she ended up falling for him, only to discover he was after her money – or something else. Even if his motivations were true, they could be all wrong for each other. Hadn't Rose seen the results of impulsive weddings over and over with her parents? It's why they had to wait, to make sure they knew each other properly and weren't walking into a terrible mistake.

'There's no need for you to buy anything new.' Aurora pointed to her suitcase in the back of the Citroën. 'I've plenty of dresses for *leonessa* in here.'

'What does that mean?' Luna asked, glancing over her shoulder towards the man who was whispering urgently with Ben.

She recognised him immediately from the picture Ben had showed her. He was just as handsome in the flesh, a little swarthier than Ben. Not quite as tall, or as good-looking as Ben, but Rose considered that to be a point in his favour. Dazzling people with your lucky DNA was bordering on rude. He broke off his conversation and gazed at Luna as if he knew she was looking at him – his whole face suddenly lighting up.

'It means lioness, *tesoro*,' Marco said, pacing towards her, his gaze intense.

'And that means darling,' Luna told Rose. 'Lioness.' She nodded studying Rose. 'That fits.'

'It is apt.' Ben eyed her too, although his expression was

more playful. 'Mostly because you're never sure if she's going to ignore you or wrestle you to the ground so she can bite off your head.'

'You already know her so well.' Luna laughed and reached out to grab her fiancé's hand, tugging him closer. 'This is Marco,' she said, skirting her arm around his lean waist and spinning him until they were facing. 'And this is my best friend, Rose. It's essential you love each other as much as I love you.'

Marco gave Rose a tentative smile, but it was clear from his guarded expression that Ben had already filled him in on her intentions and was concerned. She should have seen it coming, but it was still disappointing because it meant she was going to have to work extra hard to get the groom on side.

'It's a pleasure to meet you,' Marco said formally, offering Rose his hand. 'We've got a table set up on the terrace for the five of us. Unfortunately, the rest of my family aren't available this afternoon. Wedding plans,' he added, his eyes filled with meaning. 'But we'll see them all at the family villa later for our engagement celebrations.'

'We're all staying there,' Luna gushed. 'It's absolutely huge!'

She grabbed Rose's hand and propelled her until they were trotting up the steps at speed, heading towards the entrance of the restaurant. 'You'll get to meet everyone later and I know you're going to love them all. Just wait until you try the food. I've already put on three pounds.' She tapped a palm on her flat stomach.

Rose tried to keep up, but her foot caught in the long skirt halfway up the steps. 'No!' she yelped just as Ben appeared from nowhere and grabbed her elbow, pulling her upwards just before her head crashed into the tiles.

'Thank you,' Rose rasped, and Luna echoed her agreement.

'He's your very own prince charming,' she gushed.

'Hardly,' Rose huffed. 'I really need to get some clothes that fit.'

Ben insisted on holding on to her until they reached the top and then Rose shook off his hand, irritated by the tingles left shooting across her skin.

She was *not* going to let herself be attracted to him.

'I'm sorry about last night,' Ben whispered as Marco caught up with Luna and guided her ahead of them, leading them through the busy restaurant towards the table on the terrace that Rose had seen earlier.

She paused when they got outside to gaze at the view. It was spectacular. On the right of the balcony were fields of twisty, blooming, grape vines heavy with fruit – on the left, a crisscross of hills filled with pink, orange and green plants and trees were framed by a stunning blue cloudless sky.

She took in a deep breath before turning back to Ben. 'Sorry about lying to me, or sorry you got caught?' she asked coldly, taking a seat at the end of the table, closest to the view. Luna headed towards the chair opposite, but somehow Ben beat her to it.

'Why doesn't Aunt Aurora sit next to Ben, then I'll sit beside Rose and you can be at the head of the table?' Marco suggested to Luna. 'It means we'll all get to see how beautiful my fiancée is and you'll get the most magnificent view of us all.'

Luna beamed at him and sat, gathering Coco close. Rose could see her friend from here, but there would be no chance of a private conversation. Were the two men trying to separate them?

Ben leaned forward again as Aurora began to chat with Marco and Luna. 'I guess I'm sorry about both,' he said, answering her earlier question, his voice low.

'You're not going to stop me from speaking to Luna,' she said, glancing at her friend who was now talking animatedly, waving her arms as she recounted a story.

Ben shrugged. 'You strike me as the type of person who

usually gets what she wants. But for now, can we please lay down our swords and enjoy lunch?'

'I suppose,' Rose muttered, sighing. 'We do need to eat.' Soldiers didn't go into battle without a full stomach, and she wouldn't be at her best if she was hungry.

A waiter appeared from nowhere and began to pile the table with large platters of delicious-looking food. 'I haven't ordered anything,' Rose told him.

'We've chosen all our best dishes for you to sample,' Marco said before he pinched his nose, looking like he was going to sneeze. 'Try it all, see what you enjoy.'

'We're thinking of serving a lot of this at our wedding,' Luna said excitedly from the end of the table. 'It would be wonderful if you could tell us what your favourites dishes are. I refused to organise anything until you arrived.'

'You shouldn't rely on me...' Rose said tentatively. 'You know how I am with strange food.' She believed in sticking with what you knew. That way there was less chance of getting it wrong.

Luna laughed. 'Well, I asked Mum, and she said a bowl of cereal, so I think you'll be more help than that.' She tickled the demon under the chin as Marco suddenly sneezed, swiping tears from his eyes.

'Where is your mum?' Rose asked, talking loudly so Luna could hear above the din.

'It's taking her a while to get off the island. Apparently, the ferry's been out of action, but someone's promised to take her in their boat.' Luna shrugged. 'The only problem is she's not sure when they'll be able to do it. So she's just waiting at the moment. She's bringing my grandmother's sapphire necklace; it's my borrowed, old and blue.' She smiled shyly. 'I know I'm being superstitious.'

'She'll get here, *cara*,' Marco said, patting her arm. 'You'll have your jewellery, I guarantee it.'

'But what if she can't make it?' Rose asked reasonably. 'Surely it makes sense to delay things until you're sure she's going to arrive?'

Perhaps persuading Luna to postpone the wedding would be easier than Rose had imagined. If Deborah couldn't get here in time, surely they'd have no choice?

'I'm sorry, but it's not going to be possible.' Marco frowned.

'Sadly, it's not.' Luna nodded. 'We plan to hold the wedding on the same day as Marco's parents married,' she explained. 'Which is in four days.'

'It is a lucky day for the Marinos,' Marco said, picking up his wine. 'My grandparents also wed on this day and their parents before them. It is important to my family, and it cannot be changed.' His voice was firm.

Luna smiled at Rose. 'I'm not worried, Mum won't let me down. She'll get here somehow – fate will be on her side.'

'Indeed, it will,' Aurora agreed. 'Aldo says she will definitely be on time.'

Rose pursed her lips. The special date explained Luna and Marco's haste. It also meant her plans for an alternative wedding in Brighton would definitely be rejected. But whether Deborah would be there was another matter altogether.

'So now you understand why everything's happening so quickly,' Luna said, beaming.

'I suppose.' Rose shrugged. They could still have done it on the same date in a year, but she wasn't sure Luna would want to hear that argument.

She leaned back in her seat as the food began to pile up, filling every available space on the table. When the waiter had finished, he began to explain what everything was, pointing at each of the plates as he spoke. 'Polenta crostini with tuna; cala-mari with garlic aioli and a lemon wedge; olive and caper bread; bruschetta; antipasto with bean dip; mozzarella and balsamic vinegar; meat, olives and cheese.' He tried his best to speak in

English, but his Italian accent was heavy, making some of the words difficult to understand.

Rose was pleased when he performed a dramatic flick of his wrist and left just as another man arrived loaded with empty plates. He doled them out as a woman dressed in a tight black suit arrived and began to fill their glasses with crisp white wine and sparkling water.

Rose noticed she took extra care filling Ben's, hovering around him for longer than necessary. He glanced up at her a couple of times, speaking quietly and even winking once. He was obviously incorrigible when it came to women. Was that why his fiancée had decided not to go through with the wedding? Too afraid of losing his attention long term?

'It's amazing here, isn't it?' Ben asked as the waitress left and he began to tuck into the feast. Rose found herself nodding out of politeness.

She'd never been to Tuscany – partly due to her fear of being in a car on the wrong side of the road, and partly because she preferred her home comforts – and always knowing what was coming next. Also, her parents kept her busy and she was loathe to leave them alone for long without support.

She picked up a piece of calamari with her fork and glared at it suspiciously as Ben scoffed down three.

'You're supposed to eat it, not turn it to stone,' he joked when he noticed, stabbing another two.

Rose grimaced and took a bite. It tasted surprisingly good, not what she'd expected, and she quickly swallowed. 'Do you stay with Marco's family every year?' she asked, glancing at Luna who was still being monopolised.

Ben nodded. 'As I said, the Marinos are my family. I come two or three times most years with Marco and for Christmas. I used to come more regularly because my ex's family used to live close by.'

'They've moved away?' she asked.

He nodded. 'They wanted to make a fresh start.' He shrugged looking unconcerned. He looked around as a couple got up from one of the tables and someone came to clear. 'It's busy today.'

'Isn't it usually?' Rose asked sharply. 'Are the Marinos...' She paused. She didn't want to be rude. 'The restaurant does seem busy, but is that because it's July? I've heard of businesses struggling out of season, even in a place like this.'

Her mind whirred as she looked around. What if Marco had needed to get engaged to someone? What if it hadn't mattered who it was, and meeting Luna was simply a happy accident? Was the story about the date being significant simply an excuse to push through the nuptials?

Luna was about to become a very wealthy woman. Italian laws were complicated, and she hadn't had a chance to investigate what happened during a marriage or divorce.

Ben's eyes narrowed as he stared at Rose. 'Yes, it's always like this. Busy and successful. The whole family work hard and this place is a testament to that,' he said flatly. 'I'm sure once you've had a chance to get to know Marco and his family, you'll see there's really nothing for you to worry about. Luna and Marco will be very happy, and their marriage will last for years. Give them a chance.'

'I've been counselling couples for almost eight years,' Rose said as she plucked an olive from a bowl and nibbled the corner. She didn't normally like them, but this one was plump and a tantalising mixture of salty and sweet. 'Many of their marriages are in trouble and almost all of them wedded in a rush. A lot of them have wonderful families – it doesn't necessarily mean tying the knot was the right decision.'

She paused for long enough to eat the rest of her olive and to take a tiny sip of the delicious wine, considering her next words carefully. 'Most of the couples I see didn't know each other well when they embarked on their supposed lifetime together.'

'Have they all split up?' Ben asked. 'I thought you were all about saving relationships?'

She sighed. 'I'm good at what I do, but even I can't work miracles. Couples need to want to put in the work. They also have to listen to my advice and learn to be honest with themselves.' She paused as her parents flashed into her mind. Neither of them ever listened to her. She put her fork down, suddenly losing her appetite. 'I will say almost all of them wish they hadn't rushed into their marriages. Mostly they see that as the root cause of their mistakes.'

Ben scratched his head. 'My parents weren't dating for long before they got engaged.' He looked reflective. 'Speed didn't make a difference to them. They were together for over forty years – and as far as I know, they were happy for all of it. Marco's parents are similar.'

Aurora let out a sudden loud burst of laughter across the table.

He added, 'Aurora met Aldo in Vegas, and they married a week later. Their marriage is still going strong.'

Rose didn't want to tell Ben what she thought about that marriage. Aurora was wonderful, but clearly a fantasist. Or perhaps it had simply been too painful to let go of her husband? 'There are always exceptions, but I don't think we can bank on them. How long were you with your fiancée before you decided to marry?' She regretted the question when she saw the look of shock on his face. 'Sorry, I shouldn't have brought that up.'

'It's okay.' Ben waved a hand as Luna giggled and leaned closer to Aurora. He waited until their laughter died down, his easy-going expression returning. 'I knew Sophia for a year before I proposed, and we were engaged for almost another two.' He paused. 'I met her when I was visiting the Marinos, and we took it from there.'

'A holiday romance?' she asked.

'Not for me, but...' His expression remained blank. 'If we'd known each other longer, I'm not sure if it would have made a difference. She didn't feel the same way. Surprising, I know.' He flashed her a smile, and Rose wondered if it was real.

'Perhaps if she'd had more time, she would have realised it before you got to the altar,' she said gently.

'We had over three years. Besides, I'm not sure time is as important as you think. When you know, you know, and when you know it's wrong, you're probably right.' Ben shrugged.

Rose had another sip of wine and waited. Silence was the space where you learned the most interesting things. Pieces of puzzles people didn't always intend to share. It was irritating how much she wanted to get to know Ben, how much she suddenly wanted to flesh out and colour in the empty spaces of his life. Did he care, or was he just as emotionless about his relationships as he was making out?

'So you have rules that you think make relationships work?' Ben asked.

Rose took a slice of mozzarella and used a fork to push it around her plate before nodding, suddenly wary. Was he going to make fun of her?

'Yet you're not married or in a serious relationship – at least that's what you told Aunt A. Why is that?'

A waiter appeared and began to clear some of the empty plates. Another topped up Rose's wine before she could tell him she didn't want more. She picked it up and sipped, using the time to gather her thoughts. 'I haven't met the person who is right for me yet,' she said slowly. 'My rules are important, but they have to work in tandem with – rather than replace – things like chemistry and attraction.' Things that had been sadly lacking for her.

'Chemistry?' Ben checked, and when Rose looked up, his eyes were dark. 'You have a rule for that?'

'Nope. That happens by itself,' Rose said as something in her chest fizzed. She cleared her throat. 'I think a shared sense of humour is important too. You should enjoy the same things.'

Ben raised an eyebrow when Luna and Marco began to laugh, their heads bobbing together. 'Okay,' he said flatly. 'I had all those things with my ex, but my relationship still didn't last. As far as I'm concerned, there are no guarantees, although it would be easier if there were.' He paused. 'It would have saved me a fortune in caterers and rings.' He folded his arms and gave her a half smile. 'Tell me about your other rules, I'd like to know if I was missing something important.' Rose could see from Ben's expression that he was sceptical.

She sighed. An unbeliever – she dealt with them all the time. 'One.' She wriggled a finger and then sipped some water to counter the alcohol. 'You don't sleep together until you've been seeing each other for at least seven weeks.'

Ben's mouth tipped. 'Seven,' he choked. 'Why not six?'

'Years of study,' Rose said. 'By seven you'll have started to let your guard down, there will be less secrets. If there are cracks, and you're willing to look, you'll begin to see them. Time makes things more difficult to hide.'

'But what if you can't keep your hands off each other?' Ben looked more indignant than amused.

'That's where restraint comes in,' Rose said dryly. 'Instant gratification is one of the biggest curses of our generation. Lovers need to wait rather than leap in.' Her eyes tripped to Luna who was stroking Coco and gazing at Marco adoringly. 'That way we know what we're getting ourselves into. There's less chance of making a mistake.'

She'd had a front row seat for every one of her parents' disasters. It was enough to put you off love for life. Although she hadn't lost faith. If you followed the rules and met the right person, a happily ever after was possible, if not guaranteed.

'Sounds to me like you're trying to take the romance out of love,' Ben said softly.

'That's not it,' Rose shot back, picking up her wine again. This conversation was unsettling, but she didn't want to give Ben the upper hand by letting him see she was rattled. 'There's room for it, you just have to savour, take your time.'

Ben looked sympathetic. 'By denying each other.' He frowned. 'I'm not sure I like your rules.'

Which was hardly a surprise, but his words still bothered her. 'There's nothing wrong with them,' Rose said stiffly, pushing her empty wine glass into the centre of the table. She'd had enough.

'Tell me another,' Ben said.

She sat back in her chair and considered him. 'You shouldn't marry until you've been together for a year – and it's important to know exactly what you both want for the future. I have a checklist I give my clients.'

'A checklist.' Ben smirked, swallowing the rest of his wine. 'I'd love to see a copy.' His smile had returned, and his eyes were sparking with amusement.

'You're not a client, but I'm sure Marco will share it with you once I give him a copy. I just need to find a printer so I can print them from my laptop,' Rose said primly as the three waiters appeared again, carrying another mountain of food. 'We should eat.' She banked her irritation as they began to place the dishes on the table. 'Disagreements don't mix with food.'

'Is that another rule?' Ben teased as the waitress – who'd been ogling him earlier – came to refill his wine glass. He smiled up at her again and then blew a kiss. Rose swore she could hear the woman's hormones combust.

She forced her gaze back to the grape vines away from the table and took in a slow breath. Annoyingly, it was even more obvious now that she and Ben were on opposing sides and there would be no convincing him that she was right.

So be it. She just had to work out how to convince Luna to postpone her wedding without him or Marco getting in the way.

8

BEN

'I've arranged a special surprise,' Marco said as the waiters appeared again, and he pushed back his chair and stood, sweeping his gaze to take in Aurora, Luna and Rose, who was still seated opposite Ben. The table was littered with empty plates after they'd all gorged themselves on an incredible selection of desserts. Ben wasn't sure if he'd be able to move, he'd eaten so much.

Even Rose had surprised him by trying a spoonful of each – her pretty face flushing, as if she'd been embarrassed about showing her pleasure. Every bite she took had been so cautious, so careful – she'd been fascinating to watch.

He wondered now if that was another of her rules – a deliberate attempt to stop herself from leaping into anything and enjoying herself. But why was she so wary: was it just her parents? It was startling how much he wanted to know.

'What surprise?' Luna asked excitedly, rising to her feet too, still clutching Coco. Ben hadn't had a proper chance to speak to Marco, so had no idea what his friend had planned.

'A tour of the kitchen for the three of you!' Marco declared as a man Ben recognised as one of the chefs, and two waiters, strode towards the table holding a tray filled with colourful drinks. 'Here's a selection of *digestivos* for you to take with you while you're exploring.'

'Aldo and I would love to see the kitchen.' Aurora stood and rubbed her stomach. 'But I'm not sure if I could eat or drink another thing, *caro*.' Despite her declaration, she quickly grabbed a glass from the tray and took a sip. 'Well, maybe just a small Limoncello.'

'I'm not sure I can either,' Luna said, grinning at Marco and kissing him on the cheek. 'But I'll try like Aunt A. Thank you, it's a lovely idea, and I know Rose will enjoy meeting the team.' She picked up an *amaro* and a *passito* and offered both to her friend. Rose stood and went to join the two women, taking one of the drinks, before giving Marco and Ben a suspicious look.

'What about the demon? You can't take her into a kitchen,' Rose said, eyeing the dog which Luna was still carrying.

'We'll leave her with Marco.' Luna grinned. 'They can get to know each other. It's important they get on. She's going to give him the rings during the wedding ceremony.'

'She's more likely to eat him,' Rose said darkly.

Luna tried to pass the shih tzu to her fiancé, but he waved his arms and shook his head.

'I'm sorry, *tesoro*.' He blinked and then sneezed again. 'I'm allergic.'

Rose looked over at Ben, and he could read her triumphant expression. *Dammit*.

'To dogs?' Luna sounded shocked. 'But—'

'I'll take an antihistamine later. We'll work it out, *cara*,' Marco soothed, his brown eyes crinkling. 'If you love Coco, then I'm sure I will learn to love her too, eventually.' His face contorted as he fought another sneeze.

'I'll take her,' Ben offered, taking the bundle of fluff in his arms. Coco immediately settled into his chest, wagging her tail.

'We'll be waiting for you – and I'm sure Coco will do

exactly as she's asked,' Marco promised, his eyes continuing to water as he eased away from Ben. He watched the three women leave the terrace, before taking the seat Rose had just vacated.

Then Marco stared at the dog for a moment, his expression brooding before he leaned away as if trying to avoid her scent. 'We need to do something about your Rose,' he whispered.

Ben's heart skipped. 'She's not my anything,' he said roughly. Never would be – only trouble lay in that direction. Trouble he had no intention of seeking again.

His attention shifted to the other side of the terrace, to the doorway Rose had just walked through. He tried to catch of glimpse of her before he realised what he was doing.

What had got into him? He was behaving like a horny teenager. The waitress who'd been serving him wine had scribbled her mobile number on a card and sneaked it to him earlier, but he'd barely acknowledged it at the time. He'd been too caught up with teasing Rose. He'd fish the card out of his pocket later, see if she wanted to meet for a drink. That would be the best way of getting the Love Doctor out of his mind.

'Regardless – you need to help me keep her away from Luna. At least until after the wedding,' Marco muttered, falling silent as a new waiter appeared and placed cups, a jug, sugar and a coffee pot on the table before disappearing.

Marco poured them both a shot of espresso without a word. The liquid was thick and black, and Ben knew it would help clear some of the food and wine from his system. Maybe it would straighten out his wayward hormones too.

'I know I sound possessive, but Rose and Luna must not be left alone,' Marco repeated, his brown eyes worried. 'At least not until Rose has had a chance to settle in. She should get to know me and see how happy Luna is. I can't lose her – not now I've finally found my true love.'

Ben sipped his coffee and winced. 'You just sent them off together. They're going to have plenty of time to chat now.' He added a couple of sugars and a large dash of milk to his cup, leaning back in his chair and trying to relax as a cooling breeze skipped across the patio, ruffling his hair.

'No.' Marco shook his head. 'I asked the team to keep the three of them busy. They will fill them in on the history of the restaurant, the food, anything they might find remotely interesting. There will be no opportunity for alone time at all.'

Marco, looking concerned, scrubbed a hand through his thick dark brown hair. 'I know Rose is important to Luna and that she will listen to whatever her friend has to say. She's told me about Rose's job as the Love Doctor.' His forehead creased. 'How she counsels people and helps their relationships work. She has many rules, apparently.' He winced. 'Luna respects her and wants Rose's approval for our wedding.'

'Which I've told you Rose is unlikely to give,' Ben said, taking another sip from his cup.

'Si.' Marco looked unhappy. 'I don't want to interfere with their friendship. It's important to Luna.' He sighed. 'But I don't want Rose to talk her out of marrying me either.'

'She's going to try,' Ben said seriously. His friend had looked happy when his fiancée was here, but now he could see the lines of concern etched around his eyes. He knew how much Marco had been hurt by his last girlfriend and didn't want that to happen again.

'She can only try if she gets the chance,' Marco said, his unhappy expression morphing into something more determined. Ben knew that look from work – usually when Marco was trying to convince a client to choose his most innovative architectural design.

'What do you mean?' Ben asked slowly, taking another sip of the hot liquid. It was at least thirty degrees in the shade, but the coffee was still doing a good job of cooling him down.

'There are four days until the wedding,' Marco said. 'I need you to keep Rose occupied so she doesn't get a chance to talk my fiancée out of marrying me. At least until she sees for herself how well suited we are.' He tapped a finger on his chest. 'Which of course she will.'

Ben wasn't sure of anything. Rose had some very rigid ideas and was overprotective of her friend. With good reason, if her stories about Luna's previous relationships were true. He cleared his throat. 'I'll do whatever you want. But Luna will get suspicious if we lock Rose in the wine cellar and she disappears.' He laughed just in case Marco thought he was serious. His friend was clearly smitten with his new fiancée, and Ben wasn't sure how far he'd go to make sure the wedding went ahead.

'We won't have to resort to that. Women love you. I saw the new waitress earlier.' Marco waggled his eyebrows. 'Perhaps you could distract Rose with a—'

'Romance?' Ben snorted, shaking his head. 'Are you asking me to seduce the maid of honour?' He wasn't serious, but that didn't stop his idiot body from reacting favourably to the idea.

'Of course not.' Marco shrugged. 'But it wouldn't be the first time you've tempted someone. She's beautiful, serious and opinionated – exactly your type.' His dark brown eyes were lively.

'I don't have a type anymore.' Ben stared into his drink. 'I'm happy to spend time with Rose, but I'm not going to have a fling with her,' he said firmly. 'Firstly, she wouldn't be interested.' Coco let out a chirpy bark from where she was curled up on his knee, and he wondered if the dog was agreeing or warning him off.

'Secondly, it's not the right thing to do. I'm not looking for a fake date. It all sounds great on paper, but people –' Probably him, '– might get hurt.'

Thirdly, Ben liked Rose, and he'd sworn off getting involved with anyone he knew he could develop real feelings for. Still, the thought appealed – and for a nanosecond, he considered it before dismissing the idea.

Marco sagged. 'Okay, I understand, my friend. I don't want you to do anything untoward. I just thought I saw a spark between the two of you when you arrived.' He nodded. 'But will you agree to keep her busy and away from Luna, at least until she has a chance to get to know me and my family?'

'I can try,' Ben said. 'But we should be practical. Rose is going to get suspicious if she's forced to spend all her time with me. Perhaps Elena, Leonardo, Cesare, Isabella, even Aurora, might be able to keep her occupied sometimes?'

Marco nodded, looking a little less stressed. 'I spoke to Mama and Papa after you called last night. Nonno and Nonna I will speak to later, if I can get them in the same room.'

'Are they still fighting?'

'Yes.' Marco looked unhappy. 'Nonna keeps trying to talk me out of getting married.' His frown disappeared momentarily. 'On second thoughts, perhaps we should keep her away from Rose too.'

'Tell me how I can help,' Ben asked, squeezing his friend's shoulder.

'Could you two run some errands together, give me more time with Luna? Surely Rose can't disagree with that?'

Ben thought about spending more time with her, and he tried to read his mixed feelings as interest prickled his senses. 'It could work.' He nodded. 'But –' He frowned. '– I need your family to understand that Rose is on Luna's side. She isn't some terrible stranger trying to mess up your wedding.'

Marco gave him a curious look. 'You are worried about how my family see her?'

Ben shrugged, trying not to show how much he'd grown to like the woman. 'She's not the bad guy here. She's wrong about you, but that doesn't make her the enemy.'

He'd seen the odd flash of vulnerability since they'd met, and he didn't want her to somehow get hurt. She might be misguided, but Ben could tell she was coming from a good place. His parents had never pulled him into their marital squabbles. A lifetime of that could skew the way you saw love. It would definitely make you wary.

'You like her.' Marco's eyes sparkled and he suddenly grinned. 'Then I don't understand what's so wrong with my original plan.'

'I like Coco, but that doesn't mean I'm going to date the dog,' Ben said dryly. Irritated, because a part of him did like Marco's idea. Flustered, he picked up his coffee. 'Tell me about these errands,' he snapped, sipping so much that it burnt his mouth. It was strong and he'd probably be tossing and turning all night, but at least it was helping to sober him up. Not that he'd drunk much, but he still felt a little lightheaded. *And that had nothing to do with Rose.*

Marco waved a hand. 'Mama has a list of jobs. Choosing the food and wine is now done, but making the party favours, ensuring the wedding attire fits, generally keeping everyone sane. I found the rings, but Luna and I still need to get them sized. Mostly we can handle everything, but there will be the odd job.'

'Okay,' Ben said. 'I'll keep Rose busy, but you're going to have to stop Luna from looking for her too.'

'I can keep my fiancée occupied.' Marco winked. 'And if you change your mind about the romance...' He waggled his eyebrows again.

'Not going to happen,' Ben insisted. He had Rose Loveheart's measure, and he wasn't going to let her get within a mile of his body or heart.

Marco grinned. 'I've known you for a long time, *amico*, and in the words of Shakespeare, I think you doth protest a little too much...'

9

ROSE

Rose stared out of the window of the Citroën as Ben steered them down a windy, gravelly road, following Luna and Marco who was driving a yellow Alfa Romeo. She blinked, feeling weary. The tour of the restaurant kitchen had been fascinating, but the chef had insisted on getting them to try even more food and wine – and her stomach was stretched to its limit. For the first time since Aurora had loaned Rose one of her dresses, she was grateful it was so loose.

In the back of the car, Aurora muttered something about her own clothes shrinking, as Coco barked at a flock of birds.

'And there it is,' Aurora said suddenly in a hushed tone as a stunning, earth-coloured stone building appeared over the horizon. The house was flanked by a backdrop of rolling green hills and a cloudless blue sky which offset the terracotta barrel-tiled roof.

'It's beautiful,' Rose whispered, opening the passenger window as they headed through a set of wrought-iron gates. She breathed in the scent of lemon and cypress trees, and the cool spray from a goddess-shaped fountain as they passed.

'This is Villa Paradise,' Ben announced proudly as he

pulled the car in front of the huge building and stopped beside the sportscar Marco had parked. 'I sat outside for a couple of hours when I first saw it. It's an incredible piece of architecture – I dream of designing something like this myself.' He looked wistful.

'It's been in the Marino family for generations,' Aurora chimed in. 'Shall we get out? I think I spotted Cesare between some of the lemon trees.'

'That's Marco's grandad?' Rose checked, trying to recall the family from the photo Ben had shared.

'Yes. He enjoys working in the garden sometimes,' Ben told her, opening the door and getting out at the same time as Marco and Luna.

Rose got out too, absorbing a blast of pure heat which scorched her skin. She looked up at the villa again, taking in all three magnificent floors, the ornate wall accents, and the mosaic porch that led to an impressive, curved oak front door. There were pots of flowers dotted around adding splashes of pinks, yellows and vibrant blues.

'It's incredible, isn't it?' Luna said excitedly, bounding over to stand beside Rose. 'Wait until you see inside. The wedding's going to take place in the garden at the back of the villa – it's so pretty. There are trees and so many flowers and we're all going to sit outside!'

She clapped her hands and yanked Rose away from the Citroën, leading her towards the entrance of the villa. 'There's a swimming pool in the back too, and a huge olive grove – there are so many places to sit in the garden, it goes on for miles. You're going to have to come exploring with me.'

'Perhaps later, *tesoro*,' Marco said firmly. 'We've been gone a while; we should see if Mama or Papa need us to help them get ready for the engagement party.'

'Of course,' Luna said, nodding at Rose and mouthing an apology. 'Let's catch up later.'

'Can't I help?' Rose offered.

Marco shook his head firmly. 'You are a guest; my parents would not hear of it. Luna, why don't you find Mama and I'll see everyone to their rooms so they can refresh?'

'I'll come in a minute.' Aurora handed Coco to Luna, who immediately took off around the side of the house carrying the dog.

'I'm assuming Aldo and I are in the usual room?' the older woman checked and Marco nodded. 'I'm going to see if I can find Cesare first.'

Marco looked towards a cluster of angular lemon trees positioned on their right, but Rose couldn't see anyone. 'Is he hiding somewhere?' Marco asked, frowning.

'I think he's on his phone,' Aurora said. 'I'll go and see if he's okay. Aldo tells me things have got much worse.' She headed away from them, her skirts swishing, and Rose watched her go.

What was worse? She considered asking Marco, but from the look on his face guessed he wouldn't share with her.

'Is Cesare hiding?' Ben asked.

'No,' his friend said, his forehead knotting. 'I gave *Nonno* his first mobile for his birthday in January and now he's obsessed with doing crosswords. He says they keep his mind young. Mama says he disappears into the garden for hours sometimes. Of course, he could be using it to distract himself.' He looked unhappy. Rose shifted her gaze between the two men hoping one of them would elaborate.

Ben winced. 'I'm sorry,' he said.

What exactly what he was apologising for. Was something wrong with Marco's perfect family? Did Luna know about it?

'No matter,' Marco said briskly, his eyes skimming across Rose's face before he glanced at the house. 'You should follow me so I can show you where you'll be sleeping. It's a different room from your usual, Ben. We'll pick up your luggage later.'

'I've got no luggage,' Rose muttered, following him slowly as she tried to spot where Aurora had gone – wondering why the older woman had been so determined to find Marco's grandad and what exactly had got worse.

But Aurora had already been swallowed by the greenery, leaving Rose in the dark.

Rose stood on the small balcony at the end of her bedroom and gazed at the view. Villa Paradise was stunning and the grounds were extensive. From here, she could see the perfect backdrop of mountains peppered with trees. Closer to the main house was the glittering swimming pool Luna had mentioned, surrounded by umbrellas and loungers — framed by sprawling gardens of olive, cypress and lemon trees and flowering shrubs.

To the far left of the estate, two small, burnt orange stone houses sat side by side. Each had a blue wooden table and one chair which had been set away from each other on opposing patches of grass. The two gardens were separated by a thick fence panel flanked by stunning pots of pink oleander. The barrier looked new and a little out of keeping with the original buildings. Perhaps the family had begun to rent the cottages in the summer, and it was there to give their clients privacy?

She walked back inside and paced the room, picking up her skirt as Aurora's dress skimmed along the wooden floor. She needed new clothes but had more important things to worry about. Like where was Luna and when was she going to get a chance to speak to her friend alone?

She knew Luna and Marco's bedroom was on the second floor of the villa because Marco had mentioned it – while she, Ben and Aurora were all located on the top. Rose had no idea how she'd find out which of the many bedrooms belonged to her friend, she only knew she had to track her down.

She pulled her mobile from her pocket and tapped out a

quick message, checking that she hadn't already received a reply to the two she'd already sent.

Hi, Luna. Are you okay? When can we talk properly? R xx

Rose returned to look at the view and noticed what she presumed was a woman dressed in black trousers wander out of the doorway of one of the small cottages. The woman moved slowly and it was obvious, even from here, that she was elderly – but Rose couldn't see her face because she was too far away.

She carried a basket under one arm and proceeded to pick lemons off a tree to the right edge of the property. A few moments later, a tall man dressed in khaki green wandered out of the other cottage doorway. The man watched the woman for a few moments before approaching. As he did, the woman began to gesticulate angrily — then she threw the basket on the ground and stomped back inside her house.

Rose watched the scene play out, fascinated by the body language of the two people. There was anger there, but something else too, she just couldn't read it. Had she just witnessed a family feud, were they guests of the Marinos, or was this somehow connected to what Aurora had spoken about earlier?

Her senses were tingling, and she wished she could find out more. It had been over forty-eight hours since she'd last spoken with a client, and Rose was beginning to get withdrawal. She enjoyed fixing things when she could – enjoyed the feeling of satisfaction she got from bringing people together. Perhaps she could help the couple? Her phone buzzed and she stepped back inside, out of the sunlight.

Hi, Rose. I'll come and find you in a few minutes. L xx

Rose smiled, wishing she had the notes she'd packed in her suitcase. She'd have to track down a printer later. She'd prepared a folder for Luna and Marco. A series of questions designed to help them take a step back and think clearly about their impending marriage and all the potential pitfalls. She'd prepared a further list of suggested rules to follow so they could spend time getting to know each other properly over the next few months. She just had to convince them to follow it now.

Her mobile buzzed and she immediately picked up before the ring tone kicked in, expecting it to be Luna.

'Rose,' her mother said, and her heart sank. 'Are you still in Italy?' The question came out as more of an accusation than interest.

'Yes, I'm just getting settled in to Marco's family home.' There was no point in sharing the story of her lost luggage, or any of the things that had happened since she'd arrived in Nice. Rose hadn't told her mother Luna's fiancé's name and wondered if she'd ask who the man she was staying with was.

'Did you get my wedding invite before you left?' her mother shot back. 'Because you haven't RSVP'd and I need to know what time you'll be there.'

'I got it.' Rose sighed. 'Did you know Dad's getting married on the same day?'

'It wasn't a surprise.' Her mother snorted. 'Darling, you know your father's never had an original thought. Of course he's chosen the same day for his wedding. He's trying to upstage me. I hear the bride is younger than you.' She sounded bitter, and Rose went to sit on the bed. It was a four-poster crafted from walnut, with piles of puffy pillows and crisp white sheets. Matching gauzy curtains hung around the sides and they fluttered as a breeze from the overhead fan caught them. Sighing, she lay down and pressed the mobile to her ear, feeling tired suddenly. 'He'll be divorced before the cake's been cut. I need you at *my* wedding, Rose. You'll love William – we're perfect for each other. This time, I know I've got it right. You can do a speech, tell us about all the rules we need to follow.' She chuckled. She'd never taken any of Rose's advice seriously, often joking about her career.

'How long have you known William?' Rose asked flatly.

'Time isn't important,' her mother said dryly. 'When you finally allow yourself to fall in love, you'll understand that. Rose, tell me you'll be there. It won't feel like a wedding unless you are.'

Rose sighed; she didn't want to fall out with either of her parents. 'I need to talk to Dad again,' she said wearily. Usually, she had plenty of energy for conversations like these. Would at least spend a few minutes trying to show her mother the error of her ways, but the long journey here had sapped it out of her.

Someone knocked on the door of her bedroom and she sat up. 'I'm sorry, I've got to go. Luna's come to see me,' she said, feeling a wave of relief. At least she could stop one relationship disaster and save her best friend. 'I'll call when I can and let you know about the wedding, okay?'

'You'd better come to mine,' her mother snapped before hanging up.

Rose put the phone down, trying to untangle the new knot in her stomach, and opened the door, gaping when she saw Ben standing in the hallway.

'What are you doing here?' She folded her arms as something quivered in her belly, making the knot evaporate.

'Luna couldn't make it.' His forehead crinkled. 'She said she'd just sent you a text?'

'I was on the phone,' Rose said roughly, glancing towards the bed where she'd left her mobile.

'She said to tell you that she'd see you later, at the engagement party or before if she can make it,' Ben told her.

He'd showered and changed – into a dark blue shirt that made his brown eyes shades darker. He'd put on shorts too, which showcased the perfectly developed muscles of his legs. His skin was tanned, and he looked healthy and far more attractive than any mortal had a right to look. Rose sighed, irritated by her reaction to him, which was the result of unruly pheromones – nothing more.

'Marco's taken her to get her hair done for the party. It was a last-minute appointment, a surprise, which is why she didn't mention it earlier,' Ben said, avoiding looking at her. 'Luna asked me to walk you into the village.'

'Are you sure Marco didn't ask you to get me out of the way?' Rose asked suspiciously, pulling Aurora's dress back onto her shoulder as it slid off. Her linen trousers were washed and hanging in the bathroom, but she wasn't hopeful that she'd ever wear them again.

'What have you done with Aurora?' Rose checked the empty hallway behind Ben. 'Is she at the hair appointment too?'

'She's having a nap with Coco,' he said. 'She barely slept a wink last night. Lumpy bed, apparently.' His lips curved. 'If you stand in the hallway, you'll hear her arguing with Aldo. I don't know how they always seem to have so much to say to each other considering they never stop talking.' He sounded wistful.

Rose frowned when she heard another shout.

'Do you want to go to a boutique?' Ben's eyes filled with humour. 'Or are you planning to borrow Aunt A's clothes until your suitcases turn up?' The smile he gifted her was the wrong side of wicked. '*If* they ever do.'

'They'll get here. But yes please, I do want to go.' Rose puffed out a breath. She'd worn enough glitter to last a lifetime. 'I hope they have shoes.' She'd been wearing the same pair of pumps for way too long.

'There's only one way to find out,' Ben said, sweeping an arm into the corridor. Rose grabbed her handbag and mobile before following him out of the door.

10

ROSE

The village of Bellemilia was small and quaint. Multiple shops, a bakery, two restaurants, a bar and church were all positioned on a long main road following the dip of a wide valley, which was surrounded by emerald wooded hillsides. The road was cobbled, but trees had been positioned at intervals along the pavements to shade visitors from the hot sunshine. Rose almost tripped on the uneven pathway as she spotted a shop named, *Elegante*, which had two mannequins in the window dressed in stylish, expensive-looking clothes. 'Is that it?' she asked, feeling hopeful.

'That's the one,' Ben said.

'Have you been here before?' Rose asked.

'Once, a long time ago.' Ben's expression shuttered and he turned and marched through the doorway before Rose could ask more. Looking mournful, he waited for her just inside. Had he had an embarrassing fling with one of the retail assistants that he didn't want to talk about?

It was cool in the shop and Rose took a moment to enjoy the air conditioning, trying to discreetly flap the neckline of Aurora's dress to let in cool air as she scoured her surroundings.

There were racks of clothing set along both of the main walls, with smaller stands and tables positioned at intervals in between. Rose saw handbags, shoes, dresses, T-shirts, costume jewellery, trousers, swimwear and jeans. Towards the back of the store, she spotted a selection of underwear and nightwear and wanted to cheer. She appreciated Aurora's kindness but had missed being able to dress in plainer and more elegant clothes.

'You don't need to stay. I can take it from here.' Rose waved at Ben, hoping he'd take the opportunity to leave.

An older woman dressed in a bright red trouser suit appeared from the back room, her face lighting when she spotted them. 'Ben!' she said in a thick Italian accent, managing to sound both sexy and businesslike. Was anyone immune to this man's charms, aside from her?

'It's been a long time.' The woman skipped across the floor in a pair of heels that would have made Rose dizzy, and wrapped him in her arms. She was tiny but somehow managed to envelope him. Was this another of Ben's exes? Rose just stopped herself from shaking her head in irritation. Exactly how many lovers did one man need? According to her father, dozens and sometimes all at once... Was Ben cut from the same cloth?

'How are you?' The woman pulled away so she could look up into Ben's face. 'That bad?' she asked, her voice filled with sympathy which made Rose pause.

Why would anyone feel sorry for him, was he having a bad eyebrow day or something?

'It's been a busy few days,' he said gruffly. 'More importantly how are you?' He flashed her one of his trademark smiles and Rose stopped worrying. The flirt was back, the world was revolving back on its axis.

'I've become a *nonna* since I last saw you,' the woman gushed. 'I'll be at the party tonight, so I'll bore you about our *bambina* later. I will show you pictures, and you will tell me how beautiful she is and how you can't wait to have at least four of your own. I insist.' She laughed aloud when Ben paled and shook his head.

'You know that's not part of my future,' he muttered.

'Isn't it?' The woman raised an eyebrow. 'Who's this?' She turned and cocked her head, her eyes lively with interest, as she noticed Rose. Now they were facing, Rose could see she was older than she'd first thought – perhaps in her late fifties – although her elegant clothes and perfect figure made her seem younger than her years. '*La fidanzata?*'

'She's not my girlfriend.' Ben snorted. 'More like my arch-nemesis. Think Captain Hook and Peter Pan.'

'You're Peter Pan in this scenario I suppose?' Rose asked dryly. 'Never grew up, adored by women everywhere. I could go on…'

'Does that make you Wendy?' Ben teased.

'Ah! I see.' The woman looked between them and grinned. 'These are the most passionate types of relationship. I once—' She stopped and pressed a fingertip to her lips, her smile enigmatic. 'Perhaps you don't need to know the details.' She gave Rose a half smile as she looked her up and down critically, her eyes widening as she took in Aurora's dress. 'You work with Aurora Gallo and have recently shrunk and lost some weight?' she guessed.

'No!' Rose stepped closer. 'My luggage went missing on my flight to Italy, so I had to borrow her clothes. I'm going to need a new wardrobe.' She scoured the shop. 'Do you have any cream linen suits?'

The woman choked. 'I'm Madame Francesca Rossi. I once dressed the stars. I think we can do better than that. You!' She snapped a finger at Ben who was still standing beside the door. 'Why don't you take a seat, *bello*? You know where it is.'

'I'd rather go to a bar,' he pleaded. 'I'm sure it would be better if I got out of your way.'

'He doesn't need to stay,' Rose agreed firmly. 'I can make my own decisions about my wardrobe.'

'But where will we get our male perspective from?' Madame Rossi asked, prodding a chic red fingernail towards Ben and then at the grey sofa outside the changing room. 'Sit!'

Ben gave Rose a thoughtful look. 'I'm more afraid of her,' he whispered as he walked to where Francesca had pointed.

'Then I'll have to work harder on being scary,' Rose shot back. 'We don't need him,' she insisted as the older woman began to wander around the shop, scooping up various pieces in multiple colours.

'From the look of that outfit, I'd say you need all the help you can get,' Francesca joked.

'I told you, it's not my dress,' Rose insisted. 'Are you sure you don't have anything in cream?' she checked, feeling a little nervous now. She was used to being in control, but somehow this situation was getting the better of her.

Madame Rossi gave her a sympathetic look. 'You fit a forty, *si?*' she checked, her eyes scouring Aurora's dress. 'I think that is more of a forty-two.'

'Yes, I'm a twelve,' Rose confirmed, widening her eyes when the woman grabbed a dazzling navy dress with a plunging neck-line from one of the racks. There were subtle sparkles in the material. 'I'm definitely not going to wear that,' she stammered. She preferred her outfits to be more serious – so she could fade into the background and people-watch. She wasn't looking to draw attention to herself, and she definitely wasn't looking to recreate Aurora's wardrobe in a smaller size.

'Why not try it?' Francesca asked smoothly. 'It might suit you? Besides, you need something *bellissima* for the engagement party. Everyone in the village will be there.'

Rose sighed and shook her head. It was like shopping with her mother when she was a teenager. She'd never listened either. Although then Rose had been far more worried about pleasing her than herself. 'I'll try it if you find me a linen suit,' she bargained.

'*Si*. I have one in red.' Francesca flashed a wicked smile as she picked up trousers, a pair of red pyjamas and a tiny blue T-shirt which looked like it would be a perfect fit for Coco. 'You need lingerie? Of course you do.' She picked some out, studying the tiny, lacy scraps intently as they dangled from their hangers. Ben, who was sitting a few metres away from her, nodded enthusiastically as she held each of them up in turn.

Seriously? Rose could feel a blush forming on her cheeks and fought to control it. 'I prefer white, and it hardly matters if Ben approves. He's not going to see it,' she muttered as Francesca waved a crimson set.

'I don't mind offering advice. I'm very experienced in these things,' Ben said, grinning as the older woman turned and swished a heavy velvet curtain aside, exposing a pretty dressing room with four large mirrors, and a voluptuous chair. Then she hung all the items she'd chosen onto a set of hooks on the wall.

Ben, who was still sitting on the sofa facing the changing room, grinned. 'Do I get a drink while I'm waiting?' he asked.

'How about hemlock?' Rose suggested darkly. Why wouldn't he just leave?

Francesca laughed looking delighted. 'Depends how useful you are, *caro*,' she said to Ben. 'I have some for—' She stopped abruptly and waved a hand at Rose.

'Rose Loveheart,' Ben filled in. 'Also known as the Love Doctor. She's friends with Marco's bride.'

'Ah.' Francesca nodded vigorously, her short brown curls bouncing against her cheeks. 'Of course. Aurora mentioned you'd be visiting when she called me earlier in the week. We're friends too,' she explained as Rose started to ask how the two of them knew each other.

'But how did she know I was coming?' Rose gasped. She'd only found out herself two days ago.

'Aldo told her – he told her a few other things too.' Francesca's eyes sparkled as her gaze switched between Rose and Ben and then she laughed delightedly. 'I'm just teasing, *cara*. Marco messaged to tell me you were on your way.'

Rose shut her eyes for a moment. Was everyone in Italy unhinged or was it just the people who knew Marco's family? She might have to write a new set of rules just for them. 'Shall I try on the clothes?' she asked wearily, nodding towards the changing room.

'*Sì!*' Francesca clapped her hands. 'While you're there, I'll get you a drink of *Franciacorta*. That's Italy's version of champagne.'

Rose was about to say she didn't want another drink but decided better of it. She knew from her parents and clients that it was best to choose her battles. Besides, a bit of alcohol might make this more bearable. She walked into the changing room and heard Francesca swish the curtains closed. Then she stared at her reflection in the long mirror, wondering what had happened to her carefully managed life.

Since she'd met Ben, nothing had gone to plan, and no one was doing anything she asked – including her own wayward hormones. There was a tight ball of excitement in the pit of her stomach that she hadn't experienced before. Was this how Luna felt? Because Rose hated it, hated the feeling of chaos, the lack of control.

'Here, drink this.' A hand appeared through the curtain holding a delicate glass filled to the brim. Rose took it. The alcohol she'd had in the restaurant a few hours ago had worn off, so she shut her eyes and took a large gulp. She'd need Dutch courage if she was going to try on the clothes Francesca had selected. And she'd have to buy some; she didn't have much choice. From her brief walk down the high street, it was clear this was the only place to buy women's clothes and she doubted she'd get the chance to go anywhere further afield. She'd be too busy trying to advise Luna.

'Everything okay in there?' Ben shouted from outside the curtain. 'Do you need any help?'

Rose knew he was joking because she could practically hear the laughter in his voice. She narrowed her eyes at the midnight blue dress with the plunging neckline. What would he say if she put it on? Surely the surprise would wipe the smug smile from his face. He thought he knew her; it would be fun to show him he had no idea.

'I'm fine,' she shouted back, quickly taking off Aurora's dress, feeling a wave of relief when it hit the floor. She frowned at her underwear. She'd washed everything in the sink last night while she'd been wearing Ben's T-shirt and thankfully it had dried, but she'd definitely be taking most of Francesca's selection back to Villa Paradise with her, even if the styles were far smaller and more colourful than she'd normally go for. She stroked a piece of red lace – it was softer than she'd expected and the finish was stunning, so it wouldn't be a hardship.

'Are you staring at yourself in the mirror?' Ben asked, and his guess was so accurate Rose quickly checked there wasn't a gap in the curtain. When she was sure there wasn't, she turned to frown at her reflection. Then she pulled the navy dress up and over her hips.

'Francesca, can you help me with the zip please?' she shouted.

'I'm happy to step in,' Ben joked. 'Zips happen to be a speciality of mine. I practically have a degree in them.'

Rose laughed. She couldn't help it. Ben was charming and funny, a heady combination for any woman. She was pleased she was immune to his charms. Or at least aware they were all for show. He was just a pretty face – she reminded herself – shallow and self-centred and only looking for the next woman to impress. Like the last three of her mother's husbands and Luna's ex-fiancé too.

'I'm sure you do,' she said. 'But I'm guessing you're more adept at undressing women, whereas I need someone to help me put my clothes *on*. It's probably best if you stick to your usual lane,' she shot back.

'I'm willing to give it a try – in the interests of evolving,' Ben joked.

Rose chuckled again. Ben might be shallow, but he was funny. 'We wouldn't want you getting confused,' she said.

She stared at herself in the mirror, waiting for Ben to respond. Her cheeks looked flushed and there was an odd brightness in her eyes. She wasn't used to flirting. She liked her interactions with men to be more serious, preferring to find out more about them via a series of questions designed to expose their faults, than to fall into the easy back and forth of seductive conversation. But it was fun when you didn't mean it. More fun than she'd realised. Perhaps this explained why her parents both did it so much?

'I'm sure I could handle a change of pace,' he countered as the older woman slid through the curtain, somehow managing not to flash any of Rose to Ben.

'*Cara*,' Francesca gasped, clutching her hands to her collar-bone. 'The colour is spectacular on you and the sparkles divine. I really am talented.' She grinned as she approached, spinning Rose around. 'But you need to remove your bra!'

'That's a speciality of mine too,' Ben murmured from outside.

Rose ignored him. 'You want me to take it off now?' she asked, clutching the dress tighter to her chest.

'You won't need it,' Francesca said. 'The underwear will bunch under the silk, and it's cut so low you won't be able to stop it from showing.' She stared Rose down until she carefully removed and dropped it onto the chair.

Francesca nodded as she paced the room, checking Rose from the side and back, making various approving noises before quickly sliding up the zip of the dress. Then she spun Rose around to face the mirror. 'You look *magnifica!*' she declared, clapping her hands again.

Rose didn't usually get pleasure from shopping. She kept her wardrobe tidy and unimaginative – always aiming for professional. She'd never wanted to dress to attract a man based on looks alone. Which meant she preferred keeping things simple.

But for the first time in a long time, Rose wondered if that was a mistake. The navy suited her and brought out the colour of her eyes and the low neckline looked sexy, giving just enough away but not too much. It wasn't like Aurora's dress, but it did have sparkles – plus, this one cut in at the waist and dipped at the front, exposing her pale skin and making it almost shimmer in the light. She tried to take a step forward so she could see better and found herself almost tripping on the hem.

'It's a little too long,' she said, disappointed and oddly relieved that it was unsuitable.

'You just need some heels,' Francesca sang, drawing back the flap in the curtain again and disappearing.

'You have shoes?' Rose asked, turning to gaze at herself.

Perhaps it would be nice to dress up? Usually, Luna dazzled when they were out together and Rose was happy to take a back seat. She wasn't looking to outshine her friend – especially not at her own engagement party – but it might feel good to stand in the same bright light. She twisted around, trying to find the price tag, but couldn't see one. Rose had a strict monthly budget for her wardrobe updates. Looked like she might be blowing at least half a year of it today.

Francesca returned dangling a pair of glittery shoes from her fingers. 'I guessed your size – thirty-eight?'

'I'm a five, yes. I'm impressed,' Rose said, taking them and staring. They were high and the straps were dainty. 'I'm not used to wearing heels outside of work,' she said slowly. The older woman waved a hand towards the chair and indicated Rose should sit. When she did, Francesca put the shoes on her, then encouraged her to stand.

'Try walking! Slowly...' she said as Rose hitched up the skirt so she didn't accidentally tread on the material. The dress was exactly the right length now and the shoes were more comfortable than she'd anticipated. 'You will be fine after some practice.' Francesca waved a hand. 'Why don't you show Ben?'

'I don't need his opinion,' Rose spluttered.

'Is that a rule too?' Ben, who was obviously still eavesdropping, asked from the other side of the curtain.

'Yes, it's called dress for yourself and no one else,' she told him. 'Don't give up your style or change for anybody.' She frowned. She'd seen too many clients trying to change themselves for their partner. Even Luna had gone through a phase when she'd only wanted to wear cargo trousers because her latest boyfriend was obsessed with them. Luckily, she'd finished with him, although it had taken her months to see she was being manipulated.

Francesca sighed. 'Of course you should dress for yourself, *cara*.' She nodded towards the curtain. 'But it doesn't hurt to share if you look this good.'

'Is it cream?' Ben asked, his tone still teasing.

'No,' Rose said, twisting around and ripping back the curtain, feeling her stomach drop to her toes when Ben's mouth gaped and his smile disappeared.

She didn't need or want his approval – but that didn't stop the punch of satisfaction in her stomach at his reaction. It might be weak and irresponsible of her – but she decided to just enjoy it. It didn't have to be complicated. Ben wasn't even a friend.

'You look...' He trailed off as Rose stepped out into the main shop aiming to get a feel for the new outfit, to see if she'd be comfortable wearing it this evening.

'*Bellissima*,' Francesca filled in as she followed Rose out. 'So now we have an outfit for this evening, we need to get you sorted for the rest of your visit.'

'You'll need a bikini,' Ben said, his smile returning. 'And something to wear to bed. Unless you're planning on keeping my T-shirt?' he teased.

Francesca's eyebrow rose, but she looked pleased. 'Ah, this chemistry isn't in my imagination,' she cooed.

'It certainly is,' Rose countered.

'It's good.' The older woman regarded Ben as he went to sit back on the sofa. 'I never thought he'd get over Sophia.'

'He seems perfectly over her to me,' Rose said. Hadn't he been joking about the wedding presents back in the hotel? And what about all his constant flirting? Unless that was just a coping mechanism? The thought made her pause.

'Is he?' Francesca asked enigmatically before turning away. 'Why don't I pick you out some swimwear now – and you're going to need a dress for the wedding. Luna's already been in touch with some ideas,' she said loudly, leaving Rose floundering as she watched the older woman go to gather up more clothes, all the while chatting with Ben.

Was there more to the man than she'd first suspected? Did he actually have a heart, after all? Time would tell, but suddenly Rose wondered if she'd misjudged Ben. And if she had, what did that say about her?

11

ROSE

Rose stared at herself in the long mirror in her bedroom feeling nervous. She could hear soft music playing downstairs and checked her watch. The party had started ten minutes ago, but she wasn't ready to leave the safety of her room yet. She'd spent the afternoon messaging Luna to no avail, napping and trying on her new wardrobe before getting ready in the glamorous blue dress and heels. There was a knock on her door and she went to open it, expecting to find Ben.

'Luna,' she gasped, pulling her into the room before taking a moment to study her. Her friend was dressed in a silky red dress and her white-blonde hair had been piled on top of her head and woven with tiny pearl beads. 'You look beautiful,' she gasped.

Luna's eyes widened. 'I spoke to Francesca yesterday.' She looked down at Rose's dress and grinned. 'I knew she was a miracle worker. But... you've never looked more incredible. That style it just...' She trailed off, clearly unable to find the right words, and Rose wasn't sure she wanted her to. Didn't want more words to define how different she looked.

'Thank you,' she said instead, checking herself again. 'I'm not so sure about the sparkles. Do I look like Aurora?'

Luna chuckled softly. 'You look like you – only.' She cocked her head. 'A way sexier version. If I didn't know it would annoy you, I'd ask if you were dressing up for someone special?'

'This has nothing to do with Ben,' Rose grumbled.

Luna shrugged. 'He's very hot.' She grinned.

Rose shook her head, choosing to ignore the comment. 'What happened to you earlier?'

Luna's forehead creased. 'I'm sorry about that — and that I haven't answered any of your texts. We left in such a rush I forgot my phone.' Luna went to sit on the edge of Rose's bed and bounced a little, her face a picture of happiness. 'Then I had to sneak away from Marco while he was talking to one of the waitresses. He doesn't want to let me out of his sight.' Her eyes clouded. 'He's worried you're going to try to talk me out of the wedding, or at least ask me to postpone it.'

Rose sighed and went to sit beside her, cursing Ben for talking to his friend because he'd complicated everything. Then again, she couldn't really blame him; he was here to support Marco. They were just on differing sides. His loyalty to Marco was one of the things about him she couldn't help but like.

'I'm just concerned that you're both rushing into things,' she said.

'I understand why.' Luna nodded. 'Your parents have hardly inspired confidence in quick marriages. In any marriages actually.' She sighed. 'It's been a whirlwind, and I know you don't believe in love at first sight, but he's honestly the best person I've ever met. He's kind and thoughtful, everything I ever wanted. You know I don't make decisions lightly.' Her expression turned dreamy. 'But I want to marry him, Rose.'

Rose decided not to tell Luna that she'd said something similar the last time she'd met the love of her life. Just before she'd found out her fiancé was more interested in her fortune than her.

'Can we at least talk about it a little? I could do my Love Doctor thing,' she said, feigning a smile. 'I'll ask you both some questions, make sure you've thought everything through. Would it really be that awful to delay the wedding?'

'You know it would.' Luna frowned.

'Because of the date?' Rose checked. 'Surely that's just superstition. A marriage is either going to work or it isn't. I don't think matching up wedding days will stop it from being a disaster.'

Luna sighed again. 'You know, I think we need to rename you the Doom Doctor,' she teased.

Rose didn't laugh. 'I'm just looking out for you. I want to make sure you're not making a mistake.'

'I know.' Her friend nodded. 'But can we do this tomorrow? I'll speak to Marco, convince him to at least sit down with you and talk. But for tonight, can we just enjoy my engagement party, and could you switch that clever brain of yours off and enjoy yourself for a change?' She squeezed Rose's hand. 'I know why you're worried and I love you for it, but just because your parents are –' she winced, '– the way they are, and my last few partners have been less than ideal, that doesn't mean this marriage isn't going to work, or that Marco isn't a good man. There are lots of wonderful people in the world and relationships do sometimes work out...'

Rose sighed. 'I know,' she said stiffly. 'I've seen several successful ones.' Had coached couples through plenty of difficult times. But at her core she still had her doubts. 'Have you heard from your mum yet?'

Luna pulled a face. 'She's still waiting to get off the island. I'm trying not to get worried. Aurora told me she'll definitely make it...'

'Well, if anyone can, Deborah Kennedy can,' Rose

promised, feeling more in control because at least Luna had agreed to speak to her now. She squeezed her friend's hand just as there was a new knock on the door of her bedroom. She went to open it and wasn't surprised when she found Marco and Ben on the other side.

When Marco saw his bride sitting on Rose's bed, he paled. '*Tesoro*,' he croaked, striding towards her. 'I've been looking for you, I was worried.'

Luna stood and took his hand. 'You didn't need to be,' she soothed. 'I was just catching up with Rose. I said we'd sit down with her tomorrow so we can talk about the wedding, put her mind at rest.' Her eyes shone with meaning.

'*Si*.' Marco's lips pinched and he gave Rose a concerned look. 'But now we need to get downstairs. Our engagement party is about to start. People are beginning to arrive, *cara*.' As he said the words, the volume of the music hitched up.

'I just need to get Coco,' Luna said excitedly as she headed for the door. 'Aunt A's been taking care of her for me all day.'

Marco nodded and Rose saw that pinch of his lips again as he glanced at her, his face filled with unease. He looked almost vulnerable and for a moment she was tempted to reassure him, but she wasn't here to get involved emotionally.

All she wanted was for both of them to take a step back. To make sure they were making the right decision. She was used to asking tricky questions, to handling difficult situations – she could do this. No one had to get hurt. At least not for long.

Luna grabbed Marco's hand and guided him into the hallway, leaving Ben waiting for Rose. He'd dressed up in a navy suit that made him look even taller, drawing attention to his narrow hips and the breadth of his shoulders which seemed wider since Rose had seen him last. The colour suited him, along with the lilac shirt which most men wouldn't be able to pull off. He was so handsome it felt like her eyes had superglued themselves to his face. She blinked, trying to regain her composure. 'Did Francesca sell you that outfit?' she asked, clearing her throat.

Ben shook his head. 'She's only interested in women's clothes.'

'You two were made for each other,' Rose joked.

'I do have a similar fascination.' He grinned as he looked her up and down, his eyes sparkling with something other than humour this time. 'You look incredible. If your suitcases ever turn up, I might throw coffee over *all* your linen suits.'

Rose pressed a palm against her fluttering stomach, trying to calm it before something flew out. 'Shall we go downstairs?' She nodded towards the door, feeling her cheeks flame.

Ben offered Rose an arm and she smiled before taking it. 'You're ridiculously smooth – do you practise in front of a mirror in the evenings?'

'Doesn't everyone?' he asked seriously.

Rose found herself laughing again as Ben led her into the hallway, the nervousness in her stomach dissipating. Usually, she felt stressed, she didn't know why being around Ben seemed to help. He was such undemanding company. Perhaps because she wasn't trying to counsel him? She doubted he'd listen if she tried.

'I'll introduce you to the Marinos first,' he said as they walked down the main staircase into a large hallway with a light grey marble floor. Rose had passed through it a number of times since arriving and it had been spectacular already, but it hadn't looked like this. Someone had fixed pink and white flowers to the banister and ribbons and pearls had been skilfully woven in between. The effect was stunning and the glittering lights hanging around the walls made everything look romantic.

'Most of the family are outside,' Ben told Rose, leading her through the room into the garden where someone had erected a long trellis next to the large pergola and covered it with flowers and leaves. A long table had been set up underneath and it was laid with glasses, cutlery and plates. There seemed to be hundreds of settings, and Rose wondered exactly how many people the family knew.

'We're going to sit here to eat,' Ben said as he placed a palm on the small of Rose's back making her shiver, despite the layer of silk covering her skin. How would her body react if there was nothing between them? The unwelcome thought flew into her mind, and she pushed it out.

'I'll introduce you to Marco's parents first.' Ben guided her towards a huddle of people in the far corner of the garden. They were beside a table which had been laid with drinks and jugs of wine. Waiters and waitresses were serving the guests as they arrived. Suddenly, Rose longed for a glass of something cool.

A woman wearing a green dress turned as they approached. 'Rose, Ben!' Francesca boomed. 'You look *bellissima,*' she cooed at Rose. 'Ben, it's almost boring that you look like a movie-star all the time.' She rolled her eyes. 'I've been telling Marco's mama all about you, Rose.' She winked.

The woman standing beside Francesca turned and flashed Rose a beaming smile. 'I'm Elena Marino and you are clearly Luna's friend!' she said, coming to join them.

She looked just like she had in the photo. Elegant and stylish with dark brown hair that she'd swept onto the top of her head and secured with a shiny gold clip. She was the same height as Francesca and her figure was just as perfect. Rose wondered what kind of trouble the two of them must have got into when they were younger and whether they were as close as she and Luna were. Elena had obviously been to *Elegante* to get her outfit for the party. It wasn't as revealing as Rose's, but the cream silk clung to her figure and set off her smooth olive skin.

'Ben, Francesca is right, *caro,* you look gorgeous, and it *is* a little boring how unruffled you always seem. You need someone to fray those handsome edges,' Elena teased. 'It is past time you moved on...'

'I have moved on,' he muttered, earning himself a huff. Then she wrapped her arms around him, before pulling Rose into a hug too.

'You are as beautiful as Luna,' Elena gasped as she pulled away and studied Rose. 'She's told us all about you and how important you are – you are welcome in our home.' Her smile radiated happiness. 'I'm sorry this is the first time we've met since you arrived, there has been so much to do for the wedding, and there's still so much to organise.'

She wiped a hand across her brow dramatically and Francesca sniggered. 'But we're all so excited – it has to be perfect for Marco and Luna.' She glanced around before shaking her head. 'I'm not sure where my husband is, but I'll introduce you when I find him.'

'For now, take some wine,' Francesca jumped in and handed Rose a glass. 'It's *Franciacorta*,' she added with a smile. 'The same as in my boutique. You liked it.'

'Thank you.' Rose sipped as both women began to tease Ben about all the women who were in love with him. She tried not to listen – she was *not* interested – and, instead, watched the crowd which had doubled while they'd been talking.

Now there were huddles of people laughing, kids running in between the trees and ducking under the long table while guitar music played from somewhere inside the house. The air was warm, and she could smell the dry, woody scent of olive trees merging with the delicious fragrance of fresh food and wine.

Out of the corner of Rose's eye, she saw a woman emerge from around the edge of the house close to where the two houses and pool were located. She was dressed in black and as she drew closer, Rose was sure she recognised the silhouette. Was it the woman she'd seen picking lemons and then arguing with the mystery man earlier?

'We're going to sit and eat soon,' Elena said, distracting

Rose. 'But before we do, my sister Aurora wishes to do a reading for you and Luna.'

'Oh, I don't think—' Rose gasped as Marco appeared from the back of the villa clutching Coco and swiping his eyes with a tissue.

'Of course we must!' Luna said as she drew closer. 'Aunt A has been talking about it all afternoon, and everyone wants to hear what she's got to say.' Her eyes sparkled as she looked back at her fiancé, her cheeks glowing.

'Sì, we do,' Elena said, kissing Luna again, her expression adoring while her friend beamed back, her face alight.

'I can't wait for her to tell us how wonderful our marriage is going to be.' Luna sighed and the crowd began to murmur with excitement as Aurora appeared from the front of the house wearing a long, lacy green dress with a matching veil. She walked towards them slowly, her back ramrod straight, and the crowd began to whisper as the music suddenly shut off.

'We've set up a table in the olive grove,' Elena said excitedly. 'We just need to follow my sister.' She hooked an arm through Rose's and another through Luna's. 'Keep an open mind, *cara*,' she said to Rose as they began to walk. 'You don't have to believe in it to have fun, *si*?'

'Yes,' Rose said, unwilling to offend Luna's potential mother-in-law. But she was surprisingly nervous. She glanced behind her and saw the woman in black join the throng of men, women and children as they followed.

Someone had hung lights on the trees in the olive grove which meant hundreds of them twinkled like stars as they approached. Rose spotted the small table and chairs just as Aurora reached them and turned to wait. Then a man dressed in a white shirt and chinos went to join her.

'That's my husband, Leonardo. Marco's *babbo* – his father,' Elena translated as they drew closer, and Rose recognised him from the photo. There was a strong resemblance to Marco, only

Leonardo had deep lines around his eyes and cheeks suggesting he laughed often. Rose's short acquaintance with frowny Marco suggested he didn't take after his father in that regard. At least that was her impression of him. 'He's just as handsome as he was on the day we met.' Elena beamed.

'It's true, I was with her when she saw him for the first time,' Francesca whispered. 'It was love at first sight.'

Rose tried not to react. No wonder Marco had such unrealistic expectations.

She watched Leonardo kiss Luna, Francesca and then Elena on both cheeks, then he took a moment to study Rose before wrapping her in a hug and kissing her too. She tried not to stiffen. Her family weren't demonstrative, and it felt strange hugging someone you barely knew. But she liked it, despite that.

'It's excellent to meet you, Rose,' he said, his accent thick. 'Any friend of my almost daughter-in-law is already a part of our family.'

Rose frowned, unused to such immediate approval.

Leonardo took a step away from the round table and Rose could see it had been set up already with Aurora's shiny crystal ball. There was a pack of tarot cards beside it and a glowing white candle next to that. A chair had been pulled out ready for Aurora and there were two on the opposite side of the table.

'You're going to do readings for us at the same time?' Luna gasped excitedly.

'Sì,' Aurora said as she whisked the veil from her head and studied them, her eyes twinkling mischievously. 'It is unusual, but your lives have been intertwined for many years. Aldo tells me in many ways your fates are closely linked, so it seems right.'

Luna put an arm around Rose's shoulder. 'She's right,' she said. 'I've known you forever. You're the sister I never had. I don't know what I'd have done if we hadn't met.'

Rose squeezed Luna's hand feeling a little overwhelmed. She felt the same way but wasn't going to express her feelings in front of everyone. The crowd gathered around them was huge; everyone was staring, and she barely knew any of them.

The figure dressed in black broke away from the rest of the crowd and drew closer. Her face was still covered by the veil and her shoulders were hunched, suggesting she was uncomfortable about something. There was still no sign of the man she'd been arguing with earlier.

'Take a seat.' Aurora drew out her chair and lowered herself into it, her movements slow and dramatic. Then she leaned forward and gazed into the crystal ball. 'Ah,' she gasped, nodding. As soon as she did the crowd hushed until all Rose could hear was the pounding of blood in her ears.

Luna took a seat and Rose sat too, and they both watched as Aurora continued to stare into the glass muttering intermittently as her eyes rolled, widened and then narrowed again.

Finally, Aurora looked up. 'You both have many great things in your future,' she said, her voice deeper than usual. 'Issues will be resolved, wrongs will be put right. You will be happier and more settled than ever before.'

Rose relaxed – it was clear now that the reading would be positive and everyone would be happy by the end. It was a piece of theatre designed to liven up the evening and reassure, nothing more.

'What about the marriage?' Elena asked eagerly, stepping closer to the table, her hands twisting together. 'Will it be a success?'

'No marriage is a success!' The woman in black shouted, suddenly removing her veil and revealing short, powdery brown hair and a face etched with wrinkles. Her expression contorted. 'In the end the truth will come out even if it takes a lifetime to see it.'

'Nonna!' Elena complained. 'Please, not now.' She shook her head as Leonardo and Marco came to flank her.

'Isabella, not now,' Aurora warned just as Rose recognised Marco's grandmother from the photo Ben had shared with her.

'It has to be said,' Isabella snapped. 'Marriage is for fools.'

'Shall we see if the cards agree?' Aurora asked pleasantly. The crowd seemed to sigh collectively when, after a long pause, Isabella jerked her chin.

Aurora gazed into the crystal ball again, her expression serious. '*Si,*' she said slowly, squinting. 'I can see the future. There will be hurdles of course, like any marriage.' She gave the older woman a long look. 'But misunderstandings can be overcome, wrongs put right.'

'Some things can never be put right.' The woman snorted.

'If we are prepared to be understanding and flexible. If we are prepared to listen and forgive,' Aurora said.

'Why should we?' Isabella puffed angrily and Aurora turned back to Luna and Rose.

'The future looks good,' she said. Someone clapped and a few people went to slap Marco on the back.

'What about Rose?' Luna asked, nudging her arm. 'Will she meet somebody soon?'

Rose clicked her teeth. 'I'm not looking—'

'Of course you're not, you never are, but it doesn't hurt to ask,' Luna said impatiently. 'You worry about everyone else all the time – someone needs to start worrying about you.'

Aurora drew in a long breath as she stared into the ball again. Rose tried to look into it too, but all she could see was a deep wrinkle on her forehead, the sparkles from the lights dangling around the olive grove and Isabella's frown.

'It is not going to be a smooth path to love. But nothing worth having is easy,' Aurora said carefully.

'Sunshine is easy,' Isabella grumbled. 'So is music and the brush of the wind on your cheeks. Love should be easy. It should endure. No one and nothing should replace or interfere with what was once good.'

Aurora patiently puffed out her cheeks. 'Not everything should be easy. Aldo and I have fought our whole marriage, but he was the best thing that ever happened to me.' Her smile expanded. 'Still is.'

Rose gritted her teeth. Suggesting that love wasn't easy was the opposite to what she usually preached. Love should be easy – it shouldn't be filled with conflict or fights. That was a clear path to misery.

But it didn't matter what the clairvoyant said. The crowd were happy; the buzz of voices surrounding them were excited. This was about Luna enjoying her moment. This wasn't the time for Rose to spoil it.

'Do you know who the person is?' Luna whispered. 'The one Rose will fall for?'

'Whoever it is, she should avoid him,' Isabella spluttered and was immediately shushed by the crowd.

'I can guess who it might be,' Francesca chuckled. 'Opposites attract, you know…'

Rose shut her eyes and tried not to shake her head. She knew what was coming, knew it was just part of the theatre. A new happy ending for everyone to get excited about.

Aurora shrugged. 'Si, *leonessa* has met her future already.' She looked up and fixed her steely gaze on Rose who immediately lowered her eyes to the table. It was obvious to her and probably to everyone else, that Aunt A was talking about Ben.

She'd been match-making them since they'd picked her up. Rose pondered whether she should be angry before settling for resigned. People enjoyed the idea of a shiny new romance – especially at an impending wedding. It's why they were here, to enjoy the fantasy of the happily ever after. The idea of a relationship that would thrive without work.

'Tell us more about Luna and Marco,' someone in the crowd yelled. 'Will their marriage be passionate?' A roar of laughter erupted, and Luna began to cough, looking embarrassed.

'Will there be *bambini?*' Isabella asked out of the blue and everyone stopped laughing and fell silent. 'Because that is the reason for marriage. Will there?' she repeated louder this time.

'I don't know.' Aurora frowned before leaning closer to her crystal ball. She searched in it for a long time before pulling a face. 'It is unclear, all I can see is mist. Aldo says this can happen. We can't always see. It is not a problem.'

'*Bambinos* are important,' Isabella growled. 'When you are disappointed by your love, you have them to look after you.' She gave Leonardo a sharp look.

'I'm really not sure if that's what—' Luna began.

'Why don't you try to read her palm?' Marco interrupted. 'See if it has anything to say.'

Luna frowned at her fiancé but still offered Aurora her hand.

'Sorry, *cara,*' the clairvoyant said. 'This is not – what do you say? – *poof.*'

'Proof,' Ben corrected.

Despite Aurora's words, she took Luna's hand and studied it. 'The palm tells of potential – it is not a way to predict what might be in your future. I myself have three lines, but, after Aldo died—' She shrugged, looking sad.

Luna pulled her hand away and frowned down at her palm. 'I don't know what I want but—'

'It's just superstition,' Rose whispered. 'You can't let it worry you; it's obviously not real.'

'I know.' Luna sighed, but she still stared glumly at her hand. 'I'm being silly. I just hoped—'

'Don't let it spoil the evening,' Marco said as he strode to stand beside Luna and squeezed her shoulder in a show of solidarity Rose was reluctantly grateful for.

'Aldo says your marriage will be a long and happy one,' Aurora chimed in, perhaps trying to lift the dark cloud that had settled over the crowd.

'There are ways to help with these things,' Marco's *nonna* said ominously, stepping closer.

'Mama!' Leonardo shook his head. 'This is not the time,' he said gruffly.

'Then when is?' The older woman asked sharply, earning herself another warning glare from her son. 'We need to speak about these things. With Marco, as a family.'

'Not now,' Leonardo repeated.

Isabella sniffed and jerked her chin, although it was clear she wasn't happy about dropping the subject.

'I could read your tarot cards, now?' Aurora offered. 'We can see what else is in your future?'

'I think perhaps we've done enough for today,' Rose said and felt a presence behind her, knew without looking that it was Ben.

'Perhaps we could come back to it later, Aunt A,' he agreed lightly. 'I think people are getting hungry – I know I am. We could try it when the sun sets. I'm sure a little more atmosphere wouldn't hurt. Perhaps the spirits will be more willing to share their secrets then?'

Rose felt a wave of relief and gratitude, a little surprised that he'd stepped in. Ben might be frivolous, flippant and nothing like the men she usually esteemed, but he clearly had a sensitive side.

Aurora considered him for a moment, her expression thoughtful. 'Sì, *bello*,' she said eventually. 'We have plenty of time. Perhaps some food will help too. Then, we can pick up where we left off.'

Luna rose from her chair and Marco hugged her, then the both of them linked hands and signalled to their guests that they should make their way back towards the villa.

Rose held back and was surprised when Ben did too. 'So are you ready for our torrid romance?' he teased as he put his hand on her back and guided her forward. 'Because you need to know I'm quite the catch.'

She snorted as a laugh got the better of her again. Perhaps it was just relief from the tension earlier? 'I get the feeling Aurora is confident I'm going to fall at your feet,' she said.

'Is she?' he asked, and Rose could hear the smile in his voice. 'And are you going to?'

'Well, maybe if I trip over my dress again.'

Ben laughed. 'Is it okay if it's the other way around?'

The idea sent prickles of awareness skidding across Rose's skin making her humour fade. 'I'm not the type of woman men like you usually fall for,' she said stiffly.

'Men like me?' he asked, and if Rose didn't know better, she might have thought she detected a trace of hurt in Ben's tone. She checked his face, which was filled with amusement, and dismissed the idea.

Men as good-looking as Ben Pearson didn't fall for women like her – and women like her definitely didn't get involved with men like him.

But as they wandered through the olive grove and she took in a deep lungful of the woody fragrance, Rose thought she heard the sound of someone laughing and for a crazy moment wondered if Aurora had somehow heard her thoughts.

12

BEN

Ben knocked on Rose's door again, trying not to wake Aurora who was sleeping a few rooms away. The dawn sun's orange light glowed from the hallway window, warming his face, and he scrubbed a hand across his forehead, trying to help himself to wake up. It was almost five a.m. and he hadn't got to bed until after midnight. Rose had retired earlier – although she hadn't told him she was going to bed. She'd been avoiding him after the huge, noisy meal, probably because Elena and Francesca had taken to following them both around – seemingly intent on getting them to dance together, or photographing them whenever they got close. Also, Aurora had been threatening Rose and Luna with a tarot card reading, which Rose had made clear she didn't want. Ben hadn't known Rose long, but it was obvious she wasn't keen on being the centre of attention – and hated making her private life so public.

Despite that, the engagement party had been raucous and fun, and Ben had found himself seeking Rose out on a number of occasions. Even the advances of a couple of the female guests – friends of the Marinos – hadn't tempted him, which was unusual, and he wasn't sure what to make of that. Perhaps it was simply the lingering memories of his own engagement party with Sophia which had been held in her parents' old house, just a mile from here?

He knocked on Rose's door again, trying to practise what he was going to say in his mind. Marco had cornered him in his room just after he'd gone to bed, eliciting a promise that Ben had a bad feeling about. But he was in Tuscany to support his friend, and he wasn't going to back out now.

'What?' Rose asked as she opened the door, and Ben felt something in his chest wake up and flip over.

She wore the red silk pyjamas she'd brought in Francesca's shop. When Ben had seen them on the hanger, he'd thought they were too big. But the material skimmed her body, giving away the curve of her waist and hips, and the vibrant colour added a flush to her pale skin. He swallowed a wave of unwelcome lust as her forehead crunched.

'Why are you here?' she asked, glancing into the hallway, looking confused. 'Is something wrong?'

'No. Well, yes.' He sighed. 'Isabella is insisting that someone goes to pick up a wedding gift for Luna and Marco, and he asked if we could do it. The Marinos want to placate her, so she doesn't do anything to spoil the wedding.'

'Like me you mean?' Rose asked, looking annoyed.

Ben huffed. 'Not exactly. She is... old... and it's important to everyone that she's happy about the marriage. She can be... difficult.'

Rose jerked her chin. 'Right.' She sighed. 'And we need to pick up this wedding gift now?' she asked incredulously as her tired expression morphed into one of disbelief and she looked back at the clock by her bed. 'Ben, it's five a.m.'

'I know.' He pulled a face. 'She was very insistent that it was picked up today.'

'Why?' She challenged.

'I said the same thing to Marco. Isabella's superstitious. It's a

Wednesday and that's important, apparently,' Ben explained truthfully. 'It's got something to do with harnessing the best luck.' His friend had used the word 'magic', but Ben wasn't going to tell that to Rose. He wanted her company, although he wasn't sure why. 'Marco explained it to me,' he said. 'But I was too tired to take much of it in.' He swiped a hand across his face and squeezed the bridge of his nose. 'He asked if we'd do it for him as a special favour.'

'If it's so important, why can't he do it?' Rose narrowed her eyes.

Ben pulled a face. 'Marco and Luna have to have their ring fingers sized this morning. If they don't, there will be no rings.'

He watched the thoughts flicker across Rose's face and wondered if she was processing what the implications of that might be. Would she refuse to come with him in an attempt to sabotage the rings and the nuptials? He felt his breath catch in his throat as he waited for her response, expecting to be disappointed in her; hoping he wouldn't be. Which made little sense. 'Fine. But why do I need to go?' she asked eventually.

'It's complicated.' When she stared him down, Ben let out a long breath. 'The gift needs two people – a man and a woman – to transport it here.' She opened her mouth to speak, and he held up a palm. 'Again, blame superstition, not me. Isabella is convinced it's important that we both do it. To give it the most —' He shut his eyes for a moment, trying to work out the best way to explain. 'Potency.'

Rose sucked in a breath and motioned that Ben should step inside the bedroom. He followed her tentatively, breathing in her perfume, which was fresh with strawberry notes. Usually, he knew all the popular fragrances. It was one of his party tricks – guessing what women were wearing, getting close enough to see the flutter of pulse at the base of their neck as he identified its name. But he couldn't seem to get his tongue to move from the roof of his mouth and his brain was barely functioning – which meant he had no chance of guessing the brand.

'Are you okay?' Rose asked, reading his confusion.

Ben swiped a hand across his brow. 'It smells like strawberries,' he murmured, feeling stupid. 'In here, I like it.' Now he sounded like an idiot.

Rose raised an eyebrow. 'Thank you,' she said, going to move the sheets over her bed as if she didn't want him to see it unmade. Then she turned and folded her arms. 'What are we picking up exactly?'

Ben began to pace the room. 'You're not going to like it,' he said. He'd toyed with the idea of making something up but didn't feel good about that. If Rose found out he'd been lying again, she'd probably never forgive him. Besides, she'd find out as soon as they reached their destination. 'If I tell you, will you keep an open mind?'

She frowned at him. 'I'm all about an open mind,' she said flatly. 'I've spent the last couple of days with Aurora and I'm still here.'

'True.' He stopped pacing. 'There's a fertility symbol. A statue that Isabella wants us to collect so she can give it to Luna and Marco for their wedding gift. I know she's not on board with the marriage, but she's keen to have great grandchildren.'

Rose snorted. 'And her gift will somehow guarantee they have the *bambini* everyone's clearly craving?' she asked dryly. 'The Marinos do understand that Luna is a businesswoman, don't they? She may not want to have children yet. She may not ever want them.'

Ben winced. 'No one is going to try to force Marco or Luna into doing anything they don't want to do, but of course Marco is keen his family are happy. Think of it as a placebo – a way to keep Isabella off their backs. I know you're not totally happy about the wedding, but if Luna wants to go ahead, we want it to go well.' He shrugged. 'It's not going to hurt and it's kind of our duty.' He paused, aiming for maximum effect. 'I am the best man – and you are the maid of honour. We're all about helping things to run smoothly.'

'That's a low blow,' she muttered, but Ben could see lines etching their way across her forehead – guessed she was softening to the idea. 'Okay, now I understand what we're picking up and why we need to go today.' She blinked. 'But why so early?'

'It's a long drive,' he said, yawning and stretching as a wave of tiredness hit him. 'About three hours each way and it's going to get hot and the roads will be busy. If we leave now, we should be back by mid-afternoon. Which is important because you've got an appointment to help make *bomboniere* early this evening and you can't miss that.'

'I can't?' Rose asked, her eyes widening. 'What does it involve, exactly?' She sounded suspicious.

'Don't worry, it's nothing you can't handle.' He smiled. 'It's an Italian tradition, making wedding favours. I'm sure Luna will fill you in when you get the chance to speak.' If Marco allowed them to get within a mile of each other. 'The women have a party planned.'

'Luna didn't mention it,' Rose said, frowning.

Ben shrugged. Her constant doubts were becoming wearing. The fact that she didn't trust him was— He shook his head. He shouldn't care about that.

'I don't think she knew about it herself until late last night, and I'm not sure if you even had time to talk,' he said. 'Things are moving fast, there's a lot for the family to organise and not much time.'

Rose frowned. 'Deborah. Luna's mother still isn't here,' she said. 'She's not going to be able to be a part of any of this and I know she'd want to be.'

Ben didn't respond – what was he supposed to say? But

Rose looked disappointed, and he felt something knot in his chest. Why was her happiness suddenly so important to him?

'Family matters to her,' she added.

Ben nodded. 'I understand that. It's important to Marco too. That's why he wants his *nonna* to be happy. At least about this.' Also, his friend hoped it might stop her from encouraging them to not get married. The promise of a great-grandchild might placate the older woman. Not that Marco had any particular plans in that direction, but he wanted the wedding to go ahead without any more negativity.

Rose sighed. 'Fine,' she muttered, looking annoyed. 'And it's a fair point. I suppose I'm going to have to say yes.' She moved to the window and pushed open the shutters to reveal bright orange light from the early morning sun which bathed her, lighting up the red pyjamas and making Ben flex his fingers. 'Does Isabella live there?' She pointed to the two houses behind the swimming pool and Ben went to stand beside her so he could see where she was indicating. He nodded, trying not to breathe in the scent of strawberries.

'Do you know who lives in the other house?' she asked.

'Cesare Marino. Marco's *Nonno* – his grandad.'

'I remember from the picture, and Aurora saw him in the garden yesterday. I think I saw him too, but he wasn't at the party last night,' she said.

Ben nodded. Usually, Cesare loved spending time with his family and was often the life and soul, but Marco had told Ben that he was lamenting the problems in his marriage and didn't want to spoil the evening. Also, he'd got absorbed by a particularly difficult crossword, which he'd been keen to solve. 'I believe he didn't want to cause a problem at the engagement party,' Ben said.

Rose's forehead pinched. 'Cesare and Isabella are still married, but they live in different houses?' She turned to gaze at the buildings again, and Ben could almost hear the click of her brain, knew exactly what she was going to ask next.

'They've recently separated,' he said, guessing it was best to tell her what he knew. The Marinos didn't want outsiders to know about the fallout, but Leonardo had said Rose was a part of the family now. Also, after Isabella's outburst last night, it was hardly going to be a surprise. 'I'll tell you the full story in the car —' he promised. 'If we leave now, we'll be able to stop for coffee and pastries on the drive. I know this place—'

Rose frowned and cocked her head. 'Are you sure this isn't just a way of keeping me from Luna?'

'I'm sure.' Ben pursed his lips. 'Marco figures he can handle whatever you throw at him. He loves Luna and he's got no intention of letting you talk her out of marrying him.'

He didn't add that his friend wouldn't be averse to doing anything to protect his impending nuptials. The fact that he'd asked Ben to seduce Rose had proven that. But some things she didn't need to know.

'So, why's this so important?' Rose asked. 'Why has it all suddenly happened now?'

'The family were spooked by Aurora's reading,' he told her. '*Nonna* can be difficult. Especially at the moment. Everyone wants the wedding to go well. They don't want anyone kicking off, refusing to go or getting upset. If we get the statue and *Nonna* gives it to Marco and Luna, she might stop telling them they're making a mistake. It's as simple as that. It's all about keeping the peace, making sure everything runs smoothly.'

'A statue isn't going to help someone get pregnant,' Rose said seriously. 'Even if they wanted to, which they might not.'

Ben held up his palms. 'I know that. But this isn't about me, or you. It's about helping Marco – and *Luna*,' he drew out her name. 'It's about what they want. Which is to get married with everyone's blessing.'

'Not with mine.' Rose sucked in a breath and her eyes

flashed as she turned to him. 'But fine. Why don't you go and get the car ready while I get dressed and—' Her eyes narrowed. 'Make sure you pack your phone charger. I need to let Luna know where I'm going. We were supposed to be speaking about the wedding this morning, I'll have to cancel I suppose.' Her lips thinned. 'But I'll be rearranging our chat for later today.'

Ben nodded. He had a feeling whatever Marco threw at Rose, she'd eventually have that conversation, present her rules and try to talk them both out of getting married so quickly. He only hoped Marco's fiancée wouldn't back out, but he'd done all he could do for now.

'Maybe pack that new bikini and a towel,' he suggested as Rose opened the door and stood back. 'We'll pass some beautiful coastline on the journey. It's going to be hot and there are some pretty restaurants on the beach where we could stop for lunch.'

'Breakfast and lunch?' Rose huffed. 'This isn't a date.'

'We need to eat,' Ben shot back, feeling a flutter of temper. 'If it makes you feel any better, we can sit at separate tables,' he said, trying to reinstate his teasing tone.

He shouldn't be irritated by Rose's lack of trust; he had to keep things light. This wasn't personal and he had no intention of letting it become so.

'And I'm going to swim even if you don't – you're welcome to ogle me while I do.' With that, he walked through the door and shut it without waiting for Rose's response.

13

BEN

'I need to be back by four o'clock,' Rose said to Ben after sending and receiving a flurry of texts as he careered down the motorway heading for the village of Montotta, where the seller of the statue was located. 'So I can meet with Marco and Luna before we make the wedding favours. Luna says it's the only free time she's got before the wedding,' she grumbled. 'We're cutting it fine.'

'We can make that and there'll still be plenty of time for lunch and a swim,' Ben promised.

Rose sucked in a breath as a car squealed past and Ben had to stop himself from reassuring her. He saw a café on their right and quickly indicated so they could stop.

'I'm just going to pick us up some coffee and breakfast,' he said. 'Black for you I know, do you want something to eat?'

Rose pulled a face. 'I'll have whatever you're having,' she said eventually. 'That way if I don't eat it, you can finish mine.'

Ten minutes later, Ben returned with a bag and coffees for both of them. 'I had to beg the waitress for these. Italians do *not* believe in takeaways,' he complained. He hopped in the car and handed the coffee and bag to Rose before getting back onto the road again. They remained silent for a few minutes while she sipped her drink and he did the same. When the caffeine hit his brain, he began to wake up.

'You promised me a story,' Rose said abruptly, after a few more moments of silence.

'Sorry?'

'About Isabella and Cesare. You mentioned there'd been a fight?' Rose said, fiddling with the bag on her lap.

'Could you pass me something to eat first please?' Ben said. The café owner where he'd stopped would probably shoot him if he knew he was eating one of his famous *cornetti* while driving. Food was something to be savoured in Italy, but if they were going to have time to pick up the statue and make it back with a detour to the beach, they didn't have time for a leisurely breakfast.

Rose gave him a pastry and then stared at him. She seemed more relaxed at the moment, but the roads were clear and there were no cars shooting past. Ben knew that would change soon. He tasted some of the cornetto and sighed. 'I should move to Italy,' he murmured, quickly finishing it off as he remembered he'd been thinking about doing exactly that after he married Sophia, working with Marco from afar. He knew his friend planned to stay in Bristol after he married and had mentioned that he hoped Luna would join him there. Ben loved Bristol, but no one made cornetti like the Italians. 'Can I have another one please?' he begged.

Rose tutted. 'Not until you've told me some of the story.' She shifted the pastry bag to her other knee, out of his reach.

'Fine.' Ben shook his head. He was used to women falling over themselves to make him happy. He hadn't decided if Rose's reaction to him was a refreshing change or an annoyance. He did find her puzzling and wondered if that was the reason he couldn't get her out of his mind. 'I told you Marco's grandparents had separated recently.'

He caught her nod from the corner of his eye.

'I think that was clear last night – she was obviously very angry about something. How long have they been married?' She carefully picked a pastry from the bag. Ben reached for it thinking it was for him, but Rose took a bite. 'Not yet, you need to tell me more,' she muttered.

Ben chuckled. Perhaps he didn't mind her teasing him. 'Almost sixty years. There was going to be a big party for them next year. The family have been planning it for ages. Now, no one's sure if it'll happen.' He frowned. Isabella and Cesare's marriage had always been so rock solid. Something to aspire to. Ben knew he didn't want a long-term relationship, but he still believed in them, still wanted to see them work for everyone else.

'Do you know what happened?' Rose asked, twisting in her seat, making the emerald-green dress she'd brought from *Elegante* rise and expose the tiniest hint of knee. Ben forced his eyes back on the road, ignoring the tightening in his limbs and the way his heart had begun to hammer.

'Firstly, you have to understand Isabella is very superstitious,' he said.

'Which means what?' Rose drummed her fingers on the tiny patch of exposed skin, drawing his attention to it again.

Ben decided to just tell her the whole story. It was ridiculous, but perhaps Rose could help. He didn't know much about her track record with relationships, but she probably had more idea about what to do than anyone else. The Marino family were in bits about the break-up and the only light on the horizon had been Marco and Luna's wedding, but Isabella's words last night had proved the impending nuptials had changed nothing.

He sighed. 'Isabella and Cesare met when they were children. Isabella's family lived close to here and they went to the same school. They became best friends, and as they grew older, that friendship turned into love...' He paused wondering how it might feel to have known someone for your whole life, as Rose sighed.

'Well, at least it's not another story about love at first sight...' she muttered.

Ben chuckled, recalling the thump he'd felt in his chest when he'd seen Rose for the first time on the aeroplane. Although that had probably been fear – she had been angry. 'They married when they were seventeen and their marriage has lasted almost sixty years. It's truly tragic that after all that time, it might break up.'

Rose nodded. Perhaps feeling bad, she pulled another pastry from the bag and handed it to him. 'Keep your hands on the steering wheel,' she ordered sharply as he took it.

Ben quickly shoved the whole thing into his mouth.

'You need to finish this story if you want any more,' she said, taking another for herself. It was the most Ben had seen Rose eat since they'd arrived in Italy which meant she was obviously starting to relax around him. 'What's destroyed a marriage of almost sixty years – did one of them cheat?'

Ben didn't speak until he passed the next junction of the motorway, taking his time to study the red and pink flowers growing on nearby hills. The sun had moved higher in the cloudless blue sky and it was getting hot in the car, so he put the air conditioning on full. 'That's not it. I don't think either of them would even consider that. They're two people who are meant for each other; there isn't anyone else in the world for either of them.'

'So, what happened?' Rose pressed.

Ben sighed. 'Just after they met and before they decided to marry, Cesare planted an olive tree for Isabella,' Ben said. 'It was at the far edge of the field we were in last night – you need to walk to the end to find it. It was special to them.'

'So he planted a tree,' Rose recapped, sounding confused. 'I'm not sure how that ended a marriage after so many years.'

'I'm getting to that,' Ben said as a car overtook.

There were more vehicles on the road now, but Rose still seemed relaxed. Perhaps the story was keeping her from thinking about being afraid? 'An olive tree can last for hundreds of years – Cesare planted it as a symbol of their love. It was supposed to represent their future together. He proposed beside it. When Leonardo was born, it was the first place they took him. Marco too.'

'Okay,' Rose said, clearly still not understanding. 'That sounds romantic, but I'm still not sure why it's important.'

Ben winced. 'Years ago, Cesare gave up smoking – at least he said he had. But every now and again he'd take some wine and a cigarette to the tree so he could sit under it and watch the sun set.'

'Alone?' Rose asked sharply.

He nodded. 'It was an open secret among the family. Only Isabella wasn't aware, at least I don't think she was.'

'So he lied,' Rose said flatly.

'A white lie.' Ben stopped abruptly. What had he thought about colouring in untruths? 'But you're right, it was a lie,' he admitted.

'So, what happened?' Rose asked, a cornetto halfway to her mouth.

'A few months ago, he was smoking and doing a crossword on his phone, and a piece of ash from the cigarette set the tree alight. It burned all the way down before he could put the fire out.' He winced.

'So the tree is dead,' Rose said slowly.

'Yep,' Ben agreed. 'And Isabella thinks that means their marriage is too.' He shook his head. 'She's very superstitious, the tree was symbolic, and no one can convince her otherwise. She's furious, angry, hurt – even though it was an accident.'

Rose pulled a face. 'Are you sure there isn't more to it than that?'

'What do you mean?' He paused. He'd been expecting Rose to say Marco's grandmother was being unreasonable. That she should talk to her husband. Suggest some kind of rule.

'I mean a sixty-year marriage is unlikely to end just because of a tree – or a lie. My guess is she will have known he was still smoking. That can be difficult to hide,' Rose said. 'Perhaps there's more to this story?' She looked so serious Ben took a moment to reassess.

'You think so?' he said slowly, thinking about how Sophia had told him how excited she was about marrying him, how perfect they were for one another, but all the time she'd been having doubts. She hadn't told him that until the last minute. Was Isabella hiding something too? If she was, none of the family were aware.

'Is that why she's living separately from him?' Rose asked.

Ben nodded. 'After the fire, Isabella moved into one of the houses the Marinos keep for guests, and he followed. He wanted to stay close to her so he could put things right, but she won't talk to him.'

'It's difficult to fix something if you don't talk,' Rose said softly. 'If they don't get to the bottom of whatever the real problem is, how are they supposed to work on it?'

Ben shrugged. 'I'm not sure Isabella wants to fix anything.'

'That's a shame,' Rose said, frowning.

'What would the Love Doctor do if she could?' he asked hopefully.

'I didn't think you believed in what I did?' Rose muttered.

'I never said that,' Ben said. 'I just.' He frowned. 'This isn't the same as what's happening between Marco and Luna.'

'It could be their future, though.' Rose's lips pinched. 'I'd like to help, but I'm not sure there's much I can do unless Marco's grandparents are prepared to talk about what's happened. This goes beyond rules, it's about communication and honesty.' She frowned. 'It's also about being willing to admit if you're wrong and, in my experience, few people are.' Rose sighed, plucking another pastry from the bag and biting into it, keeping her eyes firmly on the road. Was she thinking about her parents again? From what he'd seen, she hadn't stopped trying with them.

'So we should give up?' Ben asked, feeling oddly disappointed. Then again, he'd done nothing but tease her since they'd met and contradicted her each time that she'd mentioned her concerns about Luna and Marco's rushed marriage. Perhaps he should have listened to her more?

'I didn't say that,' Rose said, shaking her head. 'I'll see if I can talk to them. If they'll admit whatever the real problem is, perhaps I can help. If they want me to...'

'Thank you.' Ben watched Rose out of the corner of his eye as she turned to stare out of the window looking thoughtful.

She might have some odd ideas about love. But for the first time since they'd met, he realised he trusted her. He just wasn't sure if he was happy about that.

14

———————

BEN

'I think we're almost there,' Ben said as he took a right, following the sat nav down another narrow avenue with a row of quaint-looking shops on one side and multiple leafy trees with angular shadows on the other. It was boiling outside and the sun was high, even though it was only just past nine. Which meant they had plenty of time to pick up the statue and stop at the beach before they made it back to Villa Paradise.

Rose had fallen asleep for the last half an hour, overcome by the stress of being in the car and the early morning – and Ben was beginning to feel tired too. He needed another coffee and to stretch his aching limbs before they started the return journey. He pulled over to the side of the road and parked alongside a row of cars, just as Rose woke up.

'Are we here?' she asked, blinking as she looked around. The green dress had ridden higher on her leg, exposing a new patch of creamy skin, and Ben forced himself to avert his eyes, although the rest of his body still responded.

'The shop's along here somewhere,' he said roughly, wagging a finger at the buildings. 'It's called—' He stopped and checked his mobile. Marco had texted him the details after he'd gone to bed. '*Negozio di curiosità.*' He looked up. 'That means curiosity shop.'

'Well, everything looks shut. I think we might have come too early,' Rose murmured, opening the door and getting out before walking along the pavement. She stopped when she reached the third shop down which had wide blue shutters covering half of the window at the front and a row of pots bursting with pink and white flowers on the ground.

Ben got out of the car too and took a moment to stretch, groaning as his back and legs complained about being squashed into such a tiny space.

'I think it might be this one,' Rose said, approaching the doorway and cupping her eyes so she could peer inside. 'I wish it was open. There's some gorgeous jewellery inside.'

'Marco said someone would be waiting for us, so it'll probably open soon,' Ben said as he strode to stand beside her. There was a large cabinet just in front of the window which Rose seemed to be drooling over. It was filled with various necklaces adorned with green, blue and red stones. Further into the shop he could see a record player and a pile of vinyl – some by a country singer he recognised.

'I need to tell Marco to visit,' he said, pointing to the records. 'He loves that artist.'

'Luna hates country music,' Rose said, frowning as she continued to admire the jewellery. Ben turned and looked around, deciding to ignore the new black mark on Marco and Luna's relationship.

'I wonder where the owner is,' he pondered. The street was quiet aside from a flock of chorusing birds, but there was a café a few buildings along and someone was just opening up. He considered going to get another coffee, but then Rose tapped on the door of the shop. When nothing stirred, she knocked again and placed her ear to the glass.

'Surely someone should be here by now?' she said.

'It's still early.' Ben eyed the coffee shop again. A man wearing a white apron was now outside opening a large white umbrella above a cluster of wooden tables and chairs.

'I thought we were in a hurry?' Rose asked, knocking again. But the shop remained silent.

Ben turned, fantasising that he could smell espresso. The man who'd finished opening the umbrella was now openly staring at them. He shouted something, but Ben couldn't make out the words. He was going to go and speak to him, but then the man started to point frantically at the pots by their feet.

'I think he's saying something's down here.' Ben knelt so he could look between the terracotta pots and immediately spotted a small hessian sack tucked behind one of them. Rose must have spotted it at the same time because she bent and picked it up.

'It's heavy,' she said, weighing it in both hands. 'Do you think this is it?'

Ben turned. The man outside the café was now nodding. 'I'm guessing the answer is yes.'

'There's an envelope tied to the outside,' she said, squinting at it. 'I'm not sure what it says because—'

'It's written in Italian,' Ben guessed, drawing closer to her, getting a whiff of strawberries again which merged with the smell of coffee. His heartbeat kicked up, but he ignored it. Instead, he studied the envelope, translating the words written on the outside–

For the one seeking the gift of life.

'Is it for us?' Rose asked eagerly.

'I think so.' Ben tugged the envelope from the rough string attaching it to the bag. 'I need to read it to make sure.' He tore open the top and unfolded the note inside which had been written in black twisty handwriting on yellowing paper. 'This is a bit ominous,' he joked as Rose shifted the top of the hessian sack down until it revealed a curved female figure carved from shiny white stone.

'It's lovely, and the material is so smooth,' Rose murmured, running a fingertip over the statue's head. 'What does the letter say?'

Ben studied the writing, taking his time translating the words in his mind, until he was sure he understood them. He was fluent in Italian but a little rusty on the written word.

'It starts with "For Isabella Marino", so this is definitely for us,' he said, watching as Rose twisted the statue around and studied its face. It depicted a beautiful young woman with lush curves and long wavy hair.

'You might want to put that back into the sack so it doesn't get damaged,' he said.

'Why?' Rose looked up and Ben pointed to the letter again before reading the first sentence aloud. 'It says something along the lines of, handle very carefully, the magic is powerful.'

'It's just an ornament,' Rose snorted.

'Is there no room for superstition in your rules?' he asked, keeping his voice gentle because he wasn't trying to criticise Rose, but he wasn't sure he agreed with the tight framework she'd wrapped around her world. There was no room for impulse, or for making mistakes. No room for happiness either, in his opinion. Too many rules made life dull – you could follow all of them and still end up unhappy and alone. Wasn't she living proof of that? Living for the day was the only way. That and keeping things simple.

'I prefer to stick with facts, they're less open to interpretation,' she said as she continued to run her finger over the smooth stone. 'Go on, you feel it, it's beautifully crafted. Luna will love it, I know that.'

Ben moved closer and stroked a finger over the statue, it was colder than he'd expected, but the sensation was so smooth it almost felt soft. 'It's very pretty,' he said after a few moments.

He wasn't sure what Rose expected him to say but wanted to please her. He got the feeling not many people gained Rose's approval, and he wanted to be one of the few. He wasn't ready to examine what that might mean, though.

'What else does the letter say?' Rose asked, turning the statue over so she could study it, looking intrigued.

Ben shook his head, trying to push away his attraction to her. She was so obviously immune to his looks that he didn't really know how to act.

He read the next paragraph. 'Something about the owner of the shop not being able to be here, after all, due to a family emergency. She's apologising.' Ben nodded. 'She said as she promised Isabella but only found out she couldn't be here a few hours ago, she wasn't able to let her know. She wanted to make sure we got it today, though. Marco said payment has been taken care of, so we don't have to worry about that.'

'Is that it?' Rose asked, sounding disappointed. 'I thought there'd be a story with it.'

'I've not finished reading.' He took in a long breath and scanned forward. 'Okay. Apparently, if this is given to a couple who care for one another, it'll help them to get pregnant.' He squinted as he tried to translate the next paragraph. It was difficult. 'Some of the Italian is in an older dialect, but the gist is—' His heart thumped hard and he took a sudden step away. 'If you touch the statue, it could make you more fertile. Which means you're more likely to get pregnant, or in my case more likely to get someone pregnant.' Oh boy. He flexed his fingers. 'I'm not sure how long the magic lasts. Perhaps we should put it away?' He looked up and saw Rose's hand had stilled over the statue's head.

'More fertile?' she checked. 'That's ridiculous.' Despite her words, she abruptly righted the statue and pulled the hessian bag up and over its head. 'I think you should take it.' She held it out, transferring her weight from foot to foot as if she were standing on hot coals. 'Marco asked you to collect it. I'm not superstitious but—'

Ben waved his hands feeling flustered. 'Neither am I.' He took another big step towards the car. 'Besides you're already holding onto it.'

'Go on,' she muttered, holding it out again, but Ben shook his head. 'Don't be a coward.'

'Nope.' He wasn't going near the thing. His fingertips were still tingling from where he'd already touched it.

Rose pursed her lips and cocked her head, narrowing her eyes. 'Why not, if you're not superstitious, surely there's no reason not to?'

She held the bag closer to him, a slight smile playing at the edge of her mouth and Ben shook his head again. He'd been around the Marino family enough to know he wasn't going near it anytime soon. Or ever, in fact.

When he was younger, before his wedding, he'd dreamed of having a family, of living an ordinary life, but since the almost wedding, he'd realised some things weren't meant for him. Children were one of them. He'd be the best godfather in the world, if he was lucky to be asked, but that was all. He wasn't interested in having a relationship and nothing, not even magic, would fix that.

'It's probably better if neither of us touches it again. Just to be safe.' He pointed towards the Citroën, feeling unsettled. 'Why don't we put it into the boot of the car and cover it with something. We can get Marco to get it out when we get back. After all, it's a gift for him and Luna,' he said wickedly.

Rose sucked in a breath but didn't argue, instead she headed for the car and indicated he should open the boot quickly. When Ben did, she quickly placed the statue in the back, pulling her hands away as if it had suddenly grown hot. 'There's nothing here to cover it with,' she said.

'Where's the *cornetti* bag?' Ben asked.

'In the footwell. I was waiting until I saw a bin.' Rose went to collect it. It was just big enough to slide the statue into and Ben helped, taking care not to handle the hessian bag for long and making sure he didn't touch the stone at all. Why take the chance?

'If anyone sees it, they'll assume it's filled with litter,' he told her.

Rose scraped her hands over her hips as if she were trying to clean away the feel of the stone, and Ben found himself doing the same – until he caught Rose watching him.

'Shall we go to that beach you mentioned?' she asked, scrubbing her hands over her hips again, making Ben wonder if she was trying to peel off her own skin. 'I think I might want to go for that swim, after all.'

'Salt water's good for breaking spells,' Ben teased, giving Rose a knowing look.

'Is it?' she asked brusquely, avoiding his gaze. 'I've no idea what you mean.'

The beach looked empty and as Ben followed Rose from where he'd parked the car, he took in a deep breath. Marco had brought him here when he'd first visited the Marinos a year after they'd met. Ben had been staying in Bristol for the summer holidays after completing the first year of his degree while his friend planned to spend the time in Tuscany. With both of his parents dead, he had nowhere else to go.

On impulse, Marco had bought him a ticket and asked Ben to join him on the trip and their friendship had been cemented during that summer. Ben had never met a family like the Marinos. They'd been so open and friendly, and he'd been absorbed into the fold like a second son. Until Ben had met them, he hadn't understood how close families could be. It had given him hope and ultimately it had made him believe he could have the same. Much later, he'd realised not everyone got to have the happy ever after – and he was okay with that. He really was.

'Are you hungry?' Ben asked Rose, working hard to keep pace with her as they marched down the final bank of glittering sand onto the flat of the main beach. 'There's a café down that way.' He pointed right. He was famished but wanted to swim some of his energy off first.

'Not yet,' Rose said, looking around. 'It's not very busy, is it?'

'It's mid-week and it's still early. This place will be heaving in a few hours,' he told her sliding his bag from his shoulder and dropping it onto the hot sand. Then he lifted his T-shirt over his head and saw Rose's eyes widen as she took him in.

She swallowed and Ben saw a pulse throb at the bottom of her throat, tried not to get pleasure from it, or to react to her obvious awareness of him. Until this moment, he hadn't known if she felt the same pull as him.

'You're going to get undressed here?' she squeaked. Ben had to fight a smile. It was the first time he'd seen the Love Doctor so flustered and he liked it. Liked that he could do that to her.

'You don't have to look,' he said, slowly unzipping his shorts, intent on teasing her.

'Seriously?' Rose yelled as Ben dropped them, revealing his navy swimming trunks. He bit down on a grin as he slid the shorts off and watched Rose's eyes widen as she tried to muffle a gasp.

Someone behind them began to clap and when Ben turned, he saw two women wearing bikinis lying on a towel staring at him with obvious interest. He hadn't noticed them before, too focused on Rose. A few weeks ago, he'd have waved and gone to speak with them, but he wasn't really interested now.

'Are you his girlfriend?' one of the women – who was obviously a native English speaker – asked Rose, raising an eyebrow.

'Because if my man looked like that, I wouldn't let him strip in public for fear of a stampede...'

'Oh, he's not my boyfriend. He's just someone I bumped into in the car park, thinks he's Magic Mike, apparently,' Rose said mildly. She turned back to Ben, and as he began to apply sunscreen to his chest, folded her arms. 'Are you hoping someone will drop money into a hat for you?' she hissed. 'I'm sure if you take the trunks off too, you'll make enough for lunch. Yours anyway...'

'Ouch.' Ben laughed as one of the women whistled.

'Your friend's right, you should take them off. I've got some change unless you take credit cards?' The woman heckled, giggling and signalling that he should continue.

Ben shook his head and flashed them a smile before turning to Rose. 'You said you wanted to come in,' he said as she shifted from foot to foot. She was wearing sandals and the emerald-green dress and looked more beautiful than Ben had ever seen her. More uncertain too.

'That was before you started to draw a crowd,' she whispered. 'I might wait until your fan club loses interest.' She nodded pointedly towards the two young women who were still staring openly. 'I know they aren't looking at me, but...'

Ben sighed. He hadn't intended to make such a spectacle of himself. He was just trying to unsettle Rose, but he didn't normally show off. What was it about her that made him behave so out of character?

'I'm going in. They'll forget me once I do. See you in there,' he said and then took off.

The water was cool and refreshing as Ben ran in, relishing the splash against his thighs as he got deeper, trying to forget that Rose was watching, hoping she'd relent and join him.

She needed to loosen up. He'd never met anyone so uptight. But there was still something about her that called to him. Perhaps it was because of how determined she was to protect

Luna? Or maybe it was because she wanted to fix everyone's relationships – while tying herself up in so many rules it made it impossible to have one of her own.

She was vulnerable underneath all those serious edges, but it was clear few people saw that. Ben wasn't sure why he could. He only knew that Rose was the first woman he'd met in a long time who'd made him question his desire to stay emotionally single. But whether that was the result of too much sun, a magical statue or his reaction to being part of a wedding again, he wasn't sure.

When Ben turned, he saw Rose. She stopped swimming and stood, her chin resting above the waves as she floated both arms at her sides, helping herself to stay balanced as the sea lapped around them.

'You made it,' he said, grinning.

'Your audience got distracted by someone selling ice cream,' she told him, flicking a piece of wet hair from her face. 'I'm afraid they didn't leave you enough coins for lunch.'

'I must be losing my touch,' he joked. 'Could be the statue's energy interfering with my own.'

She fluttered her fingertips above the waves before swiping seawater from her eyes. 'You don't think there's any truth to the statue story, do you?' For the first time since they'd met, Rose looked concerned for someone other than Luna.

'No, but are you—' Ben had to stop himself from asking if there was someone special in her life. She'd mentioned there wasn't a boyfriend on the scene. It seemed unlikely, but he still felt a twinge of jealousy at the idea.

'I'm single, so I'm not worried about me.' Her eyes fluttered over his face. 'But what about you? I'm assuming there's no one significant.'

'I don't really do serious,' he murmured, but the words were a reflex and left a bad taste in his mouth.

She didn't look surprised. 'After today, you might want to be extra careful with your... acquaintances,' she said, her tone serious. 'Obviously, you're welcome to do whatever you want, but...' She pulled a face.

Ben nodded. 'I'm not looking to get anyone pregnant.' Something inside his heart lurched. He hadn't said those words aloud before, hadn't quite acknowledged what they might mean. Rose stared at him and her face changed – he saw sympathy in her eyes and wished he could wash it away. 'Which is the right decision,' he said, trying not to snap. 'I'm not looking for serious.' There was that bad taste again.

Rose nodded and didn't push. She stared at him a little more, floating her hands on the water, letting the lull of the waves push them from side to side. Ben watched her silently as she drifted back and forth, which meant when the wave hit his shoulders, he wasn't expecting it. It propelled him forward, right into Rose.

'Sorry,' he said as his body hit hers. He might have flattened her, if she hadn't immediately placed the palm of her right hand flat against his chest, making his insides go haywire.

The wave subsided, but instead of taking her hand away, Rose left it resting on his skin. Everything inside Ben began to hum, as every molecule of his body reacted to her touch. He hadn't felt this turned on in years, and it shocked him. Was this the statue's doing or was his resolve of the last two years wavering?

Rose must have realised she was still touching him because she gasped and abruptly withdrew her palm. 'That's not me, it's got to be the fertility statue,' she murmured, reading his mind. 'Looks like I need to spend some time in the salt water until the effects wear off.' She took a wide step backwards, just as another wave crashed onto Ben's shoulders shoving him forward as if nature itself were trying to push them together.

'Or it could just be the tide,' he croaked, wondering if she was right because all he wanted to do right now was pick Rose up and bury his face in her neck before licking her senseless.

He carefully eased backwards, trying to move sideways as awareness continued to course through him. 'We shouldn't stand like this or I'm going to end up pushing you over.'

Rose moved until they were facing again, only this time with their shoulders towards the waves. She took in a deep breath and looked up at the sky. He watched as she absorbed the sunlight, wondering if he'd ever seen anything more beautiful.

'I haven't been to the beach for years,' she confided. 'I'm guessing you come here often to pose?' She opened her eyes again and gave Ben a look that was someway between serious and amused, making him feel ashamed.

'You really think I'm shallow, don't you?' he asked.

'Of course I don't,' Rose said, flushing. 'I'm sorry, I was just teasing. I'm not very good at it,' she admitted. 'I—'

'It's okay... I'm wondering if perhaps you're right.' The realisation, on top of the acknowledgement of his growing feelings, was unsettling.

'I'm not,' Rose said, stepping a little closer to him, holding up a palm again and dropping it just before it touched Ben's chest. She looked like she was going to say more, but then someone shrieked as they dived into the water and a crowd – including the two women from earlier – were suddenly swimming around them, splashing and laughing.

'We should probably get out, you don't want to be late for your party favours and I want to eat before we go...' Ben pointed towards the beach, feeling a sudden need to retreat.

He wasn't used to having these feelings, wasn't ready – but for the first time in a long time, Ben wondered if with Rose, he could be?

15

ROSE

Rose watched Ben steer the Citroën out of the car park and tried to make herself comfortable. They'd had fun on the beach aside from that strange moment in the water, when she'd thought she might have hurt his feelings. Then the moment had passed as quickly as it had arrived, and he'd morphed back into the man she recognised. Fun and sexy with no hint of depth. Only this time Rose wasn't sure she was seeing the truth.

She didn't know what to make of Ben now. When they'd met, she'd thought he was vain and shallow, but now she suspected that might have been a mistake. He'd even asked if she felt that way and she'd waved it off, but it was clear he was a little hurt by her opinion of him and she felt embarrassed.

As a psychologist she shouldn't have jumped to such an instant and negative conclusion based on looks alone. It was clear that Ben had a lot more to him than she'd assumed, but Rose wasn't sure she was ready to explore it. Wasn't sure she wanted to open doors that she might want to go through.

They joined the main highway and a car whizzed past, making her flinch. The road was busy. Probably because it was still lunchtime, and she felt her insides twist.

Her fear of being in a car was limiting her life – she'd thought about talking to someone about it, but it had never felt like the right time. What was she so afraid of? Rose wasn't sure she wanted to examine that now either. What did it say about her? A psychologist who was afraid to look inside her own mind was hardly qualified to look into anyone else's. Perhaps it was time for her to open herself up a little?

'How long till we get there?' she asked, her voice pinched. They'd eaten at the beach just before they'd left, so she wasn't hungry and there was no excuse to stop, but she wasn't looking forward to the journey. Another car sped past, and Rose gripped the edge of her seat as blood pumped loudly in her ears.

'Probably two hours,' Ben said kindly. 'Feel free to sleep – you'll need your energy for the wedding favours later.' He began to speed up and overtook a couple of cars. Rose swallowed, trying not to let the sensation of being out of control affect her. But she could feel her heart pounding in her chest, the nausea building up inside her throat. She heard her mother's ringtone, Elvis Presley's 'Can't Help Falling in Love', start playing, but her mobile was in her handbag, so she decided to ignore it. Her mother would just be chasing her decision about the wedding and Rose had no answer for her yet.

She was tired of being stuck in the middle of her parents' relationships. But didn't feel right about walking away. What would they do if their latest marriages fell into chaos again and she wasn't there to pick up the pieces?

'You're uncomfortable,' Ben guessed, glancing at her.

'I'll feel a lot better if you kept your eyes on the road,' she said with feeling.

She saw him nod and fix his eyes ahead as another car overtook and squealed past. Rose closed her eyes, then opened them again because it was harder not to watch and she didn't want to sleep.

Sunshine beat down on the windscreen and even though

the air conditioning was on full, the car was boiling. The heat seemed to bring out Ben's scent – a combination of salt from the sea and the coconut sunscreen she'd seen him use. It made her whole body tingle, made her want to leap across the car so she could bury her face in his neck. But Rose wasn't sure she wanted to acknowledge that either. He was Marco's best friend – and in her quest to dissuade Luna from marrying in such a hurry, he was supposed to be her arch-rival. It was easier that way. Way easier to ignore the attraction between them.

'Do you want me to distract you?' Ben asked after a few tense moments.

'How?' Rose flinched as another car flew past at rocket speed.

Ben thought for a moment. 'Usually, I'd flirt with you,' he said, smiling ruefully. 'But I think you'd see through all my usual tricks.'

'You have tricks?' Rose found herself bantering, surprised by how easy it was to slip into. One of her exes had once accused her of being robotic – an insult that had cut deep at the time although Rose had soon decided he was wrong. Now she wasn't so sure. She was in a different league to Ben, who interacted with people so easily. She felt her cheeks flush as the impulse to flirt back got the better of her. 'Try me,' she challenged.

Ben raised an eyebrow. 'You asked for it,' he said, sounding surprised. 'You look pretty today.'

Rose snorted. 'Is that the best you can do?' she asked. There was a beep behind them, and she twisted around and saw a massive blue bus bearing down before it swerved into the other lane. She sucked in a breath and jerked forward linking her fingers together, feeling her nails dig into her palms.

'I was barely trying, don't give up on me yet,' he joked, ignoring the bus as it disappeared into the distance.

Rose found herself smiling even as three more cars zoomed

past in quick succession, making her breath catch on its journey from her lungs. 'Bring it on.' She forced the words out keeping her tone playful, bemused by her own behaviour. What had got into her – was it the statue again, or was that just an excuse they were both using, unwilling to take responsibility for feelings they didn't want?

Ben looked amused although there was something strange about the set of his shoulders now – it was almost as if he was disappointed. 'Your brain fascinates me,' he attempted.

'Nice try,' she said lightly even though the compliment had made her flush. 'Looks are, after all, a lucky hand of fate, whereas intelligence can be earned and cultivated. You guessed right that it would please me. Bravo.'

'I said I was good.' Ben's tone was amused, but again there was something off about it. Was this something to do with what she'd said at the beach?

'Do women always fall for your charms?' Rose asked, leaning back in her seat and trying to relax, hoping Ben would too. The scenery was beautiful and she looked out of the window, admiring the mountains in the distance and the vibrant colours of the flowers and trees. She caught a waft of Ben's sunscreen again and opened the window a crack so she could feel the breeze on her cheeks.

Ben frowned. 'It's not a game. I'm just trying to make them feel good about themselves. I don't...' He sighed, clearly searching for the right words. 'I'm not pandering to my ego and I'm not indiscriminate.' He fell silent and Rose let him think. Wondered if this is what had been bothering him. Was disturbed that her opinion of him mattered. Did that mean she mattered? Because if she did, that would be bad for both of them.

'I know you're not,' Rose said because somehow, she did. Ben was a strange mixture of real and unreal. On the surface you got what you saw: a stunning face, perfect body. A veritable

Adonis who seemed happy to deliver whatever you wanted to hear. There were plenty of people vying for his attention. But underneath Rose was beginning to suspect he was much more. That perhaps he'd been pretending and was struggling with that now.

'I'm not sure why it's important to me that you know that,' he opened up, wincing.

'I do know, Ben,' Rose admitted. 'It's just we're on opposite sides here and it's easier if I paint you as someone I can't respect.' The car fell silent, and Rose wasn't sure who was more surprised by her honesty.

'Well, okay,' he said eventually, sounding less troubled. 'So, what does that mean?'

'I'm not sure I want to talk about this anymore,' Rose shot back. She had an odd feeling in her chest, a bubble of fear she wasn't ready to let burst. Who knew what might happen if it did?

Ben wasn't the type of man she'd ever thought she'd allow herself to have feelings for. But she did, and this was happening too fast. She had to slow things down – that's what she'd advise her clients to do. It was time to follow her own counsel.

A car suddenly shot up behind them and beeped its horn loudly, making Rose flinch and then turn, instantly forgetting her troubling feelings for Ben.

'That car's too close.' She could hear the tremor in her voice and tried to relax. They weren't going round the roundabout the wrong way now. Her father wasn't driving and screaming at the same time. She was perfectly safe. It was the first time she'd acknowledged that she trusted Ben. Even though it was too soon. According to her rules, about six weeks too early.

'Relax,' he murmured. 'It's just Italian drivers. Nothing to worry about.'

Another car appeared from nowhere and skidded up beside them spraying grit, matching the speed of the car behind. Rose could see the driver of the new car shaking his fist at the person behind them. She swallowed, gripping the sides of the seat again as her hands went clammy. 'This isn't good.'

'We're just going to stay in our own lane minding our own business,' Ben reassured, reaching out to lightly squeeze her shoulder. 'Don't worry.'

Rose didn't bother to respond. She appreciated his attempt to calm her but knew it wasn't going to work. The car behind began to beep its horn, and Ben put his foot down making the Citroën shoot forward, away from the other two.

'We'll get off the motorway soon,' he promised.

Rose made herself relax and sank into her chair and shut her eyes. She listened to the soothing sound of the wind blowing through the crack in the window and indulged herself by inhaling Ben's scent.

'Dammit!' Ben's curse made Rose jerk her eyes open just as the first car drove up too. As soon as it did, the other car pulled up beside it, so close they almost bumped wing mirrors. 'I'm not sure I can shake them.' He still tried, putting his foot down and speeding up.

'Maybe slow down,' Rose suggested. 'They might be trying to race us; it could be a game.'

Ben did as she suggested, but the car behind just got closer.

'I think we're in the wrong place at the wrong time. They're using us as a buffer. I'm just going to stay where I am till we get off. It won't be long.' He seemed relaxed which made her feel better.

Rose nodded and sank into the seat trying to remain calm. She'd barely been in the car over the last few years – it was easier to use buses and trains in London – which made this whole thing far more upsetting.

'I think it's going to hit us. The idiot is swerving,' Ben suddenly yelled.

Rose closed her eyes, and they were still shut when she

heard the crunch of metal bumping into metal, and when she opened them again, she saw the car behind had been shoved into the other lane. The momentum spun them forward as the other two cars sped away, chasing each other. Ben braked, but the Citroën started to skid.

'Hold on, I can't stop,' he shouted.

Everything seemed to still as Ben gripped the steering wheel, his hands going white. Rose pressed her fingers tight into the leather seat, practically peeling off the material as the car continued to slide. She couldn't believe this was happening. One moment they were driving along flanked by the two cars, and the next the Citroën was heading left, skidding on the surface of the road.

'Please just stop it!' Rose screamed as the car continued to spiral forward, seemingly still ignoring the fact that Ben had applied the brakes.

'I'm trying.' They left the safety of the tarmac and were now bumping their way along dusty stones. There was a solid wall of shrubbery in front of them and they were hurtling towards it even though Ben was pumping the brakes.

Rose knew she was going to die. She'd barely lived, and her life was about to end on a busy road in Tuscany. She had no rules for this – no rules to make it better, none to help it make sense. Today had been wonderful and she wanted more of them. More sun, more sea, more early mornings filled with espresso and sunshine. More days of flirting and the low hum of attraction. All those tantalising possibilities, all that freedom to feel. The realisation that she'd locked herself down so tightly had her choking down a sob.

'It's okay,' Ben said, reaching for her. It was only when Rose realised that he'd taken off her seatbelt and pulled her onto his lap that it was over. That they'd somehow stopped, and she was still alive.

Ben was stroking her shoulders making soothing noises. She

could smell the sea again and the coconut sunscreen she'd watched him sliding onto his perfect torso and legs before averting her eyes. Her blood was pumping fast around her body making her limbs and face heat – but whether it was a result of fear or being in Ben's arms she didn't know. Wasn't entirely sure she cared.

'It's not okay,' Rose somehow managed to choke.

Ben squeezed her shoulders and pulled her into his chest, wrapping his arms around her trying to absorb her shaking. 'You're okay, I'm okay; even the car's in one piece, just about. Although I think the car hire company might blacklist me.' He began to stroke a slow hand down Rose's back and she trembled, burying her face into his T-shirt, inhaling deeply. She couldn't seem to stop herself.

'It's not okay,' she whispered again. She pulled back and stared into Ben's face. His cheeks were flushed, and those deep brown eyes were distressed. It was then that Rose realised he'd been afraid too.

'Do you have a rule for a near-death experience?' he asked, his voice husky.

Rose thought about his question, all the while breathing him in. If he'd asked the same thing an hour ago, she'd have said something about being more careful, or that her usual rule was to stick with taking buses and trains because they were safer. But she had no answer for him, so she simply slid a hand into Ben's hair and grasped a fistful before tipping his face down and capturing his mouth with hers. The move was unlike her, but in this moment, Rose didn't care.

If Ben was surprised, he didn't show it. He didn't fight her off and he didn't pull away. No, he simply ran with it, putting all of those kissing miles he had on the clock to excellent use. He was an amazing kisser, and his mouth knew exactly what it was doing. In a world where you could be anything, why wouldn't you want to be king of the kiss?

Rose started to have second thoughts, began to wonder if this was a good idea, but then Ben adjusted the stroke of his clever tongue, somehow sliding her closer as he angled her chin.

Dear God, he was so good at this. How much practice had he had, exactly? Could you get a degree in kissing – and if you could, should she get one too? Make up for all the time she'd wasted.

Rose's insides were fluttering and she briefly wondered if someone had slipped a kaleidoscope of butterflies into her stomach. The sensation was... well, she liked it. But it was so far out of her comfort zone that she felt pressure to fight it. Ben stroked a gentle hand down her side and across her waist and Rose shifted, forcing herself to find the strength to pull away. When she did, he stared at her with the oddest expression. One Rose wasn't sure she wanted to allow herself to understand.

'Are you okay?' Ben asked, watching her intently.

Rose scrambled off his lap, somehow making it over the gear stick and into the passenger seat again. She pushed the skirt of her dress down and brushed a hand through her hair trying to tidy herself up. 'I'm fine,' she said, although she didn't sound it. 'That was just adrenaline and the effects of the fertility statue, right?'

Ben stared at her. Then he nodded, smiling, but not before she saw his jaw flex. 'Sure, and I was trying to distract you. I'm guessing it worked.' He studied her as if he were trying to take every millimetre of her in. 'You look... in control. More like your usual self.'

Was it her imagination or did he look disappointed? He broke eye contact and glanced around. They'd stopped about a metre from the shrubbery. There were cars flying past on the motorway clearly oblivious to what had just happened, and Rose realised their engines were roaring. She just hadn't noticed.

She jerked her chin. 'You look calm too.'

He shrugged. 'Physical contact is...' He didn't finish. Instead, he opened the door and got out of the car, then wandered round it, taking his time to check the bodywork and tyres. After a minute, Rose got out too.

'Does everything look okay?' she asked, following him. She had the oddest desire to wrap her arms around him, to lean in and smell coconuts again.

'There's a slight dent in the back, but the car's okay.' He nodded, giving her a look she couldn't read. She sensed an edge to him now, had a feeling she'd disappointed him again. 'What about the statue? Do you think we should check it?'

'I think we'll leave that for Marco,' Ben said brusquely. 'We've had enough danger for one day.'

He turned and walked back to the car, opened the door and got inside. Rose paused for a moment before joining him, trying to work out what had just happened and why pulling away from their kiss suddenly felt like it had been a mistake.

16

ROSE

Ben parked the Citroën outside of Villa Paradise and Rose hopped out and was immediately greeted by Luna, who was waiting by the front door holding a glass of bubbles.

'Are you okay after the accident?' Luna asked, handing Rose the glass, looking between her and Ben, a deep groove marring her forehead. 'Is the car fixed?'

'The car rescue service came and I'm fine,' Rose lied, finishing the drink in one, trying not to look at Ben.

'Really?' Luna raised an eyebrow as Rose handed her back the empty glass.

'Shall I get changed and meet you somewhere?' Rose asked, skipping up the steps, aware she needed time alone to digest what had happened and to work out what it meant, or at least how she felt about it.

'We're in the garden,' Luna shouted after her, sounding worried. 'Don't you want to talk to me and Marco about the wedding first?'

Rose winced and shook her head, aware of how odd this probably seemed. 'I don't think we have time.' In truth, her mind was too jumbled. How could she talk about rules, or give advice about love after what had just happened? She'd just kissed Ben Pearson, broken all her rules, wrapped herself around him when they barely knew each other. Now she had feelings she couldn't explain, an ache in her chest that wouldn't go away. How was she supposed to counsel anyone on restraint now?

Suddenly, all the things she believed and trusted were crumbling away – and she wasn't sure how to find solid ground again. She shouldn't be attracted to a man like Ben, but she was. She shouldn't like him either, but did. It had been easy to blame adrenaline or the effects of a fertility statue – but Rose knew she was kidding herself.

'We could make time,' Luna said tentatively, looking anxious. 'I thought you were concerned we were rushing into things?'

'Later,' Rose promised. Although she wasn't convinced that she'd be feeling differently then.

Luna frowned. 'Your mum and dad both called me while you were gone,' she confided, looking even more concerned. 'They were asking if you'd made a decision about their weddings.' She pulled a face. 'Apparently, you need to choose between them which you haven't mentioned to me. What's going on, Rose?' She sounded hurt.

'Nothing...' Rose sighed. At least nothing she was going to get into now. She had to make plenty of decisions, but for the first time in years, she had no idea which way to turn.

It was wrong – delaying and avoiding would only end up creating more problems – but for some reason, she couldn't focus. The clarity she'd spent a lifetime relying on was gone. 'I'll see you in a minute,' she mumbled, before charging into the villa and up the stairs.

．　．　．

Rose could hear the buzz of women's voices over the low hum of music when she wandered down the steps and into the garden twenty minutes later. She'd showered, changed and done her makeup so felt less frazzled. Her parents had both called while she'd been getting ready in her room, but she'd let them go to voicemail, still too conflicted to speak to either of them. Usually, she hit her problems head on – it was another of her rules – but she still couldn't seem to make a decision about anything.

What if all the rules she'd spent a lifetime creating were wrong? What if she was all the things she'd been accused of over the years – naïve, misguided even clueless – what then?

'Rose!' Luna said, suddenly jumping up from the table under the pagoda where she was sitting with Aurora, Elena and Francesca.

'You look beautiful, *leonessa*,' Aurora said, getting up too so she could give Rose an enthusiastic kiss on each cheek. 'We've been waiting for you.' She pointed to the table which had been covered with crafting equipment. 'I'm happy we're going to be able to catch up again.' She nodded at Rose. 'There was a lot unsaid last night. Aldo has so many things he still wants to share with you.'

Rose's stomach sank. She wasn't looking for more revelations – and despite not believing in Aldo, she was still a little afraid he could somehow read her mind.

'You look stunning,' Francesca chimed in as she indicated the chair opposite to where she was sitting. 'The red dress really suits you. I am a genius,' she joked.

'You are,' Elena agreed.

'Thank you,' Rose said, discreetly searching the area for Ben before taking the seat and perusing the bowls laid out in front of them which were filled with different coloured almonds, white tulle, pots of pink ribbon and cardboard hearts. Wine glasses sat at each of the place settings, and bottles of prosecco and red and white wine were peppered in between the bulging crafting bowls.

'Where's Ben?' Francesca asked, glancing around and Rose did too.

'This is a woman only event, remember,' Aurora said. 'He's with Marco, Leonardo and Cesare organising a big surprise.'

'A surprise?' Luna asked, looking around. 'What surprise?'

'Now, it wouldn't be a surprise if we told you that, would it, *cara*?' Aurora chuckled.

Rose heard the demon let out a low growl and glanced around in time to see Isabella leading Coco around the house towards them. She was carrying the pastry bag they'd hidden the statue in. Rose had almost forgotten about it in all the excitement. Had Ben handed it over when she'd been changing her clothes?

Was Marco's *nonna* going to give Luna her present now? Rose winced. This wasn't the right time – Luna didn't need the pressure of family expectations being laid on her, especially in front of a crowd.

'We should start with a toast,' Elena said, greeting her mother-in-law, holding up her drink and grinning at Luna. 'To the bride.' Everyone picked up their glasses and quickly toasted. 'We will make the *bomboniere* together now. For those of you who have never made them before.' She smiled at Rose. 'You need to make a bag with the tulle and fill it with five almonds, then you will decorate them.' She pointed to the pots on the table.

'Why five almonds?' Rose asked, studying the bowls.

'Because they signify health, wealth, happiness, fertility, and longevity,' Elena said. 'So please ensure you include them all. We don't want our bride and groom to miss out on any, do we?' She smiled.

'Almonds won't make a marriage happy, and it won't make it last,' Isabella grumbled as she pulled up a chair and sat, thumping the pastry bag down on the table in front of her. 'There's only one reason to have a wedding.' She looked meaningfully at the pastry bag.

'*Nonna*...' Elena sighed before turning to Rose. 'Isabella would obviously like to thank you for picking up the wedding gift for her. I'm sure Marco and Luna will appreciate it although she might want to wait until they are alone to give it to them.' She gave her mother-in-law a pointed look.

'What is it?' Luna whispered to Rose. 'I was hoping for a crate of puppies or some special tea.'

'My son might not appreciate either of those,' Elena joked.

'It is neither.' Isabella frowned. 'Do you want it now?' she growled at Luna.

'Why don't we wait until Marco arrives? I asked the men to join us after they set up their surprise. They are going to help us make the *bomboniere*,' Elena told them.

The older woman frowned. 'Usually, only the women make them.'

'Today we're trying something new.' Elena shrugged. 'Why don't we get started? There are plastic gloves beside your plates,' she said. 'If you can pull them on, then *Nonna*, I'm sure you won't mind demonstrating? There's plenty of tulle, pearl stems and ribbon. Please be generous – we want them to look pretty for our guests!'

Isabella got slowly to her feet. 'I do this for Marco and Luna and the *bambini* to come,' she said grandly.

'Okay,' Luna said carefully, glancing at Rose and looking worried as Coco hopped onto her lap and then curled into a ball.

Isabella delicately picked up two pieces of tulle. Rose watched as she nimbly put two small circles together before making a pouch and filling it with five colourful almonds.

Then she pushed the edges together and twisted pink, white and baby blue ribbons around the top before tying them off. She continued to work on it, gradually building it up with more strings of ribbon and adding pearl stems too. Then she silently finished the whole thing off with a white heart which someone had written *Luna & Marco* onto in swirly gold lettering.

'Now it's our turn,' Elena said as Isabella placed the party favour into a bowl in the centre of the table and then sat silently. '*Nonna* made these for me and Leonardo when we married and now, dear Marco and Luna, it's your turn.' Elena grinned as she took her seat too.

'I'm going to need plenty of this,' Francesca muttered as she sipped more wine. 'I'm good at choosing and matching clothes and styles to people, but when it comes to craft, I'm all fingers and thumbs.' She picked up a couple of pieces of the tulle and Rose watched her work before picking up two pieces of the material too.

'Take your time,' Elena said when Rose cursed as one of the almonds skidded across the table.

'That was the happiness almond,' Isabella said sourly, earning herself an indulgent tut from Elena.

Rose carefully put the five almonds into the centre of the material. Why did people believe in traditions like this? Was it easier than putting in the work required to make a relationship thrive?

For years, her parents had hoped for a magic solution – a new partner, fiancé, husband or wife had been used like a sticking plaster – but fundamentally neither had been prepared to put in any hard work. Investing in a new lover was easier than working on the relationship they already had. No matter how hard Rose tried, they never listened. Why did she keep expecting them to? Did she really believe her rules could fix anything?

'You look preoccupied,' Luna said, nudging Rose's shoulder and leaning closer. 'Something wrong?'

She shook her head. 'I'm just thinking,' she said, studying her friend's face. 'You don't look very happy either.'

'Everyone in this family is obsessed with babies,' Luna complained. 'Marco and I have barely talked about having a family. We want time to spend together without the pressure of knowing what comes next. I talked to him about asking everyone to lay off, but he doesn't want to rock the boat.'

Rose opened her mouth to offer help, to give Luna the benefit of her experience and rules, then shut it. Was she really qualified to give advice on this?

'Ah!' Elena suddenly spotted something over Rose's shoulder and clapped. 'You're here!' When Rose turned, she saw Ben, Leonardo, Cesare and Marco walking towards them looking pleased with themselves.

'What have you been up to?' Luna asked, getting up to hug her fiancé.

'It's a surprise,' Marco said, swirling an arm around her waist and tugging her close. 'Give it a few minutes and you'll see exactly what we've been up to.' He kissed her cheek.

'Now you're both here, you can have your gift,' Isabella said, rising slowly and grabbing the pastry bag before ceremonially handing it to Luna.

Cesare winced. 'Is this the right time, *amore*?' he checked.

'Go back to your crosswords, old man, you've barely looked up from them for six months, so you have no idea what's been happening under your nose,' the older woman muttered. 'Open it!' she ordered, waving a hand at Luna who started to pull the gift from the bag, before tugging down the hessian sack and rubbing her hands over the statue.

'Oh, um, I'm not sure you should do that,' Rose said, waving her hand, but was silenced by a hiss from Isabella.

'It's beautiful,' Luna gushed, holding the figure up so she could look at it properly. 'Such an amazing piece of art.' She glanced at Marco. 'When I move to Bristol, I'll make sure there's a special place for it so we can see it every day.'

'What does it mean?' Marco asked, squeezing Luna's shoulder before looking suspiciously at his grandmother. 'It's not just an ornament, is it?' He sounded annoyed.

'Isn't it?' Luna asked, her hand stilling over the stone.

'It's a—' Aurora glanced at Isabella and winced. 'Aldo says it's a *facility* statue, is that correct, *Nonna?*'

'Fertility,' Elena corrected, shaking her head. '*Nonna*…'

'It is very powerful,' the older woman said, gleefully pointing at Luna whose eyes had now widened to twice their normal size. 'Touch it once and—'

'It will help you get pregnant,' Elena finished off.

'Oh, well, that's not quite what I had in mind!' Luna exclaimed, immediately trying to shove the statue into Marco's hands.

'I can't. It works on me too.' Her fiancé held up his palms looking panicked, leaving the stone figure teetering on the edge of Luna's fingers.

'Catch it!' Luna shrieked, lunging forward as it toppled and plunged towards the ground.

Even Rose tried to step in, aiming to snatch it out of the air before it crashed onto the floor. But she was too late, and it caught the edge of the patio and smashed. The sound of stone shattering echoed around the garden while the family stood in shocked silence.

'Oh god, I'm so sorry,' Luna said, dropping to her knees and hovering her hands over the broken figure, clearly still worried about touching the pieces.

'It is broken,' Isabella said, her voice grave as she looked around at the family. 'The magic is gone.'

'I'm so sorry,' Luna repeated, looking stricken.

'It's not your fault.' Rose knelt beside her friend and started to pick up pieces of stone.

'*Nonna*, we're so sorry,' Marco said, stepping closer to her. 'It was an accident.'

'The magic won't work now,' Isabella repeated, her voice shaking. 'There is no time to get a replacement. I will not be at your wedding,' she added stiffly. 'This is a sign.'

'It's not a sign of anything, it was an accident,' Marco insisted. 'We'll fix this, *Nonna*, it'll be all right.'

'I'm not sure we want to fix this,' Luna muttered under her breath as she helped pick up the remaining pieces, shooing away Coco who'd come to investigate the mess. The dog let out a whine before scampering under the table.

'It will take too long to fix,' the older woman repeated, shaking her head.

'It's all just superstition,' Cesare said under his breath.

'It is so much more than that,' Isabella snapped. 'There is no reason for you to marry now and no reason for me to be at the wedding if it goes ahead.'

'*Nonna*,' Marco cried.

'Isabella!' Cesare said sharply. But the older woman just shook her head and slowly wandered away from the table in the direction of the two cottages, before getting swallowed into the night.

'What just happened?' Luna asked her voice wavering, as she rose and gaped at Marco while the rest of the family huddled together and began to chatter to each other, their tones low and fretful. 'Your grandmother isn't coming to our wedding?'

'It's a temporary problem, *Nonna* will come around,' Marco soothed.

'We have two days,' Luna sounded hysterical. Her mobile beeped suddenly, and she pulled it from the pocket of her dress, striding away from everyone before reading the screen. Rose knew something was wrong as soon as Luna's mouth dropped open and she paled.

'What is it?' she asked, going to stand beside her. 'What's happened?'

Her friend gulped. 'Mum's delayed again – she can't find a flight and doesn't think she's going to get here in time for the wedding.' She swallowed shaking her head and turning to Rose, her eyes full of tears. 'We're going to have to postpone.'

17

BEN

'We have to delay,' Luna repeated earnestly to Marco. 'Everything's going wrong. Your grandmother won't come to the wedding.' She shot a devastated look in the direction Isabella had gone, before shaking her head. 'Now my mum might not get here in time. Perhaps this is a sign that we're marrying too quickly?'

Ben saw Marco's forehead furrow as his whole body stiffened. He knew his friend was stubborn and was unlikely to listen to reason, especially after his experience with his previous fiancée. Marco wanted the wedding to go ahead, which meant he'd see Luna's demands as either a challenge or an indication that she was getting cold feet.

'Of course we need to go ahead,' Marco insisted, taking a step towards Luna and stroking a hand down her cheek. '*Tesoro*, you know why the date is important. We agreed. Do we really need other people to celebrate our love? Surely all that matters is the promises we're making to each other?' His gaze momentarily fell on Rose. 'Don't you agree?' he asked.

Rose pulled a face. 'I don't know what to think,' she started. 'Would it really be that awful to wait for a few days?'

Ben winced, wishing for once that Rose could be on his friend's side.

Marco shook his head vehemently. 'It's an important date for my family. You know that. If we can't marry now, it'll have to wait until next year. If you think my *nonna* is being difficult, you've no idea how upset she'll be if we choose to wed on a different day.'

'She doesn't even believe we should get married!' Luna shot back, sounding even more frantic. 'All everyone seems to care about is whether we have babies and we haven't even discussed that properly ourselves.'

'You're getting over-emotional,' Marco said, and Ben knew despite his harsh words, he was trying to put things right. 'Think rationally, *cara*. I love you and you love me. We want to marry and everything's almost ready.' He pointed to the table filled with the materials for the wedding favours before waving a hand. 'My family has been working around the clock to make sure of it. Do you really want to let them all down?'

Luna looked stricken. 'I don't know what I want now,' she whispered.

'You need to listen to each other,' Rose said, taking a step forward until she was standing between them. 'Listening is the bedrock of every successful relationship.'

Luna nodded and Marco opened his mouth, but he didn't get a chance to say more because suddenly dozens of fireworks whizzed into the sky, lighting everything in a blaze of pinks, yellows and oranges before exploding in a series of deafening bangs.

'What the hell is that?' Luna wailed, looking around.

'Your surprise!' Marco said as another blast reverberated in the sky. But no one got the chance to admire the fireworks for long, because Coco let out a sudden pitiful yelp before galloping out from under the table and charging into the darkness.

'Dogs hate fireworks!' Luna squealed, spinning around. 'Surely you knew that. Where did she go?' She searched the inky blackness just as another dozen fireworks shot above them. Ben heard Coco yelp again and tried to see where she'd gone, but the dog had been swallowed by the night.

'Coco's either in the olive grove or she's hiding somewhere in the garden,' Marco soothed as Luna let out a sob. 'She'll be fine, *tesoro.*'

His fiancée rounded on him, clearly close to tears. 'You don't know that,' she spluttered. 'An animal could get to her. She's terrified, we need to find her now!' She stumbled onto the gravelly pathway that led further into the garden.

'But it is dark, *cara,*' Marco said, sounding frustrated. 'Surely she will come back by herself?' His words were punctuated by another loud bang and a blaze of fizzing colours. They would have been beautiful in any other circumstances, but Ben knew each blast was like a nail in the coffin of his friend's wedding. Unless he could help put this right.

'How many fireworks are going to go off exactly?' Luna asked Marco furiously as yet more rockets erupted.

'Just a few more, they are on a timer, *cara,*' Marco said. 'They're supposed to be a celebration of our love; I thought you'd enjoy them.'

'Well, I don't!' Luna complained, stumbling again as she took another few steps along the uneven pathway. Behind them the rest of the family began to spread out calling for Coco. 'I need to find her.'

'Why don't you change your shoes first?' Rose suggested. 'If you fall, you might get injured.'

'*Sì* and Marco, while Luna is changing, you go and find some torches,' Elena ordered, jogging over to join them as Leonardo and Cesare quickly disappeared into the garden. 'We should all search for Coco. It's important to your bride.'

Aurora nodded. 'Aldo says we'll find her where there is—'

She screwed up her face. 'It's difficult to understand. He is saying liquid. Something red or white. It's not completely clear.'

Luna wailed. 'She hates water. She won't even swim with me.' She turned to Rose, her eyes wide. 'Where is she?'

'Go and change into flat shoes,' Ben repeated Rose's advice. 'Then check the grounds and pool. Rose and I will go to the olive grove now. There's a lake...'

'A lake.' Luna paled, then she turned and ran towards the house, stopping momentarily as she passed Marco to shout. 'If we don't find my dog, the wedding is off!'

Ben watched Rose's face as Luna disappeared into the front of the villa, and the family began to yell more orders at one another, further forced into action by Luna's declaration, while Marco stood looking shell-shocked. Rose twisted round and pulled her phone from her pocket so she could switch on the torch and began to half trot, half run into the darkness.

'Wait!' Ben yelled, switching on his torch too as he stumbled after her. 'Don't you want to change your shoes too?' He caught up and looked down at her strappy silver sandals. He paid attention, especially when gorgeous women wore heels. 'You could trip.'

'I'm fine,' Rose said, her voice matter of fact. 'We need to find the demon now. She's not going to drown on my watch. Do you know where this lake is?' She sped up again as another firework launched into the air, lighting up the sky in an explosion of colours. 'I thought they were going to stop,' she said, sounding angry.

'The men programmed them to go off so Marco would be with Luna when they ignited. I don't think there are many left now.' As Ben said it, the sky fell silent. 'The lake is this way.' He pointed left. He knew every inch of the Marinos' property – could navigate it in the dark if necessary. 'You should hold my hand; it gets rocky somewhere around here.' He caught up until they were walking side by side.

Ben thought Rose was going to refuse; instead, she left her hand in his when he took it and linked their fingers. 'We have to find the demon.' She sounded worried. 'Luna loves that dog. We have to find her; if we don't, the wedding won't go ahead.'

Ben squeezed Rose's hand and led her on a path to their right. He knew they'd reached the edge of the olive grove – close to where Cesare had planted the tree for Isabella – and imagined he could smell burning even now.

'As much as I dislike Coco, I love her in equal measure. Coco!' Rose bellowed into the darkness.

They stopped walking and waited, listening to the silence. Ben could hear voices in the distance – recognised Aurora and Francesca's dulcet tones. But Coco didn't answer. 'Do you think she's okay?' There was a crack in Rose's voice, a hint of a tremor, and a measure of vulnerability he hadn't heard until now.

Ben squeezed her hand again. 'I think she's fine,' he said. 'I'll make sure of it.' He frowned: he hadn't made anyone a promise in a long time.

'What is that smell?' Rose tugged Ben's hand, guiding him towards the far corner of the field. 'It's like ashes. Coco!' She shouted. 'You don't think the demon would be attracted to it, do you?'

'I'm not sure. It's Isabella's tree – what's left of it.' Ben shone the light from his phone onto the charred remains of the olive stump. Cesare had cleaned up most of the debris, but he hadn't pulled out the roots. Perhaps he just couldn't bring himself to do it? Maybe admitting the tree was really gone was the same as accepting his marriage was too? Ben knew Marco had offered to do it for him, but his grandfather had said no. Instead, he'd tended to the plant daily, watering the charred remains as if he hoped it would somehow reanimate.

Rose knelt beside the stump and waved her light. 'It looks dead,' she murmured. 'No wonder Isabella's so upset.'

There was a sudden burst of loud shouts in the far distance – in the direction of the house – and she jerked her head towards it. 'Do you think they've found Coco?'

Ben listened carefully. 'I can't hear barking.' He considered retracing their steps, but the lake wasn't far, and if the dog hadn't been found, they needed to check the water just in case.

Rose nodded, looking disappointed. 'Coco would bark. Unless she couldn't.' She looked stricken.

Ben took her hand and squeezed it again, then led her in the direction of the lake. He could hear the soft whistling of crickets, could smell woody bark from the trees, and a combination of dust and hot night sky that had mingled with the familiar strawberry fragrance that made him think of Rose now.

He guided her closer and heard the quiet lap of water as the evening breeze blew across the lake. He could smell it now, but it was still too dark to see. He felt on edge, a little afraid of what they might find when they drew closer.

'Coco!' Rose shouted again as the laps grew louder. 'Where are you?'

They were greeted with silence.

Rose disentangled their hands, and Ben heard the crunch of her feet on the ground as she moved closer to the edge of the water and swept the torch light from her phone in a wide semicircle making the ripples glitter. 'I can't see far. She's not near the edge. Do you think she's here?'

Ben shoved his hands into his pockets. 'It's hard to predict what an animal will do when it's afraid.'

'Have you ever had a pet?' Rose asked, turning to him.

Ben thought about it. He didn't like to share stories from his past. What was the point? But there was something about Rose's hopeful expression in the moonlight that made him break one of his own rules. 'Never.' He paused. 'My parents were elderly and needed quiet. They were sick for most of my teens and a pet wouldn't have been a good idea.' He waited for her to sympathise, to feel sorry for him. Could feel a familiar dead-weight in his chest, expecting it to get heavier.

Rose's attention fluttered across his face and her lips pursed. Her body was still, as if she'd somehow absorbed his emotions and was trying to process them. He braced himself for her sympathy wishing he'd kept his mouth shut.

'You should start with something small. Maybe a house plant?' She studied him intently and he ground his jaw surprised.

'A plant?' He could feel the heavy weight lighten.

Rose nodded. 'I'd suggest a cactus. They're difficult to kill and don't take much effort.'

'Is that supposed to prepare me for being a pet owner?' he asked, amused.

'It's supposed to prepare you for letting yourself get close to something.' She studied him, then nodded. 'If you keep that alive, you'll be ready for something like a hamster. It's important to take things slowly and work yourself up.'

'Another rule.' Ben grinned. 'I'd rather have a dog, something manly with big teeth.' His amusement faded as he looked across the lake. He'd almost forgotten about Coco, he'd got so caught up in flirting. Clearly, they both had. 'I think we should go back to the villa.'

Rose looked surprised. 'But we haven't checked all the way round the lake yet.'

Ben took a step closer to her, caught another whiff of straw-berries and clenched his hands. 'I don't think she's here. Coco was frightened. Instinct made her run, but it's in her nature to find somewhere safe. Safe isn't a dark and cold lake, safe is with Luna or somewhere in the villa.'

Rose stared at him. 'You're right,' she said, looking surprised. 'I had a gerbil called Biscuit once.' She frowned changing the subject so quickly it took him a moment to catch up. Rose didn't give much of herself away either – so he appreciated the confidence. Even if the change in subject was odd.

'What happened to it?' Ben could see from her face that something had.

Rose broke eye contact. 'She died. I got her for Christmas and my parents had a fight.' She paused. 'Can't remember why – it was probably the food, or wine, my mother's dress or maybe it was that the presents she got were too expensive or just wrong.' She shrugged. 'They screamed at each other for almost an hour. It was so loud I hid under my bed. And the next time I checked on Biscuit, she was dead. Dad took her back to the pet shop to complain and they said she'd likely suffered heart failure. It can happen with too much noise. Not all of us can handle the stress.' She straightened her shoulders as if confirming she could. She was a strong woman – but with too much weight, even strong things broke. He knew that from designing buildings.

'Can any of us?' Ben asked, wondering how many times Rose had needed to be strong. Perhaps she followed all of her strict rules to stay sane?

'Sometimes, you don't have a choice,' Rose said. 'If we go back to the villa, where should we check?' She began to walk, retracing their steps. It was darker than before, and he contemplated taking her hand again. But now Ben wasn't sure who needed the contact more and he wasn't sure he was ready to give in to this powerful need to touch her.

They walked in silence, then Rose suddenly stopped and turned so she could look up at him. 'I was wrong...'

'About what?' Ben asked.

Rose gave him a shy smile. 'About the cactus. I think you might be ready for a spider plant.'

18

———

BEN

Marco was searching through shrubbery in the garden when Ben and Rose got back to the villa. 'Did you find Coco?' he asked eagerly, frowning when he saw she wasn't with them.

'I'm sorry,' Ben said. 'The good news is I don't think she's in the lake.'

Aurora's voice suddenly boomed in the darkness, as she shouted for the dog again, making Ben jump.

'Everyone's been walking through the garden and further afield,' Marco said. 'There's no sign of Coco. Luna's beside herself.' He frowned. 'She's still threatening to call off the wedding. I can't believe she'd even say that.' He looked upset. 'Over a dog too.'

'I think it's over more than that,' Rose murmured. 'I've known her a long time and when she's anxious or worried, she lashes out.' She blinked. 'We have to find Coco, then you both need to talk about what just happened. If you do, I'm sure you'll be able to find a solution.' She patted Marco on the shoulder, but his friend still looked unhappy.

'Where haven't you looked?' Ben asked – because the fastest way to fix things was to find Coco.

His friend shrugged. 'Cesare is searching around the main garden now. We haven't checked all of the olive groves. Luna checked around the cars. The rest of us have scaled every inch of the rest of the garden. But the dog's small and could be hiding. I wouldn't put it past her.' His mouth pinched.

'Aldo says she's somewhere near liquid, remember!' Aurora reminded them from wherever she was searching in the garden. 'Aren't there red and white flowers near the swimming pool? I'm searching there next.'

'What about the inside of the house?' Ben pointed to the back of the villa where a set of patio doors hung open. Coco could easily have sneaked in while they were searching for her.

Marco pulled a face. 'We've been in and out of the house. If Coco was in there, we'd surely know. Someone would have seen her.'

Rose glanced between them. 'We'll check again just to make sure.' She began to make her way towards the house as Marco stared after her.

'Is this a trick?' he asked suspiciously.

'No. She wants to find Coco. We all do.' His voice came out sharper than he'd intended.

A furrow appeared in Marco's forehead as he stared at Ben. 'You like her,' he murmured. 'It's been a long time...'

Ben's stomach clenched. 'She's a good person. There's nothing more to it than that.' He was lying. The kiss in the car and its lingering effects had proved that. Then again, did he really want to put himself out there again? He was perfectly happy with his life as it was. But as Ben followed Rose towards the villa, he had a bad feeling he was just kidding himself.

'Coco!' Rose shouted as she made her way through the front door. Ben heard Luna yelling for the dog outside, could hear echoes from the rest of the Marino family as they continued to search. 'She's got to be somewhere,' Rose muttered as she opened a door underneath the staircase before dodging a broom handle as it fell out.

Ben picked it up and placed it back inside, shutting the door. 'I know the dog is precocious, but I don't think even she can open closed doors by herself.'

Rose jerked her chin before spinning around to stare at him, her blueberry eyes flashing. 'But Coco can. The demon got into my larder last week. I was working with a client, and she'd eaten through half a packet of ginger biscuits before I realised.'

Her mouth pinched, creating the perfect bow and something inside Ben's chest fluttered. He swallowed the feeling, suppressing a potent need to reach for her, to kiss her again.

He cleared his throat. 'Then we need to check all the rooms in the villa.' He marched down the corridor, opened the door and peered into the kitchen. 'She's not here...'

Rose nodded, then turned and walked hurriedly away. 'Where does this lead?' She opened the next door. 'Coco?' She sighed at the answering silence. 'An office.' She shut it again. 'What now?'

'The next door along leads to a wine cellar. It's usually locked, though.'

Rose strode to it, heels tapping on the tiles. 'It's unlocked. What if someone left it open accidentally? If I was a terrified demon, I might decide to hide in here.' She walked inside without waiting and Ben glanced around before following.

'Coco!' Rose shouted in the distance and Ben heard a tentative bark. 'She's here!'

He let the door close behind him and ran down the steps to join her. There was an internal door between the stairs and main cellar, and it swung shut as he joined Rose.

He'd been in the cellar before, choosing bottles of red and white wine when he'd been staying with Marco. The rustic chandelier hanging overhead gave out a little light which meant he could see Rose kneeling at the end of the room rubbing Coco's head while the dog made happy chirping sounds.

'She must have been terrified because she's not biting me. It's okay,' Rose cooed. 'It seems even demons are afraid of the dark. See, she's being nice.' She looked around at the rows and rows of wine bottles laying in wooden racks covering most of the four walls.

There was a circular wooden table and four heavy wooden chairs in the centre of the room. Ben had been down here many times choosing wine or testing bottles with his friend, so he wasn't surprised to see someone had left out clean wine glasses and a corkscrew. 'Liquid that's red and white,' Rose said. 'Aurora was right.'

'Let's go and tell Marco and Luna that we've found Coco,' Ben suggested, pointing to the door and encouraging Rose to go first. Now they were alone in this small space he was beginning to notice her again, and the chemistry he'd been attempting to ignore was making itself known. He smelled strawberries and waved a hand hoping she'd lead. He watched Rose stroke Coco one last time before rising and heading to the door. The dog followed and Ben brought up the rear.

Rose grasped the handle making the door rattle. 'It's stuck,' she said, jerking it up and down. 'Is something wrong with it?'

'Let me check.' Ben moved closer, trying not to step on Coco who'd begun to scratch the wooden panelling. 'I can't hear a click.' He tried again. 'I've got an awful feeling Marco told me the lock has been sticking.' He got his mobile out and dialled Marco, but it went to voicemail.

'When you get this, please can you come and let us out of the wine cellar? The lock's jammed, but the good news is we've found Coco.' Ben hung up. 'Do you want to try Luna?'

The dog whined. 'I can try.' Rose called and left a message too before trying the handle again. The door rattled but didn't budge.

'What do we do, sit and wait?' Rose glanced at the table. 'They could be ages.'

'Even if no one picks up the messages, they're bound to want more wine at some point,' Ben said.

'You're right.' Rose nodded, looking calmer. 'Or Aldo will tell Aurora where we are,' she joked. 'Besides, everyone's still looking for Coco.' The dog barked. 'It's only a matter of time before someone else decides to search the house.'

The chandelier flashed, and the lights went off, leaving the room in darkness. Coco growled and Rose let out a distressed hum just before they flashed back on again.

'That happens sometimes. Why don't we get comfortable? We can have a glass of wine, wait it out.' He indicated the table and went to pull out a chair for Rose before going to study the wine on the racks.

'Won't it be the wrong temperature?'

'Probably, but the wine will still taste good.' Ben pondered the racks. 'How do you feel about red?' He pulled out a bottle of Barolo and placed it on the table. 'It's my favourite.'

'Mine too.' Rose frowned and he wondered if it was because that meant they had something in common. 'But won't the Marinos mind?' She studied the label as Ben picked up the corkscrew.

'If they were here, they'd insist we have a drink to pass the time.' He took the bottle from her and uncorked it before pouring a little of the liquid into both glasses, then picked his up and sniffed. It smelled amazing. He sipped from his glass as he slid the other to Rose. She frowned at it before nodding and taking a seat. Ben watched her for a beat, then drew out the chair opposite.

'It's good!' She frowned at the door. Coco was lying beside it with her head on her paws. 'I've never seen the demon so quiet. It's crazy, but I think I'd rather she was biting me.'

'I'm sure it won't be long before your limbs are in danger again,' Ben joked, watching Rose take another drink.

'What's taking them so long?' she grumbled.

'There's a lot of ground to cover and they won't be thinking about looking for us yet.' Ben didn't add that he thought it might be a while. No one would be expecting the dog to be down here, and they were probably too busy to check their mobiles. His eyes flicked to Rose; he couldn't seem to stop himself. He could see goosebumps on her skin; watched her rub her palms over her forearms. *Dammit.* 'Are you cold?' Ben looked down at his own clothes. He was wearing a short-sleeved shirt and jeans. 'I'd offer to lend you something else to wear, but...'

Rose gazed at him. 'I think I've borrowed enough clothes for one holiday. And I have to admit I think Aurora's suit me better than yours would.' She gave him a half smile even as she shivered. Then she picked up the wine glass and took another sip. 'Besides, I've got this really excellent wine to keep me warm.' She finished the glass.

Almost the moment she put it back on the table, the lights went out. Coco let out a distressed rumbling sound and Rose whimpered.

'What's happening?' Her voice wobbled.

'Give it a minute,' Ben said.

After a few moments of silence, Rose whispered, 'Are you sure they'll come back on?'

'They always do,' Ben said. 'I've been coming here for eight years, and this has happened numerous times.'

'Should we put one of our mobile torches on?' Rose whispered. 'Although I'm only on about ten per cent.'

Ben thought about his half-used battery. 'Let's leave it for a bit. We might need light later. No use in using all the power now.'

They both fell silent again. Ben could hear Coco fidgeting, could hear a soft chattering sound. It took a minute before he realised Rose was shivering. He shifted his chair around the table aiming to get closer to her, feeling his way in the darkness. When their chairs collided, Rose yelped.

'It's me,' Ben said.

'I realise that. What I don't understand is what you're doing?' The words were delivered through a wave of chatters.

'You're cold,' Ben said, feeling awkward.

'So you think we should share body heat?' Rose asked after a pause.

Ben was about to move, but then he heard the sound of her chair scraping against the floor and suddenly her arm was pressing into his. Bare skin against bare skin. Ben's reaction was instantaneous, and he had to force himself to still. Every cell of his body was suddenly tense, and all of him, from his head through to his fingertips and toes seemed to be topping a hundred degrees.

Rose shivered again and Ben could feel the stroke of goose-bumps rising on her skin.

'How long do you think we're going to be down here?' She asked through a fresh bout of shivers. 'It's getting colder.' Beside the door, Coco let out a low growl of agreement.

'You could hug the dog?' he suggested, only half joking. He'd offer to hug her, but if he touched her again, he wasn't sure he'd be able to stop.

Rose cleared her throat. 'I think I'll take my chances with the hypothermia,' she muttered. 'I'm not sure if you noticed, but Coco doesn't usually like me.'

'She's a fool.' Ben was surprised by the vehemence in his tone.

'Not everyone does...' Rose admitted. 'Some have accused me of being too uptight.'

Ben frowned into the darkness. 'Some, or one?'

Rose didn't say anything for a moment. 'It was an ex-boyfriend. Sometimes, I'm not sure that my parents are that keen on me either. Then again, I think I've become more of a marriage guidance counsellor than a daughter.' She paused. 'Not that either of them listen to me.'

'I guess no one likes having their mistakes pointed out,' he said.

Rose coughed awkwardly. 'Well, I've made a career out of doing exactly that, perhaps that explains where I've been going wrong.'

'Have you done something wrong, though?' Ben asked. 'Or is it just everybody else?' He grinned and hoped Rose could hear he was joking. 'If it makes any difference, I like you,' he added, wondering if revealing that had been a mistake. Then again, wasn't it obvious from the way he'd kissed her in the car?

Rose fell silent. 'Don't you say that to all the girls?'

'Not really,' Ben murmured.

Her body relaxed against his. 'Would you... I mean, would you put your arm around me please?' She sounded tense.

'Of course.' He decided not to tease and wrapped an arm around her shoulders. Rose was still shivering, so he tightened his grip. 'You're freezing.' She tried to pull away. 'Let me warm you.'

She didn't move – but continued to tremble. 'I don't think the wine helped,' she said as her teeth rattled more violently.

Ben wanted to wrap her in something, hated feeling so helpless. 'Stand up,' he said suddenly. 'I've got an idea.' He pulled his mobile from his pocket and switched on the torch, illuminating the room.

Roses eyes widened. 'I thought we were preserving batteries?'

'We'll save yours.' What there was of it.

'If only there was an app to create heat,' she said wistfully.

'There is, I suppose.' He put on a random music track. 'Do you like dancing?' He stood and held out his hand.

'Dancing?' Rose looked horrified. 'I thought you were going to try to pick the lock.'

Ben shook his head. 'Can't be done. We can however dance. The movement will help warm us up.'

Rose grimaced and, for a moment, he thought she was going to refuse. Then she shrugged. 'You know I once suggested dancing to a client as a way of fixing their relationship.' She took his hand and stood, as the track changed, skipping to 'Dancing Queen' by Abba.

Rose's lips tightened as Ben led her to the empty space beside the table. A crease marred her forehead as he began to wriggle his body in time to the music, encouraging her to do the same. She didn't – but she did watch, making him feel self-conscious.

'What happened?' he asked, shaking his hips, hoping Rose would either join in or laugh. She did neither, but there was something about her expression that made him wonder if she wanted to.

Rose's lips pinched and the crease deepened. 'She refused; said she'd feel too silly.' She paused. 'The relationship broke up a few weeks later. She wanted to change but wasn't willing to step out of her comfort zone, so she lost someone she cared about.' She winced. 'I think there might be a lesson there for me. I get it – if I don't want to be cold, I should dance.'

Ben grinned. 'Dance or hug the dog – it's up to you. I've no idea how long we're going to be stuck down here.' He didn't mention the other option, the one that involved the sharing of body heat. Wasn't sure he wanted to think about that himself – but his wretched brain wouldn't let go of the idea.

Rose gave him an odd look, one that made him think she could read his mind – or perhaps she just had the same idea. It was too dark to tell if she was blushing, but Ben suspected he might be.

She wriggled her arms suddenly, shaking her head even as

she shifted from foot to foot, her pretty dress shimmering around her thighs. 'If this is all a devious plot to get me to make a fool out of myself, I guess it's working.' She rolled her eyes, then spun round in a small circle, her movements gaining traction even though it was obvious she was embarrassed.

Ben moved closer and spiralled his hands above his head, wobbling his torso. He was warmer now and hoped Rose was too. She giggled as she watched and he jiggled and writhed, delighted with the belly laugh she suddenly let out.

Then Rose slowly began to match his movements, twirling her arms around her head, spinning around – even as the track changed and 'Pump up the Jam' filled the cellar. 'I can't believe I'm doing this,' she choked. 'If my clients could see me now.' Her feet faltered and Ben wondered if she was going to stop.

'Perhaps they'd wonder if you'd made up a new set of rules?' Ben suggested, wriggling his hips again, hoping she'd join in.

'What kind?' She was still moving and Ben wanted to grab her hand. To hold her.

'The ones about living life to the fullest – leaving your doubts behind. The ones about having fun while you can, before it's too late.' He gave in to his urge to touch her, reached out and linked their fingers, then put his arm in the air so he could spin her.

Rose laughed. 'Smooth.'

'I'm just practising my seduction technique for the wedding. Isn't it the best man's job to seduce the maid of honour?' He spun her again and pressed their bodies together before stepping away, a little unnerved at the fire suddenly burning in his belly. He swallowed, then ignored reason, and the scream in his head that was yelling at him to *For God's sake stop* – and did it again.

'You don't need any practice, Ben,' Rose said, a little out of breath as he tucked her close to his chest. It was dim in the room, but there was enough light from his phone to pick out the flush on her cheeks.

'Does that mean it's working?' he asked, his voice a little husky as he tugged her closer. It caught him off-guard how much he wanted to kiss her. But he had to fight it. He wasn't looking for this. Didn't want it – did he?

'It's working.' Rose laughed, pulling away and moving under his arm in time to the music. She stepped away and then pressed her body against his again.

He could feel her slim frame through the spectacular dress, tried not to imagine how it might look without it. Did she know what she was doing to him?

'I'm getting warmer.'

'So am I.' His voice sounded strained, probably because he was positively boiling on the inside now. The track changed again, and the beat slowed, and Ben's wiggles morphed into something more sensual. He expected Rose to retreat. Surely, she had rules about slow dancing with a stranger? He almost hoped she did.

Instead, her grip tightened as she slowed and guided herself closer until they were facing each other, swaying, still holding hands. Then she looked up, straight into his eyes. 'I've been thinking about my rules,' she said uncertainly.

'The ones about dancing?' Ben asked. He expected her to step away, to demand they stop the music and somehow try to open the cellar door. Instead, she cocked her head still gazing at him intently.

'I do have some: you should avoid touching each other or holding hands.' She looked down at where theirs were still linked. 'At least until you know each other properly. Dancing can be intimate; not everyone understands that.' Had her voice grown gravelly, and what did that mean? 'Sometimes, it's better to avoid it. There's no telling where it might lead.'

Ben stopped swaying and looked at her confused. 'Do you

want us to stop?' He was disappointed, but it was probably for the best.

She shook her head. 'No, I don't.' She pulled in a deep breath and let it out. 'Do you think there's such a thing as too many rules?'

Ben searched for an answer as she began to dance again. 'What do you mean?' He was out of his depth, with no idea of what Rose wanted from him. She continued to shimmy, and he mirrored her in time to the music. Every time she jiggled an arm, foot or hip – even her mouth – he did the same. It wasn't intentional – it was more that his body was communicating with hers. That the chemistry between them had given up waiting for either of them to make a move. They'd simply been hijacked by their own impatient hormones.

'I mean do they work, do we need them, or are they just a way of staying safe – of protecting ourselves from chaos and pain?' She studied him, her blueberry eyes serious.

Ben shrugged. He didn't know what she wanted him to say, so he danced and waited, trying not to second-guess her, knowing she'd explain. Thinking – hoping – that he already knew what she was thinking.

Rose studied him and then hitched in a new breath. 'The thing is, I don't know either. But I do want to know what you're supposed to do if suddenly, instead of safety, it's chaos you crave...'

19

ROSE

Rose hitched in another breath when Ben suddenly stopped dancing and his forehead creased, his beautiful brown eyes watching her intently. 'Chaos?' He closed the distance between them until they were standing and staring at one another, the tips of their shoes just touching. 'I can do chaos.'

His beautiful mouth tipped up in one corner and Rose felt her stomach go choppy –as if she'd just dived into the ocean, leaving behind the safety of solid ground. She sucked in a breath again as her brain – the rational bit anyway – screamed that she should get herself to land again. *Pronto.* Before she did something she was going to regret.

But she knew it was already too late.

Ben placed a fingertip at the edge of her jaw, and she flinched in surprise, making him pull away. 'I'm sorry,' he said, frowning.

She shook her head and took a step closer. 'No, I'm sorry – you just surprised me. I'm jumpy.' She cupped a hand around his cheek and stroked the peppery stubble. It had been a long time since she'd touched a man, but it felt good. Ben felt good. And he was so incredible to look at – she hadn't allowed herself to stare at him before, but to hell with it, she was going to look her fill now.

Ben guided his fingertips back to her jaw and tipped her chin again so he could look into her eyes. 'I don't know what you're asking for, Rose,' he said softly, his gaze zigzagging across her face.

He did know – she could tell from the rigid set of his shoulders, from the way his eyes had darkened, and his body had angled itself even closer to her.

'You want me to spell it out?' she asked, trying to keep the reluctance out of her voice.

'I don't want to get this wrong,' he said, his tone and expression frustrated. So unlike the man she'd spent the last few days getting to know. He'd always seemed so confident and sure of himself.

Her stomach knotted – was she wrong about Ben; had she misread him somehow?

'And now you're pulling away,' he said, taking a tiny step closer, sounding disappointed. Until their chests were brushing together.

'I'm not,' she said, even though she was thinking about it. All her usual doubts were cascading into her brain like a firework display. A kaleidoscope of her parents' disastrous relationships was playing at the back of her brain. She swallowed, pushing the noise away. 'Is it enough to say I want this?' Her chest tightened as she took the final plunge. 'I just want to put my rules back in a folder. Maybe I want to pretend they don't exist. Live out the fantasy, or at least dip my toe in.' For a while anyway.

'So I'm an experiment?' The hurt that flashed across Ben's face made her knees go wobbly.

'Of course not!' She muttered. 'You're the first person I've ever wanted to ignore my rules for.' She squashed her hands in frustration. She was doing this wrong. Without her rules, she was in untested waters. Clearly drowning.

Ben must have liked what she said because he nodded. 'So we dance and take this slowly.' He took her hand again. The track changed once more, and the music grew sultry. Rose didn't recognise the song, but she could hear heartache and longing, could almost feel the same emotions reflected inside herself.

Ben pulled her closer until their hips were pressed against each other. He was taller, but somehow, they seemed to fit. She let him guide her – so tired of always being in control, of making the rules and giving advice. Especially when it felt like it made no difference.

The only advice she was going to give now was to herself. To embrace chaos, to forget the rules, to chase whatever made her happy and to forget everything else.

'Are you sure this is what you want?' Ben whispered, nudging her hair aside and pressing his mouth to her ear so he could stroke his lips against the skin underneath. Rose shivered, only this time it had nothing to do with the cold.

'We could have died earlier. I know I'm being dramatic,' she muttered.

'You?' he teased, pulling her closer still and swinging them both in a small circle in time to the music. Rose saw Coco look up from where she was lying by the door, her doggy expression content but a little confused. 'I'd never call you dramatic, Rose.'

'What would you call me?' she asked, returning his nuzzle by stroking the top of her nose along his sharp jawline. He smelled incredible, of olive groves and sunshine – with some kind of aftershave mixed in there too. It reminded her of sex and bad decisions – things she usually avoided, but now she couldn't stay away.

He whisked her round again, then dipped her, making her feel like a contestant on *Strictly Come Dancing*. This man had all the moves, and she was seriously out of her depth. But that wasn't going to stop her. He righted her again and smiled, his grin setting her insides alight. 'You're loyal and hard-working. You care about other people and put them first. Sometimes, to your own detriment.'

The answering smile that had been hovering on her lips disappeared. That was all true, but it made her sound so... 'Boring,' she muttered. 'A lot like a dog – biddable and well trained.' Her eyes flashed to Coco who looked up at her. 'Present company excepted of course; no one would ever accuse you either of those.'

Ben chuckled. 'It's quite unnerving how you can take something that's meant as a compliment and turn it into an insult. Is that a psychiatrist thing?'

'It's a listening thing,' she said sourly as Ben dipped her down before whirling them both around as the song on Ben's mobile changed again.

'Then it's time we stopped talking and try to communicate some other way,' he said, bringing them both to a slow stop, then circling his arms around her waist and pulling her closer to him. Now this was more like it. This is what she'd been dreaming about.

'I can get behind that.' She pressed her body against his, relishing the feel of him. He was muscular, she'd expected that, she just hadn't anticipated the way he'd set her skin alight until she felt like every inch of her was ablaze. She wound her arms around his neck, fighting an almost impossible urge to rip off his shirt so she could explore all that perfect landscape of hard muscle. She'd touched him when they'd been in the sea, but that had been an accident, or the lingering effects of the fertility statue; her plans tonight were deliberate.

She'd spent years drilling the difference between lust and love into her clients, but tonight, she wanted to give herself over to uncomplicated pleasure and desire.

But it was a lot more powerful than she'd anticipated.

Ben made the first move and caught her mouth in a slow, deliberate kiss. Rose had been intending to kiss him first, but as usual her head had got in the way. Thinking versus doing, rules versus going with the flow. It was the story of her life. At least her life until now. That was about to change.

The kiss started out slow – Ben had clearly decided to take his time. Perhaps he didn't want to overwhelm her? But that's exactly what Rose wanted. She wanted to be claimed, to lose herself and let go.

If there was a rule tonight, it was that there were no rules. She reached up and pushed her hand into his hair, pulled him closer and deepened the kiss. What had begun as restrained soon turned fiery.

To Ben's credit, he didn't try to pull away or make them slow down; he followed her agenda, letting his hand stray lower until it was cupping her bottom. She dropped her own and did the same, tracing the firm globe of his buttock. *God* he was so gorgeous. The blueprint for the perfect man, physically anyway. And now she was objectifying him and that was wrong. She frowned without breaking off their kiss.

'Is this okay?' Ben pulled away so he could speak.

'It's not enough,' she whispered.

Beside the door she heard Coco make a low grunting sound. 'Someone's going to find us soon.' It was only a matter of time. That, or the demon was going to get antsy. It was a miracle that she hadn't already. 'I want...' She swallowed – the next words were going to take all of her bravery to share.

Ben didn't interrupt or ask, he simply waited for her to finish. But his eyes were fixed on her mouth – his expression ravenous. It was enough to make her insides melt like a handful of marshmallows on a bonfire. 'I want more...' she rasped.

For a moment, she wondered if he was going to ask how much more. Instead, he nodded and captured her mouth in a kiss again. This time, he didn't hold back. This time, he dived straight in, using all his kissing miles to destroy her. He began to guide her backwards towards the table and chairs, as his lips travelled to her neck, tracing every curve and dip, exploring every inch of her skin. She was trembling by the time her legs hit the first piece of furniture. Then Ben growled and shoved the chair aside, easing her further back until she was perched on the edge of the table.

'This much more?' he whispered.

'No, way more than this,' she rasped as he hitched her up until she was sitting on the edge of the table. Then he slowly eased her legs open and situated himself in between. Her heart was hammering so hard that she could hear it, or maybe it was all that blood rushing through her ears?

It was so loud it almost drowned out the next slow song as it played from Ben's mobile. He stopped and placed a hand on either side of her hips, penning her in, as he leaned closer and looked into her eyes.

'How much more, Rose?' he asked again. 'I'm serious.' He looked it, and that only made him more appealing – if that were possible.

'I want everything.' Her heart, which had been hammering until now, began to pummel and pound, leaving her breathless. As if to punctuate her point – and to make sure Ben understood – she began to undo the buttons on his shorts before leaning forward and stroking her hands over his smooth skin. He was beautiful, hard but soft at the same time. Like he'd been carved out of clouds, a miracle of physical engineering. For a moment, Rose wondered if she was imagining him. Where were his flaws? Everyone had some – physically and emotionally. She had plenty. Or perhaps Ben's were simply that he was unable to commit? Or just too damaged to want to.

Ben tugged at the thin straps of her dress pushing them downwards, making her insides go haywire. Then he pushed the rest of the dress to her waist before setting to work on her bra. Rose felt it fall away, and the knot in her chest tightened as he gazed down.

'You're beautiful,' he said huskily.

'You always know the exact right thing to say.' She tried to keep her voice light. She didn't want to engage, wasn't looking to fall for this man. He was too far out of her league, and he'd never take her – or the idea of them – seriously. This was just an exercise in breaking the rules – perhaps because she needed to know she could?

'I get it wrong more often than you'd think,' Ben rasped as he stepped closer and pushed her skirt over her knees and up her thighs, making everything inside her effervesce. She was shivering again; goosebumps were obviously her language of need.

'This isn't very romantic for our first time,' he said, frowning.

Did that matter to him? Rose looked around at the dim room. The light from his phone gave it a rosy glow – almost as if someone were burning candles. 'It's not bad. The lighting is perfect,' she said. 'I don't think the other guest is going to disturb us either.' She nodded towards the door where Coco was now resting, her eyes closed, her tail flicking from side to side.

'I mean, the bed's a bit hard, but I don't think it's going to matter.' She wriggled, grinning up at him. 'At least I'm hoping you're going to take my mind off that – and soon.'

He beamed down at her, making something in her chest crack open just a little, letting in a flood of unexpected warmth.

'I'll do my best,' he murmured, stepping closer. Then he caught her mouth in another slow kiss, allowing her to explore his body with her hands. He was firm and hard in all the right places – a testament to his exceptional DNA.

She paused so she could undo the buttons on his shirt before pushing it off and letting it drop to the floor. She thought she heard the patter of paws but was too busy mapping Ben's chest with her lips to look up and see what the demon was up to. She knew if the shih tzu wasn't whining or barking, she was okay.

Ben pushed the skirt of her dress up higher, exposing the tops of her thighs and the tiniest hint of underwear before dropping to his knees. Rose placed both of her hands on the table and leaned back so she could watch him dab tiny kisses from her knee upwards making her skin explode in more goosebumps. 'May I?' he asked, looking up suddenly and pinning her with his brown eyes before pointing to her red thong. The one he'd helped Francesca pick out.

'Of course,' she croaked, starting to ease herself forward in an attempt to help. But Ben suddenly moved her closer to the edge of the table and whipped them off before she could move. 'You're quite the expert,' she observed, trying to keep the dismay out of her tone.

'I think it has more to do with eagerness than experience,' he murmured, settling her on the edge of the table before kneeling down and getting to work.

After that Rose had no words – her brain was filled with too much sensation for her to form a coherent thought, let alone a sentence. Her whole body was rocking and heating, flexing and climbing, pulsing and tingling until she thought she wouldn't be able to stand it anymore.

She pushed her hands into Ben's hair, holding on tight as her pleasure reached its peak sending her over the edge of some imaginary rollercoaster that seemed to last hours. When she finally returned to solid ground, the need inside her was only partly quenched. So when Ben made his way to his feet again, she grabbed him and pulled him down, settling him over her on the table.

'More,' she demanded, still a long way from satisfied. If she was going to break the rules, she was going to do it properly. Go all the way. Squash all her doubts and insecurities. Finally experience everything she'd been hiding from. So she knew what she'd been missing. Perhaps it would help to educate her on all the things she clearly didn't understand?

'Now...' Ben pulled back a little so he could gaze down her. He didn't say anything this time. Rose had been expecting empty words, had braced herself to ignore them. Instead, he kissed her softly on the mouth before stroking a slow hand up her leg. Then he stopped suddenly and pulled back, as his forehead creased. 'Protection,' he murmured. 'I haven't got any.'

Rose winced. She was about to ask him why. Surely, a man who looked like that would always be prepared? Only, that wasn't fair.

'I'm...' She felt her cheeks heat. 'I have a coil and I haven't—' Did she really want to tell him how long it had been? 'It's been a while.' She frowned, suddenly uncomfortable, because she didn't really want to hear a potted history of Ben's sex life.

He gazed down at her, looking surprised and a little unsure.

How many women had Ben slept with recently? 'Is it that many?' she blurted, ignoring the spear of jealousy as it lodged itself in her throat.

Ben laughed – but it didn't sound like a laugh. It was more of a choke and was there a hint of hurt in this expression too? No. She'd imagined that, surely.

'Actually, it's been two years for me.' There was something about the pitch of his voice that told her he was telling the truth. 'I don't want to talk about it,' he murmured.

Rose nodded. She wanted to explore that further – how could he possibly have abstained for that long? But she wasn't here to talk either – she was here to do. 'Then we're okay,' she said, tugging him back down on top of her, capturing his mouth this time leaving him no doubt as to what she wanted from him. Or that she wanted it now.

Ben must have agreed because a few seconds later he was

inside her and they were moving together. He had a forearm pressed on the table making sure he didn't lean on her too much, and she appreciated his thoughtfulness, even though it still surprised her.

She shut her eyes trying not to overthink, trying to just enjoy this moment. There was a lot to enjoy. She reached up and hugged Ben tightly, wrapped her legs around him moving in sync. It didn't take long before she was on the rollercoaster again, then she was diving and swooping, kissing him so fiercely she wasn't sure she'd be able to stop. And then he joined her on the ride, groaning into her mouth. Until they both seem to land, breathing heavily, their hearts seemingly hammering in sync.

But as the world stilled and their breath calmed, Rose thought she could hear voices coming from somewhere.

'Oh damn!' she yelped, trying to sit up.

Then Coco began to bark and Ben shot up, pulling away from her and immediately trying to help her put her clothes back on.

'I think someone picked their message up,' Ben said, urgently helping her fasten her bra before searching the ground. 'I can't find your underwear.' He sounded annoyed.

'Don't worry about it – you need to get dressed,' she said hastily.

He was still mostly naked and looked glorious – but he managed to pull up his trousers and fasten them just as Marco opened the door.

'You're here!' he said, coming inside, leaving the door wide open. 'We've been looking for you – Aurora's searching upstairs, she went looking for red-and-white bubble bath. We thought you might have got locked in the bathroom or something. Then I saw your message. Thank goodness you found the dog.' He didn't sound very happy about it and sneezed suddenly, then wiped his eyes as he looked around.

'What happened to the lights?' he asked as his eyes adjusted to the darkness.

'They went off,' Ben said as Marco studied him.

'What on earth happened to your shirt?' Ben moved so he was standing in front of Rose, hiding her from view. 'Oh...' Marco coughed looking embarrassed.

Rose had just managed to pull up the straps of her dress when she heard another set of footsteps on the stairs – and then Luna came charging into the cellar and immediately sank to her knees so she could hug Coco.

'You found her!' she cooed. 'I don't know how I'm ever going to thank you, Rose. I can't believe you got stuck down here – Elena mentioned there's been a problem with the lock.'

She grabbed something from Coco's mouth and frowned. 'What's this?' she asked, waving a pair of red lacy pants just as the overhead lights decided to switch themselves back on, illuminating a half-naked Ben as he suddenly zeroed in on his shirt which was tucked under the table.

'Oh...' Luna murmured, widening her clear blue eyes which ping-ponged between Ben and Rose. 'Did you both get too hot?' she asked, shooting a shocked look at Rose who felt her cheeks flame. Ben picked up the shirt, quickly pulled it on and did it up.

'Can I have those please?' Ben asked patiently, holding out his hand for Rose's underwear.

Luna handed them to him and watched Ben put them in his pocket. Marco let out an irritated huff and muttered something under his breath about Luna ogling the best man.

She gave her fiancé a disappointed look. 'At least he helped find Coco and he wasn't responsible for terrifying her either.'

'I didn't realise the fireworks would upset her; I know nothing about dogs,' Marco muttered through gritted teeth, making it clear the argument they'd started in the garden had festered. 'We need to get back to making the wedding favours,' he added, pointing towards the stairs.

'Why bother, since after tonight, I'm not sure there's going to be a wedding,' Luna shot back before scooping up Coco and disappearing through the open doorway, offering a quick glance at Rose that told her she'd have to explain herself at some point.

'*Tesoro!*' Marco shot Ben a crestfallen look, before he sneezed again and followed Luna.

'Are they going to be okay?' Ben asked, jerking his head towards the door without taking his eyes off Rose.

She nodded. 'Luna's tired and that's probably just a reaction to what happened tonight. I'll speak to her,' she promised, realising Ben was still staring at her, his eyes dark and filled with meaning.

'That was...' He fell silent, his gaze a little unsure.

'I know...' She gulped, suddenly hesitant about what to say. Then Ben reached into his pocket and handed her the red thong. She scrunched it in her hand like a talisman, a physical reminder of what they'd just done.

It had been more than she'd been expecting. But the sudden abrupt appearance of their friends seemed to have changed everything. Especially since it appeared the wedding was still in trouble.

'It was.' Ben gazed at her, his mouth tightening as he scoured her face.

'Yep.' Rose studied him, wondering what he was thinking.

'We should probably see if we can talk to Luna and Marco now...' He turned and signalled that they should leave, letting Rose walk ahead. She climbed the steps, her mind spinning, all the while aware that Ben was behind her.

What had meant to be a toe in the water, suddenly felt like so much more. She began to run, faster now, wondering if she'd just made a huge mistake – or if that had just been the beginning...

20

ROSE

'Are you there?' Rose knocked on Marco and Luna's bedroom door for the third time and waited before pressing her ear to the wood, only to be greeted by dull silence. She'd called and texted Luna multiple times after seeing her in the wine cellar the evening before but hadn't heard back. Where was she and was her best friend okay? She'd never seen Luna like this, had never known her to disappear and ignore her messages.

Guessing she must be outside, Rose spun around and headed downstairs. She knew Luna often went for long walks with Coco when she was mulling over problems. After everything that had happened last night, she was probably still confused.

Rose wasn't sure how to advise her friend yet. She'd come to Italy to encourage her to delay the wedding, but now she wasn't sure if that was the right thing to do.

Marco might not be perfect, but it was clear he adored Luna – she could do a lot worse than marry a man like him. It was obvious now that the Marinos were wealthy in their own right, so her concerns about him being after Luna's inheritance were probably unfounded. Her rigid ideas about relationships had brought her – and Luna – nothing but grief, so perhaps it was time to let them go and make sure this wedding went ahead?

'*Leonessa!*' Aurora exclaimed as soon as Rose headed outside. She shielded her eyes from the bright sunlight and saw the older woman sitting at the long table in the garden where they'd been making *bomboniere*.

Everything had been cleared away — perhaps in an attempt to forget about what had happened with Isabella and Coco? Aurora waved and then poured liquid from a green pot into a delicate cup. 'Come and sit with me, have some coffee,' she said.

'I can't stop for long.' Rose searched the garden for Luna before pulling out a chair. 'Have you seen Luna this morning?' she asked, just stopping herself from enquiring about Ben too. She hadn't seen or heard from him since leaving the cellar and wasn't sure what to expect when she did.

Would he regret what had happened between them? He'd told her that he hadn't been with anyone for two years, but had he been telling the truth? Or was it just another line? Her stomach tightened at the thought.

'Aldo says she's out walking somewhere,' Aurora said, passing Rose the full cup. 'He says you should go to the lake next.'

Rose sipped some of the hot liquid, relishing the sharp bitter taste. 'Did he tell you how Luna's feeling?' she asked, wondering if the older woman had seen her in passing.

Aurora sighed, tugging her sparkly shawl tighter. 'I'm not sure any of us can know that, *cara*. Aldo kept me up for most of the night worrying about her. He can foresee more problems with the wedding, but he believes everything will sort itself out in the end.'

Rose nodded. She wasn't so sure of that.

'I hear a lot happened with you last night too?' Aurora added, flashing Rose a bright smile, making her stomach turn over. Did Aurora somehow know what had happened with Ben in the cellar — had Marco blabbed? She bristled. It had been a private moment, not something she wanted casually discussed, especially since it had been so out of character for her. 'How do you know?' she asked sharply.

'I just do.' Aurora tapped her temple, her expression suddenly serious. '*Leonessa* – you care about him.' Rose was about to refute the observation or ask the clairvoyant who she was talking about, but when Aurora shook her head, the words died on her lips. Was it that easy to see? The idea that it was shocked her.

She shrugged. Admitting she had feelings for Ben made her uncomfortable. It was the last thing she'd been looking for and she didn't know how he felt. Giving someone all that power over you was dangerous – a sure path to getting hurt.

'Aldo says you have a great future together,' Aurora shared.

Rose sighed. The Marinos believed in happy ever afters – why not? The family clearly had enough of them. Aside from what was happening with Isabella and Cesare – and Rose wondered if that was a mere blip? But her experience was different. She had no illusions – although the squeeze in her stomach told her she did have hope.

'I'm not sure Ben feels that way. I'm afraid he's more invested in being casual,' she said, flushing because she wasn't sure why she'd confided in her so suddenly.

'Sophia was never right for him.' Aurora's eyes glittered. 'She made him feel like he wasn't worth anything. Like he didn't matter. That he was nothing more than a handsome face – something to be admired and, how do you say?' She cocked her head like she was listening to someone. 'Cottaged – no...' she huffed. 'Coveted.' She nodded. 'But never loved. She was wrong. He is a good man and deserves someone who adores him. When he finds that, he will give her his whole heart.'

Rose frowned. Hadn't she thought the same as his ex when she'd first met Ben – that he was just a pretty face? But the last few days had shown her another side to him – one she really liked. Should she drop her guard?

'When we are hurt, sometimes we try to protect ourselves.' Aurora sighed as she studied Rose's face. 'But the heart wants what the heart wants, and you both need to give in to it.' Her mouth tightened. 'To stop being so afraid and embrace what you deserve.'

'You know better than anyone, not everyone gets what they want or deserve,' Rose said sorrowfully. 'Life isn't a set of scales that automatically balances because it's fair. You didn't get your happily ever after,' she added tentatively. Whether she believed Aldo was real or not, it was clear Aurora had lost the love of her life and there was nothing fair about that.

The clairvoyant shrugged. 'I am happy. I have spent the last forty years with Aldo. Some might call it an unconventional relationship; others think I'm delusional.' She flashed a knowing smile, making Rose flush. 'But it's the right life for me.'

Rose thought it was an odd and lonely life but didn't verbalise that. She was, however, impressed by Aurora's stoicism and hadn't appreciated quite how amazing Marco's aunt was until this moment.

'I think I'm lucky,' Aurora added huskily, her voice filled with emotion. 'But if Aldo could be here with me physically.' Her eyes bored into Rose's. 'I wouldn't bother myself with petty concerns like following rules or waiting for the perfect time. If he were here, I would grab that man with both arms. And I would never let him go.' Her voice cracked and she stopped for long enough to pick up her cup and swallow the last gulp of coffee.

'I'm so sorry—' Rose said soberly, feeling a weight settle in her chest.

'So you should get going now,' Aurora interrupted before she could say anything more, tipping her cup towards the olive grove. 'There is someone you need to speak with this morning.'

'Luna, I know,' Rose agreed, finishing her coffee in one before rising from her chair. 'I need to find out what's going on. We have a wedding to get back on track.'

Aurora winked. 'All in good time, *leonessa* – and just so you know, the spirits are on your side.'

Bemused, Rose nodded, before heading into the gardens.

'Luna,' Rose called as she made her way through the olive grove, passing the table and chairs which had been left out after Aurora's reading. It had only been a few days ago, but so much had changed. All the things she'd spent a lifetime believing, the rules she'd spent her career crafting felt like they were crumbling underfoot. She continued to walk, inhaling the scent of coffee, sun cream and the charred remains of Isabella's olive tree. It's how she knew she was walking in the right direction. Perhaps her friend had headed for the lake?

She turned a corner and immediately saw Ben standing by the water, kicking his heels on the ground. He was wearing a navy T-shirt that hugged his large frame and fresh shorts that showcased his long, tanned legs. She swallowed, remembering how it had felt to run her hands over his skin, before stopping in her tracks acknowledging the tingle of pleasure in her stomach that she got from simply seeing him. The feeling made her want to run.

'Rose.' Ben turned suddenly as if he'd sensed she was standing there. He looked surprised, but his lips curved as he drew closer. 'I was expecting Marco. I wanted to see what's happening with the wedding.' He glanced behind her. 'Aurora told me he was walking around here. But I'm happy to see you instead.' He leaned down and kissed Rose's cheek, surprising her because it felt so natural.

Rose couldn't stop herself from beaming back. 'She told me Luna was here too – I came looking for her,' she blurted. 'I keep calling her mobile, but she's ignoring me and she wasn't in her room this morning. But—' She stopped and swallowed realising she'd been masking her feelings with words. Remembering what Aurora had said. 'I'm happy to see you too.'

'Ah.' Ben smiled down at her. 'That's good to know. I think Aunt A sent us both here deliberately so we'd talk. She's sneaky – or perhaps it's Aldo, I really can't tell anymore.' His brown eyes warmed and Rose felt herself flush. 'I will say I'm pleased we bumped into each other. I wanted to talk to you last night before we were interrupted.'

Rose braced herself. 'It all happened so fast,' she murmured. 'I know you're not looking for anything serious.'

Ben held up a palm. 'Rose, I like you. Probably more than I should.' He flexed his jaw looking anxious. 'I've avoided having feelings for anyone since Sophia.' He sighed. 'But I'm beginning to realise I might want more.'

'With me?' Rose asked, more than a little shocked.

'With you.' He nodded, gazing at her intently. 'It's a lot to take in, I get that. Especially with all your rules, and I know it's happening too fast. I'm guessing we've hopped to week seven or eight?'

More like six months. 'I like you too,' Rose said stiffly. 'I mean – more than I should and yes, it's definitely happening too quickly, but—' She swallowed as her mobile buzzed. 'That's Luna,' she said, reading the screen. 'She wants to meet me to talk. I'm sorry.'

Ben nodded before reaching out and linking their fingers, making Rose's stomach turn over. 'I am the best man and you are the maid of honour – so duty first is the right call. Shall we go now, and we can talk about this again later?'

Rose blew out a breath as she allowed herself to be led away from the lake towards the olive grove. The smell of ash grew stronger as they approached Isabella and Cesare's tree. Ben stopped just before they passed and dropped Rose's hand.

'Is that—' He went to kneel beside the charred remains. 'A root?' His voice rose with pleasure and surprise.

Rose went to crouch beside him and studied the tiny green shoot. 'Looks like it,' she said. 'Does that mean it's somehow reviving?'

'Could be.' Ben turned to smile at her. 'Seems we're witnessing a miracle – perhaps this might be what we need to help put the wedding back together. Will you talk to Isabella now?'

'Okay.' Rose shrugged as they both got up and took the hot, gravelly path leading towards Villa Paradise. In her experience, relationships didn't mend that easily, and she had a gnawing suspicion that Marco's grandparents' problems might be about more than just a tree.

21

———

ROSE

'Ben, can you talk?' Marco yelled across the garden as they approached Villa Paradise holding hands. He gave Rose and then Ben a considering look as they drew closer. 'Have you spoken to Luna today?'

'Not yet.' Rose shook her head, taking in Marco's grey pallor, how morose he looked. It was obvious he was devastated that Luna had threatened to call off the wedding and from the look of him, nothing had changed. 'She just texted. I'm about to meet her inside.' She pointed towards the villa.

'Thank the gods she's still here.' Marco looked relieved. 'She slept in another bedroom last night,' he muttered. 'When I went to find her this morning, she and the dog were gone. I was afraid she might have left. I need to apologise,' he said, turning in the direction of the house, but Ben placed a gentle arm on his shoulder and turned him back.

'Not now... Let Rose speak to her first.'

Marco sighed but nodded. 'I didn't mean what I said, if she really wants to delay the wedding, well...' He drifted off, clearly dismayed at the idea.

'She was upset,' Rose began.

Marco shrugged. 'And I'll do whatever I can to fix that. I'll speak to *Nonna*, see what I can do to get Luna's mum here on time. Perhaps there's a way to make the wedding happen?' His eyes widened.

'There could be. But there's a lot to talk about first.' She glanced towards the house again. Was her friend watching them now, waiting for her? 'Let me find Luna while you both catch up. I'll see if I can convince her to at least sit down and discuss things with you. Last night was probably a knee-jerk reaction, I'm hoping in the cold light of day she'll reconsider.'

'So you'll convince her to go ahead with the wedding?' Marco asked.

Rose grimaced. 'I'll get her to talk to you. I just want her to be happy; that's all I've ever wanted.' She wasn't going to browbeat Luna into getting married – her friend had to make her own choices – but she'd make sure she'd fully considered her options. Remind her how strong her feelings for Marco were. The last couple of days with Ben had given Rose an insight into how wonderful caring for someone could be. Of course that was what she wanted for Luna too.

'Do you think she'll change her mind?' Marco asked.

'Luna was upset last night, unwilling to talk,' Rose said, still surprised her friend hadn't answered any of her messages. 'Now she's had a chance to sleep on it, she'll be in a better headspace. If she wants to go ahead, I'll do what I can to remove any obstacles. If she wants to marry you, I'll be a hundred per cent behind it.'

'Thank you for talking to her, for not telling her I'm an unworthy idiot and that she should back out,' Marco said, his shoulders relaxing a notch. 'I mean it.' Then he turned his attention back to Ben. 'Shall we sit in the garden?' he asked, tipping his head towards the villa. 'In our usual spot?'

'Later.' Ben gave Rose a quick wink before they both walked around the side of the house.

. . .

'Luna,' Rose said as she reached the second floor of the villa and spotted her friend sitting in a pool of sunshine on the staircase that led to Rose's floor. Coco growled as she approached but didn't budge.

Her friend looked as tired and pale as Marco had, and Rose quickly dropped onto the step beside her. 'Are you okay?' she asked, ignoring the shih tzu as she tried to nip at her dress. 'I've been trying to speak to you since last night.' She patted Luna's knee, just managing to save her fingers from Coco's snapping jaws. Clearly, their short truce in the cellar was over.

Luna sighed. 'I needed time to think. I'm sorry.' She gave Rose a dim smile. 'Besides, from what I saw last night, you had better things to do than talk to me. Was that real or did I imagine it?' She looked surprised.

Rose laughed. 'It was real. I'm not sure what happened. But—'

'Oh, I can guess.' Luna let out a lusty chuckle. 'But the real question is, do you want it to happen again?'

Rose shrugged. 'Ben said he'd like it to. If I'm honest, I think I would too, but...' She sucked in a breath. 'It's moving a little fast. I need to slow things down. I don't want to get into a situation like my parents and make a mistake.' Just the thought had her insides curling into themselves.

'Looks like you ignored a few dozen of your Love Doctor rules,' Luna said indulgently.

'I'm sorry.' Rose grimaced. Her friend had lived through hours of sermons about the importance of taking things slowly, about the dangers of rushing into love. Then in one single night Rose had broken every single rule she'd ever preached or made up. Did that make her a hypocrite?

Luna placed a palm on Rose's knee. 'I'm happy for you. You deserve to meet someone, and you've spent far too long running from love — trying not to be like your parents. But Rose — you aren't. I only hope Ben deserves you. He's certainly hot enough.' She waggled her eyebrows.

Rose smiled. 'But what about you? You were angry last night.'

'I was.' Luna drew in a long breath. 'Everything felt like it was falling apart. I still feel like Marco's trying so hard to please his family that he's lost sight of what *we* want. Everyone seems so fixated on us having children, but I'm not ready for that yet. When his *nonna* refused to come to the wedding and Coco ran away, it felt like the final straw...' She winced.

'And what about your mum?'

Luna relaxed. 'She's finally managed to get herself on an early flight tomorrow, from London. She's in a taxi now, heading for a hotel close to Heathrow airport.' She sounded relieved. 'She called just now to tell me. When I mentioned I might cancel the wedding, she said I need to give Marco another chance.' She sighed. 'She told me not to worry about what other people want and just to focus on us. Also, she said just because Marco loves me, he doesn't have to love my dog.'

Coco growled malevolently.

'I know I don't.' Rose grinned and earned herself a laugh. 'So it sounds like you've got a few things to talk to him about?'

Luna looked embarrassed. 'I've been ignoring his calls.' She spun her engagement ring on her finger, looking unhappy.

'The key to a good relationship is communication,' Rose said primly.

'And now you sound just like your old self,' Luna teased.

Rose frowned. She didn't feel like herself at all. 'I'm just saying the only way you're likely to put things right with Marco is if you talk with him. I happen to know he's speaking with Ben in the garden now.'

'Do you really think the wedding should go ahead?' Luna

asked, looking at her suspiciously. 'Is this Ben's doing? Because you haven't been keen up until now.'

'It's not Ben exactly.' Rose pulled a face. 'Perhaps I've just realised I need to loosen up a little. Marco makes you happy and that's all I've ever wanted for you. If you want to marry him, you should forget what anyone else thinks and go ahead.' She shrugged. 'I've realised I have to stop trying to control everything – it's pretty obvious from my work with Mum and Dad that I'm not always right.'

'It's not you that's wrong.' Luna squeezed Rose's hand. 'Just as long as you remember — and that you deserve to be happy too…'

'Rose is a beautiful woman – I don't think I noticed it until now.' Marco's voice carried as Rose and Luna slowly made their way across the garden. From here, Rose could see the men were sitting on a bench overlooking the sparkling swimming pool in front of them.

'She is,' Ben said carefully.

'Wait,' Luna said, scooping Coco into her arms and tugging Rose behind a blood-red oleander situated just a few metres away from where the men were sitting.

'What are you doing?' Rose complained as Luna tugged her closer, ensuring they were both hidden. She could just make out Ben and Marco's silhouettes through the branches.

'*Shhhh*, they're talking about you.' Luna giggled, nudging Rose. 'Don't you want to know what Ben has to say?' She winked suggestively. 'I know I do.'

Rose grimaced but didn't move. Spying was definitely not something the Love Doctor would recommend, but she wouldn't mind hearing what was going on inside Ben's head. Perhaps if she eavesdropped for a few minutes, it would help her to understand what he saw in her? Or even what he really expected to happen going forward.

'I know you said Rose wasn't your type, but I wanted to thank you for keeping her occupied since you arrived,' Marco said seriously. 'When I asked you to keep her busy in the restaurant and you refused, I thought you meant it.'

A block of icy dread made itself at home in Rose's belly. What did that mean, exactly?

She glanced at Luna who was frowning too. 'Occupied?' her friend mouthed silently, grimacing.

'What do you mean?' Ben asked, sounding a little put out.

'Aside from last night.' Marco chuckled but thankfully didn't elaborate. 'You took her swimming after you picked up the wedding gift which ensured Rose and Luna didn't get time to talk. Plus, you distracted Rose by taking her shopping to Francesca's while Luna got her hair done. It's been obvious since Rose got here that she's been distracted by you. That's made it easier for the wedding plans to progress without interference.' His voice trailed off at the end, and Rose wondered if he was remembering that his almost bride was having second thoughts despite him conniving to keep them separated. 'But are you somehow responsible for her change of heart now? Is that why she's not so dead set against the wedding anymore and why she's agreed to get Luna to speak to me? I've a feeling if my fiancée decides to marry me, Rose will be a big part of the reason behind that.'

Rose winced when Luna mouthed, 'What?'

'That's not true,' she mimed. But was it?

'Rose knows her own mind,' Ben said. 'If she's coming around to the idea of you getting married, that's down to your fiancée and you. It's got nothing to do with me.'

'All I'm saying is I'm happy Rose is finally on my side. You have a magic touch with women. Perhaps you could encourage her to talk to *Nonna* next?' Marco asked.

'I think she's planning on doing exactly that,' Ben said, and Rose's stomach went into freefall.

Had this thing between them all just been an elaborate hoax? Had he always been plotting, trying to get her to make sure the wedding went ahead? Had Ben somehow staged their conversation by the lake when they'd spotted the shoot on the olive tree? A million possibilities raced through her mind. None of them good. 'She told me that she'll speak with Isabella later,' Ben added, and Marco let out a quiet cheer.

Rose bit her lip, she knew she was only hearing half a conversation, had coached enough couples to realise this might be a misunderstanding. But what if it wasn't? What if Ben had been playing her? Had everything that had happened between them just been an act – a way to encourage her to get the wedding back on track? Suddenly, she felt sick.

'What's happening?' Luna whispered, leaning closer and squeezing Rose's arm. 'What's he talking about — are you really planning on speaking to *Nonna*? What about?'

'Nothing important,' Rose croaked, swallowing a wave of bile. 'Am I hearing this correctly?' A gust of wind blew into them from nowhere making her shiver.

'You mean did Ben deliberately seduce you to stop you from ruining the wedding?' Luna asked softly, her face a picture of confusion. 'I think that's what they just said. What I can't believe is Marco would even ask that of him.' She paled. 'What kind of man am I planning on marrying?'

What kind of man had Rose let herself fall for? 'I don't know,' she croaked. This couldn't be happening. A few minutes ago, she'd been humming with excitement about a relationship that might not be real.

She'd dropped her defences, allowed herself to feel something for the first time, trusted Ben when she should have known better. She'd overturned her entire life, abandoned everything she'd built and believed in in less than four days. How could she have been such an idiot?

'I'm going to speak with Marco,' Luna suddenly snapped, and was about to reveal herself when her mobile beeped from the pocket of her dress. She juggled Coco into another arm and tugged it out. 'It's Mum,' she hissed, indicating that they should move away from the men.

'I need to take this. Then I'm going to sort this out.' Luna shot a furious look towards where Marco and Ben were still talking as she guided Rose towards the house. Rose's head was spinning, her insides pulsating with pain. She'd been so stupid. The woman with all the rules had allowed herself to be played. How had that happened? Was it just because of Ben's handsome features; had she been too flattered by his attention to see below the surface? Had she simply seen what she'd wanted to see?

When they were out of earshot, Luna quickly dialled her mother while Rose leaned her head against the cool brickwork of the villa. She felt sick, but worse, she felt gullible and foolish.

She'd spent a lifetime first witnessing and then counselling others against getting involved too quickly. Now she was reaping the devastating consequences of ignoring her own advice. She'd abandoned her rules, decided they didn't matter – and she should have known better.

Luna let out a sudden sob, and Rose jerked her head up just as her friend pushed her mobile back into her pocket.

'What's happened?' she asked, sucking in a deep breath and trying to pull herself together. She was strong and she'd get through this. Hadn't she walked her parents through all of their heartbreaks? They'd survived, even if they had simply gone and done the same thing all over again.

'That was Mum.' Luna swallowed, her face paling. 'She lost my grandmother's necklace on the way to the hotel. She's just arrived and searched everywhere, but she can't find it. She's so upset. She told me she's not getting on her flight; she's going to try to retrace her steps instead.' Her voice edged into hysteria.

'She'll find it,' Rose said more out of reflex than anything else.

'She won't. She had it in a special bag, but that's not in the taxi because she checked with them, it's nowhere. The only thing she can think is that she lost it or it got stolen on the train.' Luna's eyes flooded. 'It's gone, my grandmother's necklace is lost and my mother's not coming. If that's not a sign that this wedding should be cancelled, I don't know what is.'

Rose opened her mouth to argue, before shutting it again.

'If I'd never agreed to this wedding, we'd still have my grandmother's necklace,' Luna wailed, suddenly looking so fragile.

'You're right.' Rose sighed. 'Rushing into love always ends in disaster.'

Hadn't her parents shown her that a million times?

'So now you're blaming me?' Luna squeaked, jerking her head up as more tears streaked across her face.

'Of course not,' Rose soothed. 'But you do keep leaping into these relationships. You've known Marco for barely a month, got engaged to him in such a rush. Perhaps this is for the best.'

Rose knew she'd said the wrong thing when Luna's eyes widened.

'I need a friend right now, not a Love Doctor, or a lecture in "I told you so",' she muttered, before turning on her heels and marching away.

Rose stumbled after, her stomach in knots. 'I'm sorry,' she said. 'I'm not blaming you; I'm just upset.'

Luna stopped as she reached the front steps of the villa and Coco stood beside her growling as Rose drew closer. 'You got what you wanted. I'm not getting married and I'm going to end up alone — just like you,' her friend said, before spinning on her heels and marching into the villa.

'What's happening?' Elena asked as Luna bumped into her in the hallway just as Rose caught up. Her head was spinning. How had everything gone so wrong so quickly?

'The wedding is off!' Luna declared, before racing up the steps.

'What?' Elena cried.

'It's what?' Marco yelled, his eyes widening as he and Ben appeared from the sitting room that led from the garden. '*Tesoro*, you can't mean that?' He jerked his gaze to Rose looking angry. 'What did you do?' he moaned. Then he shook his head before bounding after Luna as she headed upstairs.

22

BEN

'What happened?' Ben asked as Elena rushed into the kitchen, shouting for Leonardo while Marco chased Luna to the second floor.

'I thought you were going to talk to Luna about saving the wedding? I'm guessing it didn't go well?' He paused, taken aback by Rose's pale face and furious expression.

'You could say that,' she said tightly, nodding towards the sitting room he'd entered the villa through seconds earlier. She marched into it, waiting until Ben followed before slamming the door. 'I don't think we need an audience,' she explained, narrowing her eyes when he opened his arms in a gesture that signalled *what the hell?*

'What's going on?'

'I like the Marino family – most of them anyway – but I'm not looking to upset them even more,' Rose spat back.

'Okay.' Ben shook his head, baffled. 'What's going on?' he repeated. Rose looked furious, but even worse, she looked upset. What could possibly have happened since they shared that moment in the gardens of the villa? Everything had been fine then. 'Is it your parents?' he guessed. 'Did they contact you about their weddings again?'

Rose's mouth pinched. 'We heard you talking to Marco in the garden,' she said darkly. 'Every... single... word...'

'What?' Ben stumbled trying to recall the conversation, wondering how Rose and Luna could possibly have overheard any of it.

They'd been sitting by the pool and Marco had offered him a beer, which Ben had refused. They'd been talking about the wedding and Marco's hopes and dreams, then the conversation had turned to Rose. *Oh dear God.*

The penny dropped and Ben's insides mirrored the movement, making him swallow a surge of dread. Dammit. 'It's not how it sounded, Rose.' He took a step towards her, but she held up a palm. 'I know some of what we said probably sounded bad.'

He winced. That was an understatement. Marco had effectively thanked him for keeping Rose out of his hair, had been celebrating the fact that Ben had slept with her. He remembered every appalling word, could feel the flush of mortification and guilt creeping up his cheeks. 'Rose, you have to know that's not what happened. Marco did ask me to keep you occupied, but I refused.'

She gave him a withering look and he let out a long breath. It had sounded awful, but surely, she must know him better than that by now? Knew there was no way he'd do any of those things to her.

'I don't know why I forgot all the rules I've spent a lifetime crafting,' she said stiffly, and Ben watched her tighten her shaking hands into fists before shoving them by her sides.

'It seems I was wrong about you, and I was wrong about Marco,' Rose continued, her eyes flashing with barely contained rage. 'Luna's right to have called off the wedding. She's a sweet and honest woman while Marco and you—' She shook her head vehemently.

Ben frowned. 'We're what?' he asked, feeling the first stirring of temper. 'You've judged me, Rose. Harshly I might add. I don't blame you for it, but you seem to have decided I'm guilty without even trying to see my side.' He waited, hoping to see a crack in her anger, a sign that she wanted to hear him out.

Rose blew out a breath. 'What would be the point. I heard everything and my ears don't lie, but in my experience people often do.' She injected the last words with enough venom that Ben was surprised he didn't immediately crash to the ground and start convulsing.

'You overheard a conversation,' he said sharply as his shoulders went rigid. 'Not all of it I might add. I expect you missed the part when I told Marco how much I cared for you. You also didn't hear the talk we had in the restaurant when I told him I wasn't going to seduce you — or trick you into staying out of Luna's way.' He held his breath, hoping at least some of his words would convince her. If she knew him at all, she'd know he was telling the truth.

'And yet you did,' Rose said quietly, the simmering temper morphing to hurt in front of his eyes, which cut far deeper than her words ever could.

'Rose – everything that happened between us was genuine,' Ben said desperately. 'And Marco truly loves Luna. He just lost his head for a while. He wants to marry her, to make her happy.'

Rose gazed at him, her expression part pity, part disgust. 'Luna and Marco won't be marrying. She heard him too, remember. He's tried to bully her into this wedding, and the date is more important than Luna's feelings, or her own mother being here. In addition to that, he asked you to keep me – her best friend – out of the way, using any means necessary. He's all wrong for her, just like you're all wrong for me.'

The words were delivered without emotion, but Ben felt

the punch of them anyway. It was as if she'd reached into his chest and used the mere power of prose to rip out what remained of his heart.

'Marco loves Luna,' Ben said softly, wondering if he should admit how deep his feelings were for Rose. Then again, she obviously didn't want to hear it, he could see that now. She'd given up on them, just like Sophia. Perhaps for different reasons, but her condemnation of him, the fact that she couldn't see beyond what she'd heard, told him everything he needed to know. She hadn't looked deeper than his skin either. She'd simply stared into the face of her own prejudice.

'I don't think Marco, or you, know what love really is,' Rose muttered, proving it.

Ben tensed. 'Everything my friend has done since arriving here has been about Luna,' he said. 'He loves her, and if you could just look beyond your experiences with your parents, your clients, if you could be a friend and not the Love Doctor for a while – I think you'd be able to see the truth.'

Rose laughed, but it didn't sound genuine. 'I'm only just starting to see things clearly now. You were always on a mission to distract me. Right from the start when you arrived on the plane looking like—' She choked on the last words, screwing up her nose as she studied him. '*That!*'

'So now the way I look is wrong?' Ben shot back, shaking his head. It wasn't the first time he'd heard it, but he expected better of Rose.

'Was spilling the coffee on me a part of your plan too?' she asked, barely looking at him as she began to pace. 'I'm not sure I can blame you for my missing luggage, but what about the flat tyre that made us late?' She stopped pacing, considering him.

Ben sighed wearily. 'You're determined to see the worst in me. Even if you hadn't heard Marco and me talking, I wonder how long it would have taken you to sabotage the wedding, and any chance of a relationship we might have had.'

'I don't know what you mean,' Rose said bitterly.

'I think you do,' Ben insisted. 'What happened between us *was* real, Rose, you're just too afraid to see it.' The knowledge of that was almost too painful to admit.

He watched her blink as she absorbed his words. 'You were always looking for a way out, or a sign that I was tricking you. I got beneath that hard shell for a while – thought there was a chance for us. But I see now, there isn't. You're always going to try to find a problem because you're absolutely terrified of love. So scared you can barely see straight.' He narrowed his eyes.

'I'm not,' she spluttered, her beautiful face contorting as she glared back at him.

'You've been so screwed up by your parents that you don't want to take a risk. You're not dealing with them either.' He sucked in a breath. 'You're trying to fix something that's broken over and over, refusing to see you're being manipulated because neither of them want a healthy marriage that lasts. Perhaps they just enjoy the attention they get from constantly messing up? And maybe it's just easier for you to watch a relationship burn from the sidelines, to criticise and find things wrong while expounding your unrealistic rules.' He sighed. 'That way you can pick away until there's nothing left. That way you never get hurt and you're never in the wrong.'

'Isn't that like you too?' Rose asked, her voice stiff. 'You're the man who got his heart broken, so decided to never allow himself to feel again.'

Ben absorbed the new blow and nodded curtly. 'Perhaps you're right. Which just means we're even more perfect for each other than I originally thought.' He shook his head. 'You've got between a couple who could have been happy. Instead of helping make sure this wedding went smoothly, you've tried to imagine every single thing that could go wrong. You're like a wrecking ball, determined to break whatever doesn't fit your rigid ideal. It's learned behaviour, you don't really believe any relationship will work. It's no wonder Luna's decided to call off the wedding.' He shook his head. 'For a Love Doctor, you really don't have a clue about love.'

'That's not true,' Rose said, her voice wavering for the first time.

'Isn't it?' Ben asked softly. He didn't know whether to feel sorry for her. All he could focus on was that he and Rose were over before they'd even begun. The first woman he'd met in two years that he'd allowed himself to have feelings for had broken his heart.

But he'd had a lucky escape – that was clear.

'I'll see you around,' Ben said curtly as he turned and headed towards the doorway that led to the garden without looking back, ignoring the piercing pain coursing through his chest.

23

———————

ROSE

Rose raced around her bedroom, throwing all her clothes into the small suitcase she'd borrowed from Luna when she arrived. It was time to head back to England, time to get back to her clients. If she thought about Ben anymore, her head – or heart – were going to explode. She wasn't running away, she just... Didn't want to be here anymore.

Her mobile pinged from the other room, and she went to pick it up. There were multiple messages from her parents. She really had to deal with them soon. Their weddings were only a few weeks away and she had to decide which one she was going to attend. Ben was wrong: they needed her help, this had nothing to do with being manipulated – and she *definitely* wasn't stuck.

Irritated, she dropped the phone back on the bed and brushed her fingertips across her temples. She had a headache starting, but it was nothing compared to the pain in her heart.

She heard a cry and spun around trying to identify the source. Then another voice yelled something in Italian. Was it Marco? It took Rose a few seconds to realise the shouting was coming from outside. She quickly went to the balcony.

From here, Rose could see Isabella and Cesare. The older man was on his hands and knees, waving towards the olive grove, while Isabella shook her head vigorously. Watching them, Rose felt a churn of sympathy. It was obvious that Marco's grandfather wanted to show off the new olive tree shoots. But it looked like Isabella was too angry with him to care.

You're like a wrecking ball, determined to break whatever doesn't fit your rigid ideal. It's learned behaviour, you don't believe any relationship will work. For a Love Doctor, you really don't have a clue about love. Ben's words echoed around Rose's mind and she choked back a tear. It wasn't true. But maybe she could prove that to herself and Ben before leaving for England? She'd promised to speak to Isabella, after all.

When Rose reached the garden, the couple were standing outside their respective houses, still glaring at each other.

'You have to tell her to come to the olive grove,' Cesare begged Rose, switching to English as he saw her approach.

'I'm not going anywhere with you,' Isabella spat back. 'Go back to your phone, old man.' With that, she turned on her heels and stumbled into the house.

Cesare let out a pitiful sigh and muttered something about being a stupid old fool, before he headed to his own house with his shoulders slumped, leaving Rose feeling wretched for them both.

The garden fell silent. What would her rules say? Rose rubbed her temples again. Get the couple to open up and talk. A marriage didn't end because of a dead olive tree – her years of experience had taught her that at least. There was definitely something else bothering Isabella, something she hadn't admitted to yet.

Rose took in a deep breath and glanced back at the villa. Her bag was packed, and it would be so much easier to find Luna and simply escape. But something was telling her it wasn't time to leave yet.

. . .

Isabella was sitting at a table in her kitchen when Rose approached the open doorway. She hovered for a moment, watching as the older woman tried to stick fragments of the broken fertility statue back together. The figure's head looked a little skew-whiff and there were a lot of pieces missing. A shard fell off and the older woman cursed and dropped her head into her hands.

'Are you okay?'

Isabella glanced up and took in Rose, her steely expression returning. '*Sì*.' She sounded defensive. 'You want coffee or wine?' she snapped, waving at the light blue chairs surrounding the small wooden table, indicating Rose should use one.

'Coffee please, black,' Rose said, pulling out the seat furthest from the statue. It might be broken, but she wasn't taking any chances.

Isabella grinned as she put a mug in front of Rose perhaps sensing her thoughts. It was the first time Rose had seen the older woman do anything but frown, and she thought she could see glimmers of the smiling woman she remembered from the photo Ben had shown her in the Citroën.

Had that just been a few days ago? It felt like a lifetime. Rose sighed.

'Problem?' Isabella asked, her eyes pinning Rose as she took her seat again. 'I heard you fighting with Ben when I was in the garden today.' She narrowed her gaze. 'He is *un brav'uomo* – a good man – this is rare.' Her eyes momentarily darted to the wall that separated her house from her husband's and she frowned.

'I'm fine,' Rose said lightly. 'But I know something's troubling you.' She let the words sink between them. She knew from her work with clients that getting people to open up took time. Time she didn't have. She didn't want to bump into Ben again which meant she needed to find Luna and leave soon. There was no point in rehashing old ground or raking over new hurts. She was simply too raw.

'I'm fine too,' Isabella said softly, her crooked mouth, signalling she knew Rose was lying.

'Okay, Ben and I did have an argument,' Rose muttered. A little tit for tat wouldn't hurt.

'*Si*,' Isabella said, her expression wily. 'As did Cesare and me.'

'About the tree,' Rose checked. 'Or something else?' She waited, but the older woman simply picked up the glue and stuck what looked like an arm back on the statue, only it was the wrong way up. 'I should give you a job as a relationship coach, you'd get everyone to talk,' Rose said grumpily after a lengthy silence. 'If I tell you, will you tell me?' she asked.

Isabella gave Rose a toothy grin, her wrinkles stretching across her face.

Rose sighed giving in. 'Marco asked Ben to keep me occupied while I was here and—' She swallowed because the idea that it had all just been a trick really hurt. 'He did.'

'Occupied.' The older woman cocked her head, her blue eyes brighter now. 'He seemed happy enough to be occupied, *leonessa*. He seemed happy with you, and this is new for him. Are you sure he listened to my foolish *nipote* – grandson,' she translated. 'Or did he do what was in his own heart?'

Rose's stomach churned and she couldn't respond. Ben's denials had fallen on deaf ears. She'd forgotten one of her biggest rules, the one that said you should hear someone out. 'You know love turns us all into idiots,' the older woman said sympathetically, reading her mind again.

'Sometimes.' Rose leaned forward. 'But Ben says I don't know anything about love.' The words almost glued themselves to her tongue, perhaps because she suspected he might be right? For all her rules, what did she really know? She'd never been in love and had spent a lifetime finding fault with it. Because she *was* afraid. Afraid of so much.

More of Ben's accusations flooded her head, filling her with shame. *Maybe it's just easier for you to watch a relationship burn from the sidelines, to criticise and find things wrong while expounding your unrealistic rules... That way you can pick and pick away until there's nothing left. That way you never get hurt and you're never in the wrong.*

Is that what she'd done with Marco and then Ben? Expected them to repeat the patterns her parents had taught her? Rose's stomach sank.

'Do any of us know about love?' Isabella asked, her eyes fixed on Rose's face. 'The question isn't what we know, it's what we're prepared to do to fix things when they break.' Her face sagged as her attention flickered to the wall again as she clearly recognised what she'd just said. '*If* things can be fixed, that is...' Her gaze drifted to the statue, and she shook her head. 'Not everything can,' she said huskily.

'Was it just about the tree burning down?' Rose blurted. 'I mean is that the only reason you and Cesare fell out?'

She had nothing to lose. Isabella was either going to open up or she wasn't, and she didn't have much time to find out.

Rose thought the older woman wasn't going to answer for a moment because she simply picked up her coffee and took a slow sip, her gaze thoughtful. 'No,' she said eventually.

'Then what is it?' Rose asked.

When Isabella raised an eyebrow, Rose sighed and her attention fixed on the statue knowing she'd have to confide too if she wanted her to talk. 'If I thought what happened with Ben was real, I'd try to fix it,' she said slowly, the words emerging from her mouth before her brain could stop them.

'If it feels real, it probably is.' Isabella sighed. 'Besides, some things are meant to be mended.' She paused. 'Ben is a good boy. He was hurt once, and he's not someone who would want to do the same to someone else. Aurora's crystal ball predicted you are supposed to be together, and she told me Aldo says the same.'

'*Aldo*,' Rose snorted, shaking her head. For a man who didn't exist he seemed to have a lot of opinions about her life.

'What upset you?' Surely, it was her turn to ask a question again?

Isabella put the glue down. 'I am sad the tree is dead, but I am sadder my husband is gone,' she confided, her cheeks flushing.

'Gone where?' Rose asked. Cesare was living next door.

'He has replaced me.' The older woman's voice was flat.

'With whom?' Rose asked. Surely, he hadn't had an affair? He didn't seem the type. Then again, her father didn't and he'd had them over and over again.

'He left me for his phone,' Isabella declared, her lips stiffening. 'There is no room for me in his life now.'

'*Ah...*' Understanding finally dawned.

Hadn't Marco mentioned he'd got the mobile for his grandad? And hadn't the family joked about his crossword obsession? Cesare had been on his phone when the tree had burned down. The link was obvious. Isabella had mentioned it enough times, Rose should have picked up on it before.

Rose grabbed the glue from the table and sucked in a breath, telling herself to be brave. She carefully plucked up the statue's foot before fixing it back on. 'You're right, some things can and should be fixed, *Nonna*. You just have to know when to try and when to walk away.'

After leaving Isabella, Rose went to speak with Cesare about Isabella's revelations and what he might need to do to put things right. He listened and nodded, but she wasn't sure if he'd do what was necessary, but for now it was out of her hands.

After that, she searched the garden, olive grove and half of the house before she finally found Marco. He was sitting on the stairs she'd found Luna on earlier with his head in his hands. Beside him on the step she saw a steaming mug.

'Marco,' Rose said as she approached and saw him look up and blink a few times. 'Do you know where Luna is?'

'No.' He picked up the full cup and stood. 'I thought she'd left with you.' He turned and gazed up the steps. 'Is she still here? I've checked all the bedrooms...' He turned back to Rose and frowned. 'Not that I expect you to tell me.' He cleared his throat, looking embarrassed. 'Luna told me what you'd overheard. I'm sorry.' He shook his head, and a flop of brown hair fell onto his forehead, making him look less polished than usual. More vulnerable. 'It was all me, not Ben.' He winced. 'I'm the imbecile.'

'Seems to be a theme,' Rose said dryly.

'You can't blame Ben for what happened,' Marco insisted. 'I know I've messed everything up with Luna.' His forehead creased. 'The irony is, I was trying so hard not to lose her that I ruined everything.' He took a small step closer. 'I love her so much; she's perfect, kind, an incredible businessperson and she always knows the right thing to say.'

'She does,' Rose agreed.

'I don't have enough words in my head to explain how much she means to me. I was afraid if we delayed getting married, if you talked her into postponing, that she'd have time to realise I'm not really good enough for her.' He sighed, sounding sad. 'I can be uptight and boring. She's so easy to be around, so much fun – I wanted to marry her from the first day we met. I want to make her happy and I can't bear the idea of not being with her for the rest of my life.' He pushed the strands of hair from his eyes, which were filled with emotion. 'I suppose I have to get used to it now.'

He grimaced. 'I knew the wedding was rushed, but once I

got the idea and she said yes to my proposal, I couldn't let it go.' His shoulders sagged. 'I just—' He sighed. 'The date doesn't really matter. I shouldn't have pushed, and I definitely shouldn't have asked Ben to keep you out of Luna's way. Especially since I know you only had her best interests at heart. Blame it on me being an idiot – please don't blame Ben,' he pleaded. 'For what it's worth, he told me he wouldn't distract you. I honestly think whatever happened between you was genuine. I've never seen him as upset as he was when you argued. Not even after Sophia.'

'I think I saw what I wanted to see,' Rose admitted. A lifetime spent watching her parents' toxic relationships had taught her to look for problems. Ben had been right. 'Rather than seeing what was there.' She sighed and watched Marco sip some of the liquid from the mug and wince.

'It's tea,' he said when she raised an eyebrow. 'I think I'm learning to like it.' He sipped again and shuddered.

Rose smiled. He was trying; he really did love her friend. How could she not have seen that? 'Do you still want to get married?' she asked and watched Marco's eyes light up.

'Of course I do,' he said emphatically. 'But Luna's determined to call off the wedding. *Nonna*'s refusing to attend, Luna's mother is going to miss her flight because she's lost her grandmother's necklace. It's hopeless. You might be the Love Doctor, but I'm not even sure you can fix all that.'

'You just worry about getting everything ready. The rest you can leave with me,' she promised.

Marco jerked his chin, looking less than convinced. But instead of commenting, he took another quick sip of tea and pulled a face.

24

ROSE

Ben was right. She'd got everything wrong. *Everything.* Rose paced across the garden shaking her head as she searched for Luna before checking her watch. It was almost midday, and she had a lot to get sorted if the wedding was going to go ahead tomorrow. As Isabella had said, some things could and should be fixed, and Rose was going to do everything she could to make sure they were.

But the first thing she had to do was call Luna's mum.

She stopped by the swimming pool and quickly dialled Deborah Kennedy's number while she watched sunlight throw multicoloured sparkles across the water.

'Rose?' Deborah answered swiftly. 'Is everything okay with Luna? She told me the wedding's been cancelled.' She sounded miserable.

'It has,' Rose said carefully. 'At least for now.'

'It's awful,' Deborah wailed. 'I feel like it's all my fault. I lost my mother's necklace and then Luna decided to call the whole thing off.'

'I know,' Rose soothed, pacing to the edge of the pool. 'But everything's going to be okay.' She was going to make sure of it.

The older woman ignored her — too caught up in her own unfolding disaster. 'I've called the taxi and train company, but either they haven't found the necklace yet or no one's handed it in.' Her voice wobbled, the emotion in it almost tangible. 'I double-checked in the hotel too, but I can't find it anywhere.' She sobbed, which was out of character for the normally calm and efficient scientist. Rose went to sit on a bench beside the pool, the one she'd seen Marco and Ben talking at just a few hours ago, trying not to go over everything she'd heard. Analysing it, remembering all of Ben's denials — how she'd ignored them — wasn't going to help fix anything. 'The necklace has been in my family for generations. Luna was supposed to wear it tomorrow. She's devastated,' Deborah sniffed.

Rose sighed. 'I'm going to put everything right. But first, I need to tell you none of this is your fault and second, I'm going to sort it, so you don't have to worry about a thing.' She pulled a face because she had no idea if she could really pull it off.

Her stomach was already in knots anticipating what she was going to have to do this afternoon, the familiar fear gnawing at her insides. She was terrified, but knew she had to finally face her fear and move on. 'You didn't cancel your flight, did you?' she checked, praying the older woman hadn't got around to it.

'No.' Deborah sighed. 'I've spent all morning trying to track the necklace down.'

'Don't cancel,' Rose ordered, momentarily shutting her eyes as a wave of relief rolled over her. At least one thing had gone her way. 'Catch the flight, but don't tell Luna you're coming yet.'

'Why not?' Deborah asked, sounding surprised.

'Because I've got a lot to do before I convince her to go ahead with the wedding,' Rose confessed. 'And she'll just tell you not to come.'

'But what about the necklace?' Deborah asked. 'She needs

something old, borrowed and blue. She won't marry Marco without it. How are you going to solve that if I can't find it?'

'Leave it with me,' Rose said, smiling as she drummed her fingers on the bench. 'The Love Doctor has a plan.' And for once it had everything to do with bringing a couple together again.

Rose paced around the Citroën clutching the car keys like an amulet. She could do this. She *wasn't* afraid. It was time to move beyond the memories of her childhood. To finally release herself from the things that had held her back for so many years. Her rules, anxieties, prejudices, everything had to change. Starting with this.

She took in a long breath as she reached for the door handle on the driver's side and almost jumped out of her skin when Coco suddenly barked.

Rose spun around, expecting to find Luna, but instead she saw Aurora standing on the driveway in a glittery orange dress. She looked magnificent.

'*Leonessa*,' the clairvoyant said approvingly. 'Aldo told me I'd find you here. You are finally facing your demon, *si*?' She nodded at the car as the shih tzu came bounding up to Rose and growled.

'Which one?' Rose asked dryly, keeping one eye on the dog's jaws. 'And where's Luna?'

'She is sleeping in my room,' the older woman soothed. 'She's upset and I said she could hide away in there and lick her, what do you say, *wombs*.'

'I think you mean wounds,' Rose said.

'Perhaps.' Aurora nodded, looking serious. 'Aldo says you are going to fix the wedding,' she added, her gaze travelling back to the car. 'You have places to go?'

Rose nodded, feeling a fresh bubble of anxiety climb up her

throat. 'I've not got much time,' she croaked, before turning and opening the driver's door. Coco let out a delighted bark and immediately scrambled onto the passenger seat. 'Get out!' Rose demanded, skirting around to the other door and yanking it open. She signalled to the dog that it needed to move, but Coco simply growled.

'It seems you will have some company on your journey. Perhaps you two need some time alone?'

'I don't know why,' Rose muttered. 'She hates me.' She signalled to the dog to move again, but Coco didn't budge. 'I haven't got time for this! If you're coming, you need to get in the back,' Rose muttered angrily, slamming the door. If the dog wanted to come, she wasn't going to try to move her — she valued her limbs too highly.

She turned back to Aurora. 'I need you to speak to Leonardo, Elena and Francesca, to tell them to make sure everything's ready for the wedding tomorrow. Marco already knows.' Rose walked around to the driver's side again, expecting the older woman to ask her more. 'It's going to go ahead.'

'Already done.' Aurora grinned.

'How? I only just decided,' Rose asked, but Aurora simply tapped her temples. '*Aldo...*' Rose muttered. Or just powerful intuition.

'Of course!' the older woman chuckled. 'Oh, and I just saw Isabella and Cesare walking towards the olive grove. I believe you had something to do with that too?'

Rose shrugged.

Cesare had obviously finally persuaded his wife to go and look at the new olive tree shoot, but Rose doubted that would fix things between them. She only hoped the older man would listen to the other advice she'd given when they'd spoken earlier. Getting Isabella to agree to go to the wedding was one of the final tasks she had to complete, but she wasn't convinced Marco's *Nonna* was ready to let go of her resentment yet.

'It's not the time to worry about that now,' she muttered, taking in a deep breath and climbing into the car before moving the seat backwards and forwards to get it in the right place. She switched on the engine and saw Aurora wave. Rose felt her chest grow heavy.

'Aldo says remember to breathe,' Aurora shouted.

'Great advice.' Rose swallowed. 'I can do this,' she murmured, switching off the airbag for the front seat because the demon was clearly not going to budge, then putting the sat nav on and programming in the address, grateful she could remember it.

When the voice said something loudly in Italian, Rose momentarily closed her eyes. 'Aldo, I don't believe you exist, but I could really use your directions right now,' she muttered as she took off the handbrake and Coco let out a joyful bark.

'Weird time to become my cheerleader,' Rose grumbled, giving the shih tzu a distrustful look. Was the dog lulling her into a false sense of security – did the demon plan to murder her on the way?

She put her foot on the accelerator, ignoring the drone of the sat nav as the voice continued to give her instructions, and she steered the car slowly down the driveway.

A car whizzed past the Citroën on the motorway and Rose had to stop herself from slamming on the brakes and screaming. She swallowed, her chest heaving, her forehead dripping with sweat, despite the air conditioning being turned up so high her hands were almost blue.

'Only an hour to go,' she croaked to Coco, checking on the dog who was curled up on the front seat looking like an angel – a fallen one in any case. She hadn't moved or made a sound since the journey had begun and her company was oddly reassuring. Which meant Rose was clearly going mad.

Rose sighed and took in a long breath. Then again, the drive so far had been uneventful, aside from the heavy traffic which just kept building. But she was tired, probably because she was so stressed. Her head hurt and she could only hope that when they arrived at their destination, she'd be able to park easily. She had to pick something up and then head back to Bellemilia in time to speak to Luna so she could convince her to go ahead with the wedding. Hopefully, she'd still have time left to speak to Isabella and Cesare too.

A car beeped behind them, getting too close, and Rose shrieked, gripping the steering wheel tighter, remembering Ben's hands clutching it in the same way. He had good hands, tanned and large, and hers seemed so small in comparison. She kept her gaze on the road, trying to concentrate on breathing as her mind wandered to the night in the cellar.

Would he ever forgive her for being such a coward, for rejecting him when he'd allowed himself to have feelings for her?

Another car shot past, its engine firing loudly, and Rose let out another loud shriek. Her brain trapezed to the moment in Paris when her parents had been arguing. She could almost hear the crunch of metal, the churn in her stomach as the car had rolled – it had been chaotic and terrifying. But perhaps the worst thing about it had been that her father had continued shouting, her mother too. Neither of them had been concerned about one another or Rose. They'd simply used the accident as a weapon – a new crime they could lay at each other's door. Were Ben and Isabella right, had she ever mattered to them, or had she always been a pawn in their relationship war?

She squealed when something rough touched her trembling arm. 'What are you doing?' she yelped when she realised Coco had moved into the centre of the car and was now licking her forearm. 'I'm not food — and eating the driver is a terrible idea. Besides, this is dangerous.'

She tried to ease the dog away with her elbow while keeping her eyes on the road. But Coco licked Rose's arm again, her rough tongue gentle.

'You are one weird dog,' Rose grumbled, giving up as the shih tzu continued to dab at her skin. The repetitive motion was soothing, and she let herself go with it, taking in a deep breath and letting it out slowly, matching the dog's movements. She continued to follow Aldo's advice as she drove, allowing herself to consider why she'd chosen to carry all that fear with her for so many years. Wondering if it was finally time to let it go.

After a few moments, Coco eased away and curled up on the front seat, leaving Rose feeling oddly bereft. 'Thank you,' she whispered as the dog began to snore.

Half an hour later, Rose pulled up in Montotta and parked in the same spot Ben had used a few metres down from the café. She let out a prayer of thanks when she saw the curiosity shop was open, and as she hopped out of the car, she called for the shih tzu to follow her inside. She had something important to collect, and time to save the wedding was running out...

25

ROSE

After hours of driving, Rose pulled into the driveway at Villa Paradise and switched off the Citroën before laying her head on the steering wheel. She waited a beat until her pulse finally steadied. Beside her in the passenger seat, Coco let out a long, contented sigh. 'We're back.' She carefully pried the bag she'd got from the curiosity shop from beside the dog and opened the door.

'You're home!' Aurora boomed, suddenly appearing from around the corner of the villa. She leaned down to pat the shih tzu, who'd exited the car out of the driver's side and immediately bounded up to say hello. 'Is your *emission* accomplished?' Aurora asked.

Rose nodded and rattled the bag. 'My mission was a complete success.' She smiled as she looked around, turning back to see the older woman holding up a mobile phone.

'This is *fantastico*. Your aura says you had a good journey,' the clairvoyant declared, beaming before pointing the phone at the dog. 'And Coco is relaxed too.' She glanced up, looking curious. 'You have put your differences behind you?' she asked. 'You both have vibrant colours – the drive was not too stressful it seems.'

'It improved,' Rose told her. She wasn't sure she'd ever love being in a car, but somehow driving to Montotta had helped her to murder a few long-held demons. She glanced at Coco. Old and new.

'What's with the phone, I thought you didn't have one?' she asked as Aurora continued to hold it up, gazing through it intently as she swept it back and forth, checking their surroundings.

'It talks to me even more than my spirits,' Aurora declared as it pinged in her hand. 'But it has aura and tarot card apps. I thought I'd try them out. Aldo says it's good for me to be part of the future.' She frowned suddenly looking mournful. 'But Luna's aura is *very* dark. Her heart is broken.'

'Hopefully, I'll be able to help with that. Where did you get the phone?' Rose asked, hoping her suspicions were correct.

'Cesare.' The older woman's forehead creased. 'He said he had no need for it anymore. Told me I can keep it. I didn't want it at first, but then Cesare told me about the apps.'

Rose nodded, trying not to smile. The chat she'd had with Marco's grandfather after speaking with Isabella had obviously reaped rewards. She'd told him about Isabella's heartbreak, how he'd been ignoring her for the past few months and encouraged him to think about parting with his phone – he'd clearly decided to listen to her advice. She glanced towards the garden. 'Do you know where he is now?'

The older woman waggled her eyebrows looking delighted. 'Sitting in the garden with Isabella. If you go now, you might catch them. Their auras are very green.' Her eyes flashed. 'That means they are *excommunicating*.'

'Do you mean *communicating*?' Rose guessed and Aurora nodded. 'I'll go and see them now, then I need to track down Luna.' Wherever her friend was hiding.

'She's still in my bedroom,' Aurora told her, putting the phone back in her billowing pocket. 'I'm about to go and see if she wants something to eat. She's starved herself all afternoon.'

'Can you tell her that I'll come and join you in a moment please? I've got some things to explain and make up for.' Rose glanced at the bag she was carrying, hoping it would be enough.

'Of course, *leonessa*.' Aurora smiled. 'We will see you soon.' She nodded at Coco and signalled towards the villa with her chin.

The dog sniffed a couple of times, before trotting up to Rose and rubbing her small body against her leg in a gesture of, what...? *Solidarity, friendship, insanity?* Baffled, Rose gazed down at her, then she watched as Coco followed the older woman inside.

Rose could see Cesare and Isabella as she wandered slowly through the garden, watching the last rays of the sun begin to disappear. They were sitting at a small table set up equidistant between their two houses. Beside the table was a pot and as Rose drew closer, she could see a tiny shoot emerging from the inside. Was it the olive tree?

'Rose,' Isabella said as she looked up and spotted her. She waved a glass of wine indicating that she should take a seat before disappearing into her house.

Cesare sat concentrating. He was gluing pieces onto the fertility statue, and it was obvious he'd been working on it for a while. The fragments that Isabella had stuck in the wrong places had been put right and the original form was beginning to re-emerge.

'You're doing a great job,' Rose said as she sat and watched him work. Were the couple still planning to give the statue to Luna and Marco? If so, she'd have to ask Marco to stage an intervention. The gift wouldn't help their cause.

Isabella returned and put a glass of crisp white wine in front of her. 'My husband is doing well.' Her eyes twinkled as she gazed at him. 'I want to thank you for speaking with us both today.' Her voice was thick with emotion.

The older man nodded. 'You helped to fix what couldn't be fixed.' He nodded to the shoot and then the statue, before beaming at his wife. 'And now we are beginning again, together. All in a new spot.' He waved his hand at the pot and then their houses.

'You gave your phone to Aurora,' Rose commented, sipping some of her drink which tasted tart and refreshing. She could hear crickets singing in the olive grove, could smell heat and sunscreen and was reminded of Ben. Her stomach did a slow somersault, but she ignored it. She might have helped to heal this couple's relationship, but she wasn't sure she'd ever mend what had broken between her and Ben. All those words that couldn't be unsaid, all that misunderstanding...

Cesare shrugged. 'I no longer need my phone. I've got more important things to keep me occupied. My wife has given me a long list of tasks.' His eyes sparkled and he picked up the glue and another piece of the statue and waved it before winking at Isabella who flushed endearingly.

Rose leaned back in her chair enjoying the sensation of a job well done. All those years of working with her parents and she'd never come close to healing any of their relationships. Perhaps it was easier when people wanted to make the changes?

'Marco came to see me earlier,' Isabella said. 'He said perhaps the statue isn't the best gift for him and Luna at the moment. He didn't want to upset me, but he said they wish to wait for their *bambini*. That getting married is just about them.' She frowned. 'Perhaps this is okay. Marriage—' She gave her husband a long look. 'Will be good for my grandson I think.'

'It's *finita*!' Cesare declared as he put down the glue. Then he carefully spun the statue around, before pushing it across the table towards Rose.

'Which is why we've decided to give it to you!' Isabella said, clapping her hands. 'To thank you for what you have done for me and Cesare.'

Rose gulped as she stared into the statue's face. It looked like it was laughing at her.

'We'll give it to you tomorrow after the wedding, once it's dry,' Isabella said. 'For now.' She glanced towards her house. 'I have things to do.' She winked at Cesare. 'And we both have a wedding outfit to find.'

Aurora opened the door to her bedroom just as Rose arrived. From where she was standing in the hallway, Rose could see Luna looking solemn sat on the bed beside Coco. Her friend jumped up as soon as she entered the room and Aurora shut the door. Then the shih tzu hopped off the bed too and came to rub herself against Rose's leg.

'Woah,' Rose said, startled. 'I'm really not sure what that behaviour means.' She stared down at the dog, baffled. 'She'd expected Coco to revert to normal as soon as they got back to the villa. This was odd.

'It means she's starting to like you,' Luna said, sounding shocked. '*Finally.* What did you do?'

Rose considered, still staring at Coco. 'The demon came for a drive with me this afternoon to keep me company. Then instead of biting, she licked me when I started to get stressed.'

'Aldo says it's because you showed her your true self — your vulnerability,' Aurora interrupted.

'You drove?' Luna gasped, her dog instantly forgotten. 'What possessed you?'

'It was about time... I've held onto that fear for far too long.' She paused absorbing the truth, considering how many years she'd wasted. 'Besides, I had something important to pick up.' She offered Luna the bag. 'I owe you an apology.'

'Why?' Luna frowned but took the package. 'I know I got upset with you earlier, but I've had time to think, and I know you've always had my best interests at heart.' She sighed and went to slump on the edge of the bed. 'The engagement all happened in such a rush. I should have listened to you. Marrying Marco tomorrow would have been an awful mistake, you were right.' She grimaced.

'I was *wrong*, Luna,' Rose said, feeling the punch of the words in her chest. The truth of them. 'I can see that so clearly now. Marco loves you.'

Luna's eyes widened to almost twice their normal size. 'Sorry?' she spluttered. 'What's happened? Did being in the car rewire your brain or something?' She frowned. 'A few hours ago, we found out the man I love asked Ben to seduce you to keep you out of the way.' Her voice rose an octave. 'Worse than that, Ben did.'

Rose felt something pinch in her chest. 'It was a misunderstanding.' She sighed as she went to sit on the bed beside her friend. 'You know I have trouble trusting people. I'm always looking for problems. I've spent a lifetime homing in on them – even the ones that weren't really there.'

When Luna opened her mouth, Rose held up a palm. 'As a psychologist I know better than anyone what the root cause of that is.' She winced. 'But how could I spend my life trying to fix relationships, when I'm not even sure I ever truly believed that a healthy one was possible?' she pondered unhappily. 'I've looked for perfection and then jabbed and criticised when I didn't find it.' She felt ashamed. 'Because there's no such thing as perfection. At least not when it comes to two people trying to make each other happy.'

She thought about Aldo and Aurora, about Isabella and

Cesare, about her clients. Their marriages weren't perfect, but somehow, despite that, they could and did thrive.

'Things can work, but you can't always rely on rigid rules. It's up to the individuals to discover the right path for them. I'm not saying I'm always wrong, I'm just saying...' She screwed up her nose as she tried to find her way through the words, to articulate everything she'd recognised since her conversation with Ben. 'I might need to ease up a little.' Her voice lowered. 'Marco loves you. You light up when you're around him and he does the same. You're supposed to be together.'

'But we're so different,' Luna complained. 'You said so yourself. He doesn't even like tea!'

Rose shrugged. 'When I saw him earlier, he was drinking a cup.' She didn't add that he still hated it. 'That tells me a lot. It means he's prepared to try it for you. He wants to make you happy. For your relationship to work. So he lost his head for a bit, made some stupid decisions. I think what really counts is that he wants to put them right.'

He was willing to learn and change, something neither of Rose's parents had ever wanted to do. Instead, they made the same mistakes over and over, continually pulling her into their mess. It had coloured everything for her. Ben was right, it was time for her to walk away.

'He wants to put them right?' Luna cooed, her face brightening.

Rose nodded. 'But he can't unless you talk to him.'

Her friend frowned. 'I suppose I could.' She swallowed, brushing a hand across her face looking unsure. 'But the wedding still can't happen tomorrow. Mum's not here, my grandmother's necklace is gone, and Isabella is refusing to come.' Tears pricked her eyes, and she blinked, shaking her head. 'That's just too much wrong for it to be right.'

'What if I told you your mum's agreed to catch her flight in the morning. She's going to arrive in plenty of time for the ceremony,' Rose said as Luna's unhappy expression changed to shocked. 'I've spoken to Marco's grandparents too.' She smiled. 'They've decided to come to the wedding, after all, together.'

Luna's jaw dropped. 'How did you pull that off?'

Rose gave Aurora a quick wink. 'Let's just say I used my intuition. Plus, I talked and they listened. There really wasn't much more to it than that.'

Luna's answering smile suddenly dimmed. 'But what about my grandmother's necklace? Even you can't do anything about that,' she said quietly.

'I can't help your mum find it if I'm still in Italy,' Rose agreed. 'But I'm hoping this might make up for it a little. I know it's not the same, but perhaps it's the start of a new tradition.' She nudged the bag that Luna had put on the bed towards her. Then watched her friend take out the velvet blue box the owner of the curiosity shop had placed inside.

Luna opened it and gasped. 'It's a sapphire necklace,' she gushed, taking the jewellery out and holding it up, watching it sparkle when the light overhead caught in the vibrant blue stones. 'It's not exactly the same as my grandmother's — but it's silver and it looks old.'

'It is... I bought it for you, it's yours.' It was the one she'd seen when she'd gone with Ben to pick up the fertility statue. If she was feeling fanciful, she might even say it was like it was meant to be. Aldo or Aurora would probably tell her the same.

Rose took a smaller box out of her pocket and opened it. 'I brought these sapphire earrings to go with it – for me.'

'It's like they were made for each other!' Luna cried, bouncing excitedly.

'I thought you could borrow them tomorrow. Something old, something blue...'

'Something borrowed,' Luna finished, grinning and then leaping forward and wrapping Rose in a hug. 'Thank you,' she whispered. 'I can't believe you put my wedding back together.'

She drew back suddenly, and her expression turned stormy. 'But what about Ben? Aren't you furious with him? Surely, you don't want to be maid of honour with him as the best man?'

Rose shrugged. 'It'll be okay. I think we got him wrong. He's a good man. Besides, I think we're both adult enough to stand side by side and watch our favourite people in the world get married.'

'Are you sure?' Luna asked.

'I'm sure.' Rose felt the churn in her stomach again. It would be hard, but she'd do it for her friend. She sighed. 'But it's up to you now, Luna. The only thing that really matters is whether you want to do this. Do you want to be with Marco for the rest of your life?'

'I do!' Luna whispered, then louder, 'I do, I do, I do!' She suddenly vaulted off the bed making Coco bark frantically. Then her friend swung open the bedroom door and bolted into the hallway, on her way to track down her fiancé.

Rose followed, pausing on the threshold and savouring Luna's happiness, as she allowed herself to wish just for a moment, that things could be different for her…

26

———

BEN

Ben stood at the end of the wedding aisle under a stunning arbour created from vibrant pink pansies, crimson dahlias and white roses. Beside him, Marco adjusted the collar of his shirt as Ben's throat tightened. Being here, waiting for his best friend's bride, should have brought back a barrage of awful memories. But he could barely summon an image of Sophia now – instead, all his mind would conjure was Rose.

He hadn't seen her since their fight. He'd returned to his bedroom, intent on packing his bags and leaving for England, only the idea of going anywhere without her was just... wrong.

Which showed he was as much of an idiot as he'd been two years ago.

Beside him, Marco fidgeted with his tie looking anxious. 'I'm so nervous,' he confided, blowing out a breath. 'Less than twenty-four hours ago, Luna was determined not to marry me, now...' His gaze returned to the end of the long aisle which had been lovingly created by the Marino family. Cesare had laid down a row of white wooden planks that ran parallel to the sparkling swimming pool. Then Elena, Aurora and Francesca had embellished the edges with multicoloured ribbons and flowers to match the ones on the arbour and *bomboniere.*

Leonardo had filled the sunny garden with rows of white chairs too, ready for guests, and they were slowly filling up with family and friends. A low buzz of excited voices overlapped in the warm fragrant air.

'Are you worried Luna won't turn up?' Ben asked as his eyes glued themselves to the villa and refused to budge just in case he caught a glimpse of Rose.

'No, but—' Marco paused. 'I'm sorry, is this bringing back bad memories? I didn't even think.' He sounded horrified.

'It's okay. I hardly remember that day now.' Ben turned and took in his friend properly. Marco was dressed in a cream suit, light blue shirt and a patterned tie which Francesca had picked out for the wedding. He looked handsome and concerned. 'You never asked me what made Luna change her mind,' Marco said thoughtfully. 'Why is that?'

Ben shrugged. His friend had burst into his bedroom late last night and gleefully informed him that the wedding was back on before disappearing into the bosom of his rejoicing family. Ben had meant to go and join them to find out more, but he'd been too heartsick. He couldn't bear putting a dampener on the celebrations so had decided to stay away.

'I...' He couldn't think of an excuse. A reason that didn't include, *I'm happy for you but talking about your wedding just makes me realise what a mess I've made of my own life.*

'It was Rose. The wedding's back on because of her,' Marco said, watching Ben's face as he absorbed the blow.

'What do you mean?' he asked, confused. 'She told me the wedding was off, that you and Luna were all wrong for each other.' That Ben was all wrong for her too – or maybe it had been the other way around? It didn't really matter now. His heart was starting to ice over again – or at least it would once he was back in Bristol. Then this whole thing would feel like a bad memory. In time, he'd forget all about Rose. At least he hoped so…

'This is *all* because of her,' Marco said passionately, waving a hand at the aisle. 'She convinced Luna to forgive me, encouraged her mother to fly to Pisa this morning.' His attention strayed to the rows of chairs. 'Deborah's in a taxi now, she should arrive any minute. I can't wait to meet her.'

'Did Luna's mum find the necklace then?' Ben asked, surprised. He'd been led to believe it was hopeless.

'No.' Marco shook his head. 'Rose drove herself to Montotta and brought a replacement for Luna to wear.'

'Hang on… Rose did what?' Ben's heartbeat skipped up and he turned to gape at the villa as if expecting her to appear and explain. 'But she's terrified of being in a car. Was she alone?' Or had she taken someone with her? He ignored the hit of jealously that it hadn't been him, as he imagined how frightened she would have been. Trying not to think about all the things that might have happened. What if she'd had an accident again? Just the idea of her getting hurt made his body go cold.

'Apparently, Coco went with her,' Marco told him, arching an eyebrow.

'Coco?' Ben choked. 'The demon from hell who hates her?' Had she gone mad?

'I know.' Marco shrugged. 'Aurora saw them just before Rose headed off. Told me she drove there and back by herself. She returned last night with an antique necklace and spoke to Luna. Told her she'd made a mistake.'

Marco paused. 'Apparently, Rose said I was an idiot – which is true.' He shrugged nonchalantly. 'But she told Luna that I loved her and she should give me another chance.' He let out a puff of air. 'Luckily, Luna did.'

Ben's head was spinning, and he felt sick as his mind began to mull all the terrible things he'd said to Rose yesterday. All those awful accusations had obviously driven her to prove him wrong. What did it mean that she had? Did it mean she cared about what he thought?

His jaw dropped when he suddenly spotted Isabella and Cesare making their way towards them across the lawn, holding hands. 'Am I dreaming?' he rasped.

He must be. None of this could be happening. He'd clearly wandered into a parallel universe, powered by Disney.

'No.' Marco chuckled. 'That was your Rose too.'

His Rose. *His.*

The words beat a tattoo in Ben's mind, branding themselves through to his insides. Rose *should* be his. Would be if he hadn't messed everything up.

'She somehow got *Nonno* to convince *Nonna* to look at the olive tree, then she got him to give up his phone because, apparently, that's what's been wrong all along,' Marco marvelled. 'Who knew?'

'She did...?' Ben shook his head feeling desolate. Rose had done all that to fix her best friend's wedding after he'd told her she didn't believe in love.

He should have been more understanding, instead he'd criticised her and left. He knew about her parents – he should have understood what drove her, why she found it so difficult to trust. She'd only ever had Luna's best interests at heart. Instead, he'd been like an open wound, desperate to protect himself by pushing her away.

'I need to speak to her. To apologise,' he said urgently, swinging his gaze back across the lawn and taking in the new guests who'd arrived and were now waiting for the wedding to begin. In the front row, Francesca waved at him and mouthed that he looked *magnifico*. 'Where is she?' he asked.

'She's with Luna. They're getting ready, so you can't talk to her yet,' Marco said, reaching out and patting him on the shoulder. 'You should relax. Everything's okay. If Luna's forgiven me, I'm sure Rose will do the same for you.'

'I doubt it,' Ben said, his voice as dry as brick dust. How could she?

Marco shrugged. 'Stranger things have happened. Besides, she's a Love Doctor – if she can't forgive the man she cares for, who can?'

'I wish that were true,' he muttered, thinking about all her rigid rules.

Then music began to play, and Ben saw Elena leading a woman who looked like an older version of Luna towards the empty chair next to Francesca, while Leonardo hefted a suit-case into the villa.

Had Deborah Kennedy arrived? He didn't get a chance to find out because the music got louder, and Marco straightened and patted his back again.

Ben mirrored his friend and turned to face the villa just in time to see Luna looking stunning in a floaty white wedding dress covered in hundreds of tiny heart-shaped sparkles walk slowly out of the patio doors — her elbow linked with Rose's.

He watched as they took their time descending the steps, his heart in his throat as he took in every detail. Rose looked beautiful. She wore the long dress Francesca had picked out for her on their shopping trip. He hadn't seen it when Rose had tried it on, but his knees went to liquid as he watched the straw-berry-coloured material flow like water around her legs and the ribbon straps of the bodice hug her elegant shoulders. Someone – Aurora perhaps – had sprinkled her collarbones and bare arms with sparkles, making her look almost unworldly. His stomach went fluttery, and he suddenly felt giddy, like all the air had left his lungs.

In his mind, Ben begged Rose to look up so he could somehow signal that he was sorry, that he'd been wrong. But she avoided his eyes.

. . .

'To the bride and groom,' Ben said, holding up his champagne glass as his audience — who were sitting at various tables dotted across the lawn — drank before starting to clap loudly. He sat again, relieved he'd completed his best man's speech. The guests had all laughed and cheered in the right places and he knew he'd done his friend proud.

But being on form – trying to remain happy and joyful — had taken its toll. *Rose still hadn't looked at him.*

Ben gazed over at her again and he felt desolate. He had to fix this somehow; it wasn't something he could brush off or joke about. He couldn't repair it with cake or a lifetime of toasters. This wasn't pretend and he couldn't fake it until he made it. Not this time. This was real — and he had to do something before it was too late.

'Um.' Ben stood abruptly, making his chair scrape on the grass as the guests fell silent. 'With the bride and groom's permission,' he said loudly. 'I wonder if it would be okay if I said a few words?' He cleared his throat feeling self-conscious. 'To Rose.'

'Hell yes,' Marco said, raising his glass.

'I thought you'd never ask!' Luna cheered.

When Ben glanced over at Rose again, he saw she was looking at him, her expression confused. Then she gave him a tentative smile and his insides reacted immediately. It was like his blood had suddenly returned, flooding every available space with warmth. What had been lying dormant – even frozen – suddenly reanimated. He felt hope creeping into his limbs. His throat still felt dry and he had a lot to say, so he took a quick sip of the champagne.

'Aldo says to say what's in your heart, *bello*,' Aurora piped up from one of the tables, waving her glass. 'Unless you want me to get my crystal ball, and tell you which words to use?'

Ben shook his head, smiling. 'That won't be necessary,' he said, turning his whole body to face Rose, trying to pretend their audience had disappeared. 'I have an apology to make. I accused you of a lot of things yesterday.' He paused when she started to shake her head looking uncomfortable.

'You don't—' she began.

'I said you were scared of love.' He took another moment to gather his thoughts, hoping the perfect words would come to him.

'Keep going!' Luna whispered in a very loud voice.

'You're doing brilliantly, *caro*,' Elena added.

Ben sucked in a breath. 'But what I should have said is that I was the one who was afraid.' He pulled a face as some of the crowd let out a hushed *ahhhh*. 'I got hurt two years ago and it was easier for me to shut down and not get close to anybody.'

'*Sophia*,' Francesca spat angrily.

'Then I met you and everything changed,' Ben said, his voice gruff. 'Suddenly, I started to feel things. I began to fall for you. Despite my best intentions.'

Rose stood abruptly too and held up a palm. 'And I ruined it.' Her cheeks glowed with embarrassment as her gaze swept across their audience before she turned back to him. 'Because you were right. I was scared. I did look for problems – with us and with Luna and Marco — and I needed you to point that out.'

He smiled at her as relief flooded his bones. 'I needed you to help me feel again,' he said, suddenly not caring that everyone was listening. 'I'm not sure anyone else could have got me to open my heart. I know it seems crazy – we've only known each other a few days – but I love you, Rose.'

'Of course you do!' Aurora boomed.

Ben put his empty glass back on the table because suddenly he wanted to be beside her, wanted to hold her and tell her everything was going to be okay.

Rose must have felt the same because she shoved back her chair. You could have heard a pin drop. None of the guests made a sound as they both walked around the table, their eyes glued on one another.

Then suddenly Rose was in Ben's arms and he was kissing her, hugging her closer, wishing they were alone. He tipped her to the ground, deepening the kiss, as everyone watching them began to clap, cheer and stamp their feet and he felt Rose's answering smile against his lips.

'I said they were meant to be together!' Ben heard Aurora yell over the din. But he didn't pull away – he couldn't – instead he continued to hold on. Knowing whatever happened from this day forward, he and Rose — *his* Love Doctor — were never going to be scared of loving each other again.

EPILOGUE
ROSE

'Luna and Marco are going to be here soon,' Rose said to Ben as she raced around their flat, making sure everything looked perfect.

She stopped and took a moment to admire the fireplace they'd added since she'd moved in with Ben three months ago. Pausing to run a hand over a frame that contained a photo from their best friends' wedding of the whole Marino family – including Ben and Rose – at the end of that special day. They'd all been giggling, high on emotion – the result of a plentiful supply of wine, food and love. Rose didn't think she'd ever been so happy.

Her mobile rang and she turned and almost tripped over the fertility statue that Isabella and Cesare had presented to her just before she and Ben had left for England. She hadn't had the heart to refuse to take it, so it had taken up pride of place beside the fireplace. Although Rose made a point of not touching it too often now it was mended – just in case.

'That was your mum,' Ben said, wandering in from the kitchen, wearing an apron and a sexy smile that made her stomach do a slow somersault. 'She wanted to tell us that she's just arrived at your dad's house and she's waiting for him, so they might be a few minutes late.'

'They're still planning on driving here together?' Rose asked, her eyes widening.

Her parents had been through a transformation since she'd refused to attend either of their weddings. They'd both gone ahead with their nuptials of course, but as predicted, neither of the marriages had lasted.

Since then, Rose had sat them down and had a stern talk about her new boundaries, including how she wasn't to be used as a pawn in their relationship battles anymore. Nor was she prepared to give them any advice. After which, they'd both changed so much she hardly recognised them.

But this was a whole new level of weird.

'Looks like it,' Ben told her, turning on his heel and heading back into the kitchen before picking up a wooden spoon from one of the counters. Rose followed, taking a moment to admire the new blue cabinets and oak breakfast bar in the centre of what had once been a separate kitchen and dining area but had recently been knocked through. Being engaged to an architect had certainly paid dividends.

'You don't think they're going to get back together, do you?' Rose asked, feeling a sudden tightness grip her chest.

Ben smiled at her indulgently. 'Even if they do, it's not your problem anymore remember. That's your new number one rule.' He repeated her new mantra for about the five hundredth time.

Rose nodded and walked up beside him so she could admire the bubbling pot of Bolognese that she knew contained the secret recipe Isabella had passed down to Ben. But as she breathed in the amazing fragrance, her stomach suddenly clenched and she had to step away.

'Everything okay?' Ben asked, turning and gently pressing

their mouths together. Rose leaned into the kiss, savouring it, before pulling back.

'I'm fine. I think I'm just stressed about this lunch,' she said, pressing a hand to her belly just as her mobile went off again. She rolled her eyes. 'It's probably Mum again.'

She picked up the mobile, surprised to find Aurora's name on the screen. '*Ciao!*' she said, smiling. 'I didn't expect to hear from you today.'

'*Leonessa*, I wanted to be the first to congratulate you,' the clairvoyant boomed from the other end of Cesare's mobile.

'On what?' Rose asked, widening her eyes at Ben who'd obviously heard.

'On the *bambino* you are carrying, of course!' Aurora said excitedly. 'Aldo just told me you are expecting.'

A LETTER FROM DONNA

I want to say a huge thank you for choosing to read *A Very Italian Wedding*. If you enjoyed it and want to keep up to date with all my latest releases, just sign up at the following link. Your email address will never be shared and you can unsubscribe at any time. Also, you'll receive a copy of my free short story, *The Christmas Mix Up*!

www.bookouture.com/donna-ashcroft

I hope you adored *A Very Italian Wedding*, my hot, comical and fast-paced romp to Italy for a glorious Italian wedding. Did you enjoy meeting Ben Pearson, a man who closed his heart to love after it was broken? And did you warm to Rose Loveheart, the prickly love therapist who was so damaged by her parents' disastrous marriages that she created a set of rigid rules to ensure she (and her clients) never got hurt? Poor Rose, I think we all knew that was unlikely to work out!

When I came up with the idea for the story, I was really excited to throw Ben and Rose into a situation that would immediately spark plenty of conflict. Asking them both to attend their respective best friend's wedding was the perfect solution. Obviously, Rose was always going to want to talk her friend, Luna, out of the rushed nuptials, while Ben was equally intent on ensuring Marco's marriage went ahead and his heart remained intact.

I hope you enjoyed reading all the resulting sparky conflict and that it made you laugh. The myriad collection of characters were intended to be both frustrating and loveable. From Luna and Marco, the intended bride and groom; to Marco's fabulous clairvoyant Aunt Aurora and the spirit of her husband Aldo; to the rest of the Marino family — not to mention Luna's shih tzu, Coco, and her love–hate (mostly hate) relationship with Rose. There were plenty of learnings for the hero and heroine, but hopefully for the supporting characters too.

If you did enjoy your journey to Italy and the resulting messy but poignant love stories, then it would be wonderful if you could please leave a short review. Not only do I want to know what you thought, it might encourage a new reader to pick up my book for the first time.

I really love hearing from my readers – you can get in touch with me on social media or via my beautiful website.

Grazie,

Donna Ashcroft

www.donna-writes.co.uk

 facebook.com/DonnaAshcroftAuthor

 x.com/Donnashc

 instagram.com/donnaashcroftauthor

ACKNOWLEDGEMENTS

I have been very blessed in my life with many lovely friends and an incredible family. But I wanted to give my kids a special mention here. They are both amazing people and if I could write them their own love stories, the ones they deserve, then they would be just like one of my romances: filled with colourful characters, warm and quirky pets, supportive friends and the perfect happily ever after.

This is also a reminder to them that they need to read my books — and that they can skip over the bedroom scenes if they want!

I want to say a big thanks to my wonderful writing community, there are many of you, but I wanted to name a few. Firstly, my best writing buddy in the world, Jules Wake, Anita Chapman, Liz Finn, Sarah Bennett, Bella Osborne, Pernille Hughes, Karen King, Suzanne Snow, Verity Bright, Clare Wartnaby, Rachel Lake, Erin Green, Ian Wilfred, Ruby Basu, Liney Hogg, Nancy Peach, Lizzie Lamb, Lauren Forsythe, Caroline Roberts, Olivia Beirne, Kim Nash, Kerry Kennedy and Susan Buchanan.

Gorgeous friends, family and supporters, thank you for all your support, reviews and general championing. Jackie Campbell, Julie Anderson, Eva Abraham, Soo Cieszynska, Fiona Jenkins, Andy Ayres, Alison Phillips, Kirsty Oughton, Emma Crowley, Caroline Kelly, Lucie Klarnerova, Sue Ward, Kirsty Egan-Carter, Tess Thorpe, Amanda Baker, Claire Hornbuckle, Tricia Osborne, Danel Munday, Linzi Stainton, Caroline Smail, Emma York, Meena Kumari, Grace Power, Cindy Wilson,

Cindy L Spear, Cindy Siler, Anne Winckworth. Plus, Dad, Mum and John, Lynda and Louis, Peter, Christelle, Lucie, Mathis, Joseph, Tanya, James, Ava, Rosie, Philip, Sonia, Muriel and Stephanie. Also, thanks to my OH, Chris (crossword lover, and the inspiration behind Cesare's addiction).

Also thank you to the wonderful Mel and Rob Harrison of Thinking Fox who look after my wonderful website and newsletters!

As always, thanks to the fabulous team at Bookouture, including my lovely editor, Ruth Jones, who is off to pastures new (I hope they're wonderful). Also, to my new editor Cerys Hadwin-Owen and the brilliant Natasha Harding. Thanks also to Lizzie Brien, Lauren Morrissette, Melanie Price, Noelle Holten, Kim Nash, Jess Readett, Lauren Finger, Hannah Snetsinger, Katherine Lenderi, Natasha Hodgson, Peta Nightingale, Richard King and Saidah Graham.

Thanks to the incredible and generous blogging community who are so supportive to me. A special thank you soooo much to the following bloggers who were part of my last two blog tours! @bluefairybugsbooks, @succaforbooks, CindyLSpear, @sue.wallace1974, openbookposts.com, Kirsty Reviews, @eric-as_bookreviews, Novels Alive, @Dianelikestoread, @apotpour-riofopinions, Page Turners Book Reviews by Caroline, @marbooks88, @annette_reads_daily, StarCrossedReviews, @musedsymphonies, @bookwormwhitlock86, Staceywh_17, Page Turners, Stardust Book Reviews, A Little Book Problem, Inspiredbypmdd, Open Book Posts, Passionate Encounters, Portable Magic, and Carla Loves to Read.

I also want to say a big thanks to all the bloggers from the Czech Republic and Netherlands for your wonderful support too.

Finally, to all of the readers who support me and read my books – I appreciate you so much, thank you. xxx

PUBLISHING TEAM

Turning a manuscript into a book requires the efforts of many people. The publishing team at Bookouture would like to acknowledge everyone who contributed to this publication.

Commercial
Lauren Morrissette
Hannah Richmond
Imogen Allport

Cover design
Debbie Clement

Data and analysis
Mark Alder
Mohamed Bussuri

Editorial
Cerys Hadwin-Owen
Lizzie Brien

Copyeditor
Natasha Hodgson

Proofreader
Catherine Lenderi

Marketing

Alex Crow
Melanie Price
Occy Carr
Cíara Rosney
Martyna Młynarska

Operations and distribution

Marina Valles
Stephanie Straub
Joe Morris

Production

Hannah Snetsinger
Mandy Kullar
Ria Clare
Nadia Michael

Publicity

Kim Nash
Noelle Holten
Jess Readett
Sarah Hardy

Rights and contracts

Peta Nightingale
Richard King
Saidah Graham